PLANET ZOLA

By John Forrest

PROLOGUE

World has moved to an era of globalization. Our lives are dependent on many products supplied by large corporations. We need TVs, computers, cars, and most of all we need substantial amount of affordable energy. If we could have it, we would even want to own servants and slaves. How could so much need be satisfied? How could so many things be supplied for such huge human population on the surface of this world?

The answer is, perhaps obvious for many, large corporations. Yes, the corporations that are rich with our money are the answer. They can certainly afford to supply us all we need, even slaves. They certainly have desire for it, too. Perhaps they are some sort of "Angels". But all comes with a price; the price that is not just the money but the inherent risks to our planet. What if one of these giant corporations turns evil; what happens, then? One morning when you woke up, what if you accidentally found out that one huge corporation has been planning to destroy all humans and end the life. Can that possibly happen? No, one would think not really. That would not happen because if it happened, media members would surely dig it out or investigators of the security forces would uncover it. Even the government officials and politicians would find it out. The corporation would be exposed in one way or another.

How could it be exposed and be stopped? If a corporation has a plan to take over the world, can media expose it? No, not if the corporation owns the media. In our era, the media often determines the government in so called democratic systems. People usually have no choice, but vote for the candidate the media present us as the best option. And it often happens that all the options presented to the voters are the same thing called with different names just like choosing a snack of French Fries or fried potatoes. It would matter none and does make no difference to the end result for what is being chosen.

If there is one or more of the large media organizations that the corporation does not own, the corporation can certainly buy few of those among the organizations to serve their purpose. If a good will government declared war against a corporation, it would usually have a short life in governing. The media would find a way to collapse those who get in the way of the corporate success.

But the story in this book is not about the media. It is about the slaves inflicted into every society all over the world by one big evil corporation. The corporation that provides the entire humanity with the technology, and comfort has secret plans.

~ _ ~ _ ~ _ ~ _ ~

Nothing happens by chance just as nothing can be destroyed or be created from nothing. Everything in the universe reverts back to the balance state; actions create reactions. The Theory of Origin proposes that the original universe was in perfect, optimal balance condition. Whenever the balance starts to change, nature uses its tools to fix or eliminate the problem, and to return to the original balance state. Nature has powerful tools including the ones easily recognized by almost everyone, such as storms, volcanoes, floods, big fires, and many others. In addition to those, it also has universal superpowers that are considered as, one in a billion chance events in the scientific environment, an event not likely to happen in our lifetime. For example, large meteors crush each other to establish reformation of the original balance state when the balance is disturbed so much that it is no longer possible to fix it by the nature's localized tools. This is similar to a human's life; when a problem in our body occurs

3

in advance stage, sometimes surgery can be the only way for us to eliminate the problem. We would have it willingly to get ourselves back to the healthy state no matter how painful the procedure is.

In the Theory of Origin, the well-known big bang theory was considered as an event for forming new solar systems, perhaps, a new universe to form smaller parts of a huge universe but not the original universe. The original universe had the energy to create the big bang events, the energy sourced from the natural events within the universe. Giant planets can crush each other with incredibly strong speed and huge forces, creating enormous energy to cause such events of the big bang in different locations to form different universes within the universe.

~ _ ~ _ ~ _ ~ _ ~

Once there was a happy town living an easy lifestyle in harmony and comfort. People could buy anything they needed in their town. When they went out for shopping, there were many shops to check around for quality and good price. They would also often get a bit of discount due to the competitive free market system in their town.

One day, a new shop opened in the town. It looked nice, with modern internal decorations. They had many varieties of products. The prices in this shop were very low, almost half the price of any other shop. People were wondering how this shop could afford to keep the prices so low. The curiosity created some doubts at first but the doubts just flitted through people's mind in short time. They quickly developed a habit of shopping in this shop. Success for this shop was imminent. Other shops could not compete with it, and they soon closed down one by one. The town's farmers and small-scale producers who sold their products in other shops all went bankrupt. This new shop was bringing the goods from somewhere else out of the town, somewhere nobody knew. By time, there was no production in the town. This was the only shop for the residents. Gradually, the shop increased the prices. The prices eventually became much more expensive than what they used to pay before this shop had come. Since this was a free market system, there was nothing to do to change the conditions. They had to live with the consequences of their choices. Soon, the market stopped bringing the good quality items. Since this was the only shop in town, residents had no choice but pay the high price for the poor quality products. Most of these products wouldn't even find any customer for any price at other cities. For the residents of this town, it was not easy to go somewhere else for shopping because the closest town was five hundred miles away. The town got poorer, and their lifestyle turned in to misery while the unknown shop owner, or perhaps owners, got richer and richer in the ideal system called free market of the capitalism.

The system established in our societies around the world worked well, or so it seemed, for many years. Nobody imagined this could happen. Could it be predicted what the world would be like in the future? How many of us could imagine a civilization on a planet far away could manipulate us with our own systems, our own rules, laws in our own earth and change our lives completely. Everything we knew in life would change, perhaps would be lost forever, before we even notice.

TABLE OF CONTENTS

PROLOGUE

CHAPTER 1: MURDER MYSTERY

CHAPTER 2: DAWN OF THE COMPANY

CHAPTER 3: IMPULSIVE ROMANCE

CHAPTER 4: CORPORATE SUCCESS

CHAPTER 5: EMERGE OF SUPERCARS

CHAPTER 6: DIRTY PLAY

CHAPTER 7: NIFFY MEETS BRAWNY

CHAPTER 8: A FOGGY CLUE

CHAPTER 9: PLANET ZOLA

CHAPTER 10: ASSASSINATIONS ON ZOLA

CHAPTER 11: TREASON

CHAPTER 12: THE PERFECT COMPANY

CHAPTER 13: SABOTAGE

CHAPTER 14: COFFEE FORTUNE-TELLER

CHAPTER 15: CHAOS

CHAPTER 16: DARK ERA

CHAPTER 17: MONARCHY ON EARTH

CHAPTER 18: A LIGHT of HOPE

CHAPTER 19: MASSACRE

CHAPTER 20: A GOOD IDEA

CHAPTER 21: DEVILS ENEMY

CHAPTER 22: THEORY OF ORIGIN

CHAPTER 1: MURDER MYSTERY

Milton was an intelligent sixteen-year-old young man who had just graduated from his high school with honors in Perth. He had devoured his studies as he was always hungry to learn more. He was interested in high-level scientific subjects, especially fuzzy logic, neural network techniques, and neural intelligence. These techniques were being studied, aiming to build machines that can learn from experience or an existing training data set to be able to make decisions. Milton would spend most of his time researching about these high-level scientific methods. Learning about these subjects became a natural part of his life, a need like eating food or sleeping. He had always felt the hunger for the high-level knowledge.

His life could be considered dull by most, as he dedicated his life to gain scientific skills. Milton would usually get up at seven in the morning even on holidays and weekends. He would rarely go to sleep at the same time as his parents since he would often work until late at night. During weekdays, his family would also get up early as his father would go to work in the morning. His mom would prepare a variety of food for breakfast. Warm smell of pancakes would fill up the kitchen with frying sound of eggplant, mushroom and sweet yellow chili peppers on the pan. She would serve the pancakes with maple syrup or homemade jam together with boiled or sunny-side up eggs. She often served the food with freshly squeezed orange juice. Milton loved his mom's cooking, as she was very keen to make delicious meals for her family. When it was on a weekend or a holiday, he would try to be quiet not to wake up his mom. He would often have cereal for breakfast and some fruits. After breakfast, he would have a cup of coffee. He was not allowed to drink coffee up until a year ago. His parents were keen about his health, and his mom believed that drinking coffee at a too young age was not a healthy choice. When he started drinking coffee about six months ago, he didn't really like the taste at first. However, the coffee made him feel more awake and more focused. He noticed his speed in reading while understanding the full contents of technical articles was much faster. He continued drinking coffee once a week, and later started to have a cup daily. He thought of coffee as a requirement to be able to focus on his hobby. So, it became his morning ritual.

His family had a two-car garage and some garden in the backyard. Three years ago, his father extended the garage to make some space for Milton. This young scientist always had a large variety of equipment collections around; two old computers, a remote-controlled car and helicopter his dad gave him several years ago on his birthday, a video camera, a car engine he got from a nearby junkyard, another engine from a laundry machine, many types of screwdrivers, a small welding machine, a voltmeter, an amperemeter, and many other tools. He also had few personal protective equipment to use, a face shield, eye-protection glasses, and a set of ear cover. He was fascinated with the way machines worked. This fascination created a strong desire in him to learn about how they were built, and controlled with computer chips. He would spend many hours dissembling and reassembling electronic and mechanical equipment.

Several months ago, he spent some time searching for universities to continue his education. He was particularly interested in the Artificial Intelligence Technologies University, which is also known as AIT, in California. The university was well-known for their research on the automation and artificial intelligence in robotics. He applied at the university to study, requesting a scholarship to cover his tuition fees with three supporting letters; one from the principal, one from his physics teacher, and another one from his math teacher at his high school. His application was successful, unsurprisingly, considering his extraordinarily high

IQ level, and soon he received a letter of acceptance. The selection committee at the university granted him not only the acceptance, but also a scholarship to help with his living cost.

He was going to fly to California two weeks later, in mid-December, to register at the university to start the winter semester in January. On a Sunday afternoon in November, Milton was walking down on Park Street next to the King's Park in Perth. As most of the weekends, he was wearing his blue jeans with a plain white T-shirt, and his walking sneakers with air-cushioned base to comfort his feet. In the city, streets were usually quiet on weekend outside the main business district. There was a nice breeze on the air gently brushing his face, a pleasant day to take a walk outdoors. There was a wall along Park Street between the park and the pedestrian pavement of the road. While walking, he was looking over the wall toward the park, at the trees, and was enjoying the view of cockatoos settling within the shadow of branches.

He was thinking of going to the entrance to take a walk in the park. Then, his attention was caught by some sounds from the park. He stopped and looked toward the sound that was coming from between the trees. He noticed three men were walking through the trees toward him on his right side when he faced the park. They were at a far distance, he could barely see them. Then, he noticed something more interesting at his left, some thirty meters away. There was a strange emptiness in between the leaves of many branches, strangely cutting through the branches. Milton couldn't understand why half of the branches were disappearing as if something was blocking the view, but there wasn't anything to block. Then, as they were getting closer to him, he noticed that the man in the middle was unconscious. The two men were carrying him toward the shadowy empty area in between the branches. He kept himself low, hiding behind the wall and watched them. The man in the middle was wearing a short-sleeved white shirt, and light blue trousers with dark brown shoes. The other two men were wearing black trousers with black T-shirts and dark glasses. They had short hair, as if they were soldiers of a highly disciplined army.

In a moment, he thought of calling the police emergency number with his cell phone. The phone had a video screen on the top surface over the numbers, which would slide forward by pressing and pushing. As his phone made little click sound, his heart beat faster thinking they might have noticed him, but he was lucky they didn't seem to hear it. He pressed the numbers 0-0-0 and the Dial button, but his phone was not working; it didn't dial the number. The phone was affected by a strong static filling the air, and he could even feel the electricity in the air. The numbers displayed on the screen were randomly changing continuously in every few seconds. The screen was getting foggy, almost unreadable. The bottom half of the numbers was turning back to the normal and the screen was flashing. He decided to try the phone's video to record them. The video seemed to work for a moment, but then stopped almost instantly. The phone's screen went all black. He noticed his heart was beating much faster than usual; he was scared and worried especially since he remembered well charging his phone's battery just last night.

When they got closer, Milton could see the face of the unconscious man clearly. He hid himself from them behind the park's wall. They passed him, and headed toward the branches. He noticed there were some spots of blood on the back of the unconscious man. Obviously, they must have hit him from the back, and knocked him unconscious. Suddenly, they disappeared into the empty part of the branches. As soon as they disappeared, there was a strong wind blowing the leaves and branches around. The unusual emptiness in between the branches was there a moment ago, but not there anymore. Now the strangely empty part was covered up with many branches and leaves. Something was preventing them from being seen, but he could not figure out what, and how.

He was confused of what had happened. He wanted to turn back to go to the city center, but he couldn't move for a while as he was puzzled and shocked by the scene. He sat down on the pavement and slowly calmed down. While sitting, he started to think, and many questions flooded in his mind: What had just happened? Why? Who were they? They looked like they might have killed him. Could he help him? He was not sure of what to do. What was all that? What happened to the man? Was he already dead? He was also confused from the view in between the branches looked empty as if something was hiding them, but why wasn't there anything at all? He could not make any sense of what he had seen.

After sitting down for a while, he got up and went back home to talk to his dad. He was living with his parents in a suburb called Victoria Park. His father worked in a bank as a financial planning manager. His mother worked part-time as a primary school teacher, spending the rest of her time at home with cleaning, cooking, and doing daily housework. Her cooking would usually contain a lot of vegetables and little bit of meat to enhance the taste. She was very keen about her family's health and would especially give attention to Milton's diet, ensuring his healthy lifestyle. For her as a mother, Milton was a special son mostly because of his noticeable intelligence. His mom noticed his interest in mechanical toys and his high intelligence even when he was a one-year-old baby. His favorite toy was his bag of attachable plastic bricks that he would build different shapes, fitting them to each other. The shapes he was making did not look like random shapes formed by attaching the parts of the toy cubes unconsciously, but they were often looking like objects resembling cars, bridges, or animals, which wasn't expected from a baby of his age. She never forgot the time when she bought the toy tricycle when he was only two years old. After seeing the toy in pieces, she thought her son had broken it on the same day he got it. Just two hours later, the tricycle appeared laying down fully intact on the carpet in the entrance of his room. Her husband was at work, and there was nobody else at home, other than Milton, to fix the toy, but thought of her two year old son fixing it didn't feel realistic for her. Then, she watched with her own eyes him taking the front wheel's nuts off, carefully putting the front wheels aside, and reattaching it again and repeating the same actions again and again, trying to ensure the wheel looked perfectly fit. It was not easy to believe for her that such a young kid, her own kid, could be doing this. Various thoughts went through her mind; perhaps there was a reason for such an unexceptional skill to be given to her son; perhaps he had a special mission to perform; but no clue of what it could be. In that day, she was excited, and could hardly wait for her husband to come home to tell about what he did.

Milton's father always tried to keep his thoughts, "realistic," and he never believed in such supernatural ideas. He would always try to explain to her how such things couldn't be possible. It was admissible for him that perhaps Milton was a smart kid, but there was nothing more to it. At the dinner table, she was keen to tell him about Milton's super skills, but she wanted to start the conversation about him first, "How was your day?"

He replied reluctantly, "It was a boring day. I had to waste most of my time in a meeting listening to an insurance seminar that had almost nothing to do with my work. I hope you had a better day."

She replied with a cheerful voice, "Yes, I had a wonderful day. I have witnessed a real miracle. Our son, Milton was able to dissemble his tricycle and reassemble it fully by himself. He took all the nuts from the front wheel, took the wheel out of its place and put it back perfectly. I could not believe my eyes at first. But he did it many times in front of my eyes. I think our son is special. I believe he has a special mission to do in life. His super genius intelligence is very unusual."

He tried to convince her about how such things cannot be possible by finding a justifiable explanation. He said, "Milton just likes to play with those types of toys that could be fit into each other and build shapes. I think there isn't anything unusual about it. His taking off the wheel of tricycle must be something that he must have accidently found out. This type of things can happen sometimes. It does not mean he has a special mission to do something great or anything like it. I just hope he would have a decent job to make a good living when he grew up."

Although they were not rich, they could maintain a decent lifestyle in their four-bedroom house. Their house had a lockup garage and a small backyard on the opposite side from the entrance. Victoria Park suburb was not far from the city. It would take about fifteen minutes by train and fifteen to twenty minutes by bus, depending on the traffic. Trains on a Sunday were usually quiet and relaxing; there would always be some empty seats available to sit down. Although his father thought him how to drive, he was not keen for Milton's getting a driver's license and owning a car at least until his 18th birthday. Milton was feeling exhausted that day and needed to calm down. While coming back home in the train, he kept thinking in his mind and trying to make sense of what he had witnessed.

On Sundays, Milton's parents would usually go out to play tennis and come home around 5:30 PM. He stayed in his room until dinner was ready. He wanted to give some time for his father to rest before telling him about the incident in the city. After they had dinner, his dad asked, "Is everything OK, son?"

It was obvious something didn't look right, and both his mom and dad could tell from his pale face. He explained them all what he witnessed that afternoon. How someone was kidnapped by two other men, and how there was an emptiness or something invisible hiding some of the branches and leaves. He also told them that he tried to call the police, but the phone didn't work. Then, he tried to take pictures and videos, but did not succeed.

His father curiously asked, "Really? How? What do you mean by emptiness in between branches and invisible? I can't say I follow you."

"I also can't make much sense of it, and I don't have an explanation for how and why, but that's what I saw."

His father's face turned serious and asked him, "OK. Perhaps the video captured something, even an instant of image could give us clues to what happened. Let's check the video, shall we?"

"Yes, let's see," said Milton and quickly got off the table. He ran to his room upstairs to get the cell phone. When he was coming down the stairs, he was looking at the cell phone's screen, and was pressing the play button, but it was obvious from his face that there wasn't anything in it.

"Nothing," he said. "There is nothing." He knew it didn't record, but he was hoping that perhaps a small instant of the picture, if it worked, could be the evidence.

His father said, "I really want to believe you, but it sounds all strange. I am sorry, son, I just don't know what to say. "

Milton noticed even his mom didn't seem to believe. "Never mind. I know what I said doesn't make much sense."

Milton didn't have any proof, and he could see that it wasn't going to be possible to convince them. He decided there wasn't much of a point to continue persuading his father. However, it was about someone's life, and he felt that he had to try to do something about it although he was not able to make sense of the event himself. He knew all that happened was real; he did see it, someone probably got beaten up, kidnapped, maybe killed, and disappeared.

He was thinking to himself there might have been a missing person reported around there, and for that, he could be taken seriously by the police. If there could be an investigation to find out what happened, something might come out. He wasn't sure of what they could possible do to confirm the events that happened. He was thinking perhaps they might have some equipment; the electrical current changes might have been recorded, perhaps, by accident. He decided to talk to the police the next day.

He was feeling totally exhausted and went to bed early that night, but it wasn't possible for him to fall asleep while his thoughts wouldn't calm down. He was continuously trying to find an explanation for himself, but he just couldn't. He would normally go study his books or work in the garage after dinner, and would continue until late night.

It took him a long time to fall asleep that night. When he woke up, it was already half past ten in the morning. He skipped breakfast and rushed to the local police station. As he was running out the door, he could hear his mom was shouting behind him from the kitchen. "Milton, you have to have your breakfast first." He pretended he didn't hear her as he thought he had to do this as soon as possible, hoping he was not already too late.

He entered the police station and walked to the front of the information desk facing the main door. He stood there silent for a few seconds as he was not sure where to start. The officer at the information desk asked, "May I help you?"

"I want to report a kidnapping I witnessed in Park Street in the city," said Milton.

She took a form from under the table, and while holding a pen to take notes, she asked, "When was it?"

"Yesterday afternoon, two men were carrying an unconscious man, and he was injured on his head."

She was looking surprisingly cool and didn't seem to get excited or did not even seem to care much. She asked without any apparent emotion, or excitement, on her face, "Did they take him with a car? How did it happen?"

He replied, "They disappeared within the leaves and branches. It looked like there was something within the branches creating an image"—he paused for a moment—"like an empty space. I couldn't see what it was. It was invisible."

She stopped writing for a moment. "Do you mean the branches and leaves were very dense, and they passed through it, and you couldn't see them?" she asked doubtfully about his story as she kept looking at the form.

"No, the branches and leaves weren't so dense although there were many leaves," he said, lowering his voice unconvincingly and continued with his normal tone of voice. "There was something invisible, and that was creating a vision

23

as if the middle of the branches were empty"—after pausing a moment—"in fact the middle part also had leaves and branches."

She stopped taking notes and lifted one of her eyebrows up. She said with a treating tone, "Look, young man, I must remind you that it is an offense to make a false reporting."

"No, no, I am not just making things up. I saw someone was in trouble and just want to help," he said, keeping his voice calm.

She looked unconvinced, "OK, but we are only responsible around this area. The events in the city fall in the city police station's authority, and that's where you should report it."

Milton wasn't sure if he should really go there. He didn't have a different, more convincing story for them. It was obvious that she was just trying to get rid of him and didn't want to deal with his, "imaginary" story. She tried to look serious while advising him to report the event in a different police station. Milton thought in his mind he had no choice but try everything he could possibly do.

He went to the city police station and explained what he had seen to a police officer. His explanations weren't taken seriously. The officer told him that nobody had been reported missing, and they weren't aware of any unusual activity in the area. They couldn't do something unless there was some sort of proof of anything wrong or unusual happening.

Milton felt unsettled, disappointed, and worried about what he had witnessed while he prepared for his flight to the United States to continue his education. The feeling of guilt has occupied his mind; the guilt that he failed the stranger was overwhelming. He could not stop thinking in his mind that it was highly likely his failure could have cost the stranger's life.

CHAPTER 2: DAWN OF THE COMPANY

When Milton arrived in California, he scanned through the airport, looking around with curiosity. He noticed the custom officers working at the airport with their unwelcoming facial expression, almost angry at people arriving.   He felt very nervous and a bit worried of the serious-looking, big muscled security officers, thinking they were treating everyone like criminals ensuring to take their fingerprints and pictures with cameras. For a moment, he felt like returning back to home, but he knew that wasn't a good idea.   He gathered all his courage and stood up in the line as wondering if they would allow him go through as they never seemed to smile to anyone. As he waited behind a long line of probably more than eighty people in front of him, he noticed a difference in the officers on the other section next to them who were stamping the passports of US citizens and green card holders. Those officers seemed like totally different people.   He noticed that the officers were not only smiling, but even asking friendly questions each time they stamped a passport. He could hear an officer's conversation.

"How was your trip, sir?" asked the officer, stamping the passport at the gate where a US passport holder was going through.

"Oh, it was very good. Thank you," the man replied as his passport got stamped.

"That's great. You have a nice day, sir," said the officer smiling in a friendly manner.

He couldn't believe how different the characters of the officers were at each side although they were working for the same department, as if they were from two distinct planets. As the line was getting shorter and shorter, he was feeling nervous about the angry-looking security officer on his line. Eventually, it was his turn to get his passport checked. The officer asked with his thick commanding voice, "Why are you here?"

Milton replied with a nervous tone as though he had done something wrong and was about to get caught, "Eee... I am here to study, sir." He repeated himself with a friendlier tone as if he was trying to melt the ice in the air unconsciously, "Yup, I came here to study."

The officer gave him a serious look, "Put all your fingers in that ink and press here on this screen, one at a time."

Milton was surprised that it wasn't even an electronic finger print machine; he had to actually dip his five fingers in a wet sponge with red ink before pressing each of his fingers on a scanner, but he didn't feel like questioning their ways. He thought this old style semi-computerized technology must be the result of a cost saving trend among most countries around the world affected from the recent economic recession. For an instant, he thought in his mind Einstein must have been wrong about Time Travel, especially in backward direction. It was already obvious to him that Time Travel to future was not only possible, but it was unavoidable and uncontrollable; nobody could speed the Time Travel up or slow it down. He could not understand why he had to dip his fingers in to the ink since the scan looked like it was connected to a computer. He thought for a moment they might have wanted to make some fun not to get too bored sitting in their small tight cabins. He carefully did exactly as he was told in silence.

"Move slightly to your right and look in to the camera," ordered the officer.

As he moved in front of the camera, he thought that it would probably be the worst picture ever in his life as he was feeling extremely tired from the long flight. Then, he thought they probably deserved getting his worst pose considering his unwelcomed treatment. When the officer stamped and put his passport on the side of his glass cabin, he relaxed and gave out a breath, murmuring to himself, "Oh, thanks God."

He arrived in his apartment near university campus by a shuttle bus. His accommodation, a two bedroom apartment, was arranged by the university at a walking distance from the campus. He was going to share the apartment with another student who arrived there a week ago from Chicago. His housemate, Assange, also registered at AIT and had similar interest to Milton. Milton felt happy to have a friend to discuss scientific topics and share ideas.

About a month later, there was a new company established based in Denver, Colorado, by a man called Bernard who was the only son of a French man and an American woman. The company name was Robo Limited selling androids to help in house work and help people in their daily lives. He used to work as a marketing manager for a toy company, making remote-controlled toy robots. He claimed that he had a breakthrough, a new discovery in Neural Artificial Intelligence systems or NAI that enabled these machines to behave consciously. This conscious characteristic was necessary for the robots to be able to learn life as they experienced and served humans just like a slave of a real person. They were produced to provide slavery service without requiring regular payment. This was a sudden and surprising development for the scientific environment from someone like Bernard as he had neither any noticeable background in robotics, nor prior publication in any journal, not even a conference paper. However, he stated that he had always been interested in robotics as a hobby in an interview published on a daily newspaper. There weren't many questions asked about how he could make such a development without some type of specialization in the technically complex science of neural intelligence systems. Media had always been a strong tool in convincing the public for anything with a little bit of information as long as it could be written using some popular, "buzz words" with concise sentence structures. It was written in a newspaper that he worked long hours almost every day for many years to develop the method. A model android display was available as proof of his skills that was pictured on the front page.

The android in the picture looked very cool with its shiny metallic outfit, standing with humanlike features except with a more solid-built appearance. It was six feet tall with a little red light in the middle of his eyes. He had little exhaust holes behind just below his ankle joints, which would fire up when it needed to speed. His little powerful engines fitted within its body. The android was fitted with wheels inside his feet that would come out under his feet when he needed to speed on a smooth surface like rollerblading without using his main engines. It also had internal radio wave receiver that could get radio broadcasting and weather forecast. The more interesting thing about the picture was its smiley looking face gesture although its' body and face looked like it was built from steel.

The major characteristic of the android was its ability to make advance logical decisions. Media was very much interested in them, and many TV presenters and news writers were already lined up to get interviews with Bernard, the president and the owner of the Robo Ltd.

As the company president and owner, he stated in a TV interview that, "conscious intelligence" was required for the robots to be able to behave like us in life so that they could help us. They obeyed the orders from the owners, and they were fully controlled by the family who owned them. These androids were able to perform functions necessary in man's life, such as cooking, shopping, washing laundry, and driving a car. There was no technical information released to the public about how they were built and how they would function.

For the first few weeks after the company was established, there was no interest from the public to buy any androids, and Bernard was feeling frustrated. While he was thinking what to do to make his androids popular and make people want it, he noticed a small article on a newspaper mentioning about a fund-raising party. Suddenly, he recognized the great opportunity to market his androids. This was a big party organized in Aspen by volunteers to help raise funds for the people in Africa who were living in poverty.

In winter, Aspen's luxuries ski resorts in Rocky Mountains would attract tourists of the elites in the society. Many celebrities and rich people attended the party called Water for All, which was also broadcasted on TV to ask for donations from the public. The party aimed to raise funds to help bring clean water in poor regions of Africa where many people, especially children, were dying from lack of clean, drinkable water. In the party, Bernard donated a robot to the fund raising committee to help them with their work in Africa's rough territory. By making this donation, he had the chance to talk about it on TV and in front of many people who can afford to pay big cash for anything if they wanted. Bernard explained the specifications of the robot on the stage. A small microphone was attached to the collar of his jacket.

"This android can walk and run like us on rough lands. It can carry heavy weight. It can do grocery shopping, drive a car, cook almost any food you like from their rich variety of recipes, wash laundry, do ironing, clean house and do many other things to help you in your daily lives."

When he stopped for a while, a lady from the crowd asked, "Does it run on a battery? How long would it go?" Some laughter was heard among the crowd.

He replied with a smiling face, "This android is built with a different technology that provides a lot of benefits with its great features. Its Energy System is one of its many great features. It has its own power generator that can run more than two hundred years without needing any external energy source. Its energy system is extremely efficient. Another great feature is its ability to perform maintenance on itself. It would never require any repair or service, at least not in our lifetime."

"Sounds better than my husband," said a lady as the crowd laughed and asked, "Can I get one too?"

Bernard was thrilled in joy to see the results of his marketing scheme right away. He smiled. "Yes, you certainly can."

Then, he got off the stage and went next to the volunteers' group representative. He took a piece of paper from his pocket and said with a low tone of voice, "There is only one little thing about this android. It cannot be dismantled. You need to sign this paper."

She looked surprised from unexpected signature requirement, "Oh, what is that for?"

Bernard replied with a calm voice, "Nothing to worry. It is just a formality really, stating that if the android is intentionally dismantled, the company will not be responsible for any damage that can be caused by the self-destruction mechanism inside the protected box where the main processing chips and power generator are located."

She looked worried. "Is this dangerous? What if some parts break by accident? Would it explode?"

"No, of course not," he said. "The protected box is made from a special type of steel, which is much tougher than the toughest steel available on Earth."

She gave a quick chuckle "you talk like it was an alien technology."

He responded "Oh of course not. I personally, assure you the box cannot be damaged accidentally. Only if extremely specialized machines and tools are used intentionally to recover the company's IP secrets, then it would self-destruct. As you would understand as all other companies, we just want to protect our Intellectual Property (IP) rights. In normal use, it is one hundred percent safe. This is a kind of confidentiality agreement to protect the company's IP. "She looked hesitant to sign the paper for a moment. Bernard assured her of its safety repeatedly. "I assure you it is extremely safe. In any case of an accident, it would recognize the accident, and that would prevent the self-destruction

35

mechanism being activated." While the lady was taking time, Bernard started to worry, thinking that her hesitation could broadcast a negative image about his android and destroy his marketing plans.

Luckily, she finally got convinced and showed her agreement, saying, "I see. It all makes sense now." She signed the paper with a smiling face as if she had intentionally given him a hard time to make a joke of some sort.

Bernard took a deep breath, relaxed and smiled back to her while he could feel cold sweat running down his neck. Then, he walked to the lady who wanted to have an android. "Well, we will have ten of them ready for sale in a few days."

The lady who asked the question was Shannon Jones, who was a well-known celebrity and a fashion icon. She was the daughter of the Jones family who were among the ten richest families in USA. Their wealth was initially created mainly from the real estate business, but they later expanded the business to jewelry and cosmetic industry. Her interests and questions about the android got others' attention too. After talking to her, Bernard got requests from five other wealthy attendants in the party. The people who were requesting the androids were not only rich enough to pay but also influential over others in the elite society. Their requests made others believe owning an android would be the next trend to show off one's wealth in the world of rich and famous.

Bernard decided to sell them for $10 million each. He knew the six people who were already asking to get it would pay almost any price regardless of the amount he would request. However, he didn't want to ask a higher price because he wanted the continuity of the sale and achieve a wide spread stability in his business.

CHAPTER 3: IMPULSIVE ROMANCE

After selling the six androids, Bernard said they had produced only ten more of this special series, and these sixteen androids were called Alpha-one series. Sale of these ten androids would be an ideal measure for the company to evaluate the market demand and the price people would be willing to pay for. They were sold almost immediately as many celebrities wanted to have such perfect slaves. Individuals weren't the only ones wanting to have them; two of them were bought by a construction company to handle moving heavy material and installation. These robots could easily pick up and carry a two hundred kilogram steel column and set it up on precision requiring places that would be difficult, costly, and time consuming with cranes or any other machines.

It was obvious from the demand of the first set of androids that there were many people who seemed to be ready to pay even a much higher price than what Bernard asked for. However, he kept the price the same since he was making more profit than he expected. By keeping the price at this level, he could sustain higher demand rates. He had big plans and huge dreams; he was aiming to infiltrate millions of slave robots into the society. He decided to put sets of twenty-five androids in the market weekly for a month as many people were ordering them. He rented a small workshop in a quiet area in Georgetown, Colorado. There were six androids and three large bulldogs guarding the workshop. The quiet location was ideal for his plans to stay out of the public eyes and out of the attention.

He later increased the weekly sales to fifty per week and then increased to one hundred. Even though the price was very high, people did not mind using their hard saved earnings to pay for it for different reasons and purposes. These androids functioned perfectly without needing any fuel, repair or service, but that wasn't the only reason for them selling so many. Just as he predicted, having one of these machines became the symbol to show off one's wealth and power thanks to Shannon Jones for igniting the move. The media was greatly helping in the sales as they were talking about it every day in almost every TV channel, all the radio stations and newspapers around the globe. Their talk about how wonderful were the slave robots serving during major new hours was such an excellent free marketing system even Bernard couldn't have planned it any better. Although all these androids were assigned varying names and serial numbers, they were all the same in functionality.

Within three months, eight hundred androids were sold, and the demand was still just keep increasing. The army also contacted Bernard to show their interest; they requested one thousand androids to help them carry out dangerous missions, like going through the high-risk fields for soldiers, clearing mines in the areas with the risk of booby traps, or going to the hot firing zone with cameras to provide information to the army. They paid half of the total cost in advance to help him produce the androids. Police organizations and fire departments in various states also ordered another thousand androids. To cope with such huge demands from organizations and the public, the company decided to build factories that could produce androids in mass quantities.

Bernard pocketed a lot more cash than what was required to build a factory. He knew well that these demands were only the initial requests that would keep increasing day by day. He decided to build the plant in Canada where they could buy as much uranium as needed from the mines there to use as an energy source to build the androids. The androids were also using uranium as a source to produce their internal energy. Their energy production system was much more efficient than any other energy production method known on earth. The androids would not produce any nuclear waste or posed no risk of any type of radioactive leaks. Robo Ltd. built the factory quickly within three months. The security at the factory was very tight. It was guarded by using many security cameras, high-tech computers, specifically built guarding androids, and trained dogs. The factory was able to produce 3000 androids daily. Humans and androids were working together at these factories

Even within the factory, nobody knew exactly how these machines functioned and how their energy generator system worked. Some of the small parts and pieces were being produced in the high-security section of the factory. This section contained a few different internal rooms that each of them had double steel doors. The parts built in these secure rooms would come in sealed steel boxes, and no one was allowed in that section except Bernard. Only a few androids would enter there to build those parts. Bernard told others that this section of the factory contained high-rate of radioactive particles, and it would be harmful to them. He would always carry a special protective suit when he wanted to get in that section and would carefully put it on before entering there. He also said that the ordinary protective suits would not help them, and his suit was unique, specially built just for this section.

In fact, there was no risk, or no sign of radiation in the section. He made it all up to ensure that others wouldn't get too curious about it and try to enter. The guardian androids wouldn't allow anyone to come closer anyway, but he wanted to make sure of that. The source and technology including the energy reactor to build the androids had to be kept secret to sustain the growth of the company with such an incredibly high profit rate in the long run.

The parts containing the energy generator and the main processing chips would come out from the top secret section of the factory in rectangular steel-cast sealed boxes. The main processing chip and the generator were mounted inside this box with some small pins, and a few extending pins outside for connection to fit into the robot's main body. These parts were built with a self-destruction mechanism, and if anyone trying to open it succeeded to create even a tiny scratch, or a slight movement of the seal, it would explode, totally burn and melt itself with the strong energy released from the uranium, leaving nothing to trace other than some worthless melted metal pieces.

The explosion caused by the self-destruction mechanism was indeed strong like a small bomb. In fact, the company released a document stating that if the sealed protection box was damaged, or even slightly scratched, it would surely cause an explosion that could be fatal to humans and any living thing around it. The harm would not only be caused by the direct impact of the explosion, but there would also be some risk of radiation that could cause harm to anyone within its proximity. Every customer would sign this form to protect the company against potentially getting sued.

The androids were indeed safe against an accidental explosion event causing harm to owners. An explosion was only reported once. In that event, a CEO working for one of the biggest banks committed suicide when one of their financial brokerage stole $50 billion of their customer's money. He scammed them by distributing some of his new customer's money to the previous customers to make it look like he was making large profits for them in Wall Street. When his scam was discovered, the customers' money was already lost. The CEO had a high level of professional integrity and moral values. He couldn't accept such a big financial scam and harm to his customers. He took his rifle and put the muzzle inside his android's throat and fired down toward his chest. The bullet damaged the security seal, and android exploded, because its processor unit didn't calculate the event as an accident. The explosion killed the banker while it destroyed the android and burned its security box.

The price of the androids was gradually reduced down to $100,000 aiming to sell to majority of the population worldwide. The demand was huge from all around the world, and one factory was not able to cope with it. Bernard opened another large factory in California, which increased the total production capacity to ten thousand androids a day and employed over fifty thousand people. The uranium needed for the factory's nuclear energy generator was being transported from Canada.

Even with the substantially increased production capacity, they were still barely catching up with the world's massive demand. Most of the countries in the world were ordering tens of thousands of them almost monthly just to use in security forces, which was not only the army, the police, and the fire departments, but also anywhere where security was needed body guards for countries' leaders, security for the government buildings like the senate building, or large organizations that required private security. In addition to the government, companies were ordering many of them to use at work in banks, production companies in plants, airlines, and even at some large shops as cashier to eliminate the shops from being robbed at nights, and shopkeepers getting shot by thieves. After all, these androids were free when all the cost savings were considered. They would never require salary payments, food, or fuel, no maintenance, no complain, and they would never get tired. They could deliver excellent performance continuously. The sale of the androids was a total success for the company and an unusually fast growth was achieved.

Since the company started to grow very quickly, Bernard opened offices in almost every state to organize the demand and ensure on time deliveries to customers. He opened some offices in Europe, one in China, and one in Japan also. He had an office in John Hancock Center, one of the most prestigious office buildings in Chicago located at the Michigan Avenue. There were eleven employees working for him. Aleyna was his personal secretary; Dr. Rick, Dr. Asimov and Dr. Schwarz were the scientists specialized in NAI and robotics; there was a finance advisor, an accountant, a company lawyer, and four document controllers to keep track of orders and sale information coming from their offices in other cities and countries.

Aleyna was quite attractive and young girl at her twenty-two. The smooth skin of her legs, her beautiful thighs and well-shaped hips would always create a pleasant environment in the office with her usual thin and tight mini skirt. She would wear a white shirt on top that had a deep slit and lace in front, which would make her look like she was an elegant swan. She was born in a small town in the northern part of Russia. Her family moved to the States when she was only two years old. Besides her attractive feminine features, she had a very warm and amicable personality that made her gain everyone's sympathy at work.

Aleyna was impressed with Bernard's success and professional manners as she got to know him shortly after he moved to the office. He would always wear dark colored suits personally tailored for him, matching mature taste in ties and shirts with silver cuff buttons. Although he was nearly at his forties, she was interested in him without caring his age. Every morning when he entered the office, she would look into his eyes with a smile and say, "good morning" from her table at the side of the entrance, facing the door. Her desk was the only one located at the entrance as she would be the first person to meet any visitor even though it was rare for anyone to come to their office from outside.

On a Thursday in the office, Bernard asked her, "Aleyna, please come to my office with the last month's report of orders and sales."

Aleyna looked at him, with a light smile as usual, and softly acknowledged, "Ok, I'll be there in a second." She grabbed a folder from the shelves and put some papers she had recently printed in and walked into his office.

"All right, how did our orders go from last month?" asked him while he was settling comfortably in his chair.

Aleyna took the chair across his table and put it next to him, and she touched his leg with hers in an accidental manner. She then leaned her head closer to him, as if trying to look at the folder closely. After taking out the papers, she started reading some number, "Well, 15,485 from Chicago, 87,946 from Washington."

He started feeling attracted to her as he was feeling the sweet smell of her Dior perfume and touch of her leg. He interrupted her reading, "Excuse me," paused for coughing lightly from nervous feelings caused of being too close to Aleyna. "It all sounds great."

"Yeah, it is good," said Aleyna as she turned to him. Her face was very close to him. Bernard, sounding a little shy, asked, "Well, are you living with your boyfriend?"

Aleyna looked at him with a smile, "No, I don't have any."

"I suppose you couldn't choose one. I am sure many young and handsome men must be chasing you as you look so fabulous."

"Wow, do you really think I look so?" said she, moving her head even closer to him.

"Well, yes, it is obvious that you are an extremely attractive and pretty looking, lovely young lady," said him while he was feeling thrilled as if he were in a job interview pressured with the questions, yet feeling the full confidence to get an offer. He felt an overwhelming urge to have a taste of her lips, but pressed strongly on his breaks to keep himself under control and could barely stop before he got driven too far by his instincts. He was always consciously considered about his business image.

Aleyna had a cheerful and mischievous look in her eyes, "Oh, I am really flattered to hear that from you. You don't look too bad yourself."

He almost whispered, "I wonder if you are free tomorrow night for dinner."

She noticed that his voice was unusually low since he didn't want anyone to know his interest on her. She thought his professional character might have required him to keep secrets, especially since she was an employee. "Sure, I'll be happy to join you," replied Aleyna with a slightly lower tone of voice not to make him feel uncomfortable.

After the work on a Friday, Bernard took her to one of his favorite cozy restaurants in Chicago in his Bugatti Veyron sixteen-cylinder sporty car. As they entered the restaurant, he first led her to the waiting bar to have a cocktail and to initiate a relaxed mood with the help of alcohol. After having a drink, they moved to their tables to have dinner. As they were eating, Aleyna talked about her family and how they moved to the United States when she was only two years old. "My mother was telling me everything would freeze up from cold in winter times in my home town. She didn't like the cold weather and snow. My father was a math teacher at a high school. He would often talk about how magical the numbers are and contained rules within themselves. Once he told me how amazing it was that when the location of digits in a number is changed, the difference with the original number would always be divisible by nine."

Bernard looked at her scratching his jaw. "Really? How?"

"Well, a simple example is 21 minus 12, for example, equals to 9 and is valid for any number. The same idea holds for all numbers such as 317 and 173. The difference is always equal to the multiples of 9" said Aleyna.

He was just listening to her without saying much about himself. He thought in his mind it was interesting to hear Aleyna, his secretary, talking about magical wonders involved in math. He silently attempted to do the calculations in his head to check if it was right but got confused quickly. Then, he got an opportunity when Aleyna excused herself to go to the bathroom to refresh her makeup. He took out his cell phone and opened the calculator applet. He calculated the difference between 317 and 173 as 144 in the calculator function carefully pressing on the each number's button and divided it by 9 to see a surprising integer number 16. He could hardly believe it was true.

He first felt disappointment on himself for failing to do a simple calculation in his head that Aleyna seemed to get instantaneously as she was talking. He thought about his success at work and found it hard to accept in his pre-judgmental mind that she was in fact quite an intelligent girl. Then, he could not avoid his mind wondering to try to find the reasons for this strange relationship within the numbers. He was supposedly making discoveries in advance robotic technologies, but not even getting very basic fundamentals of simple math calculations right further added to his self-disappointment. He knew he was never good in any scientific subject, but all his intelligence was developed in convincing people by using words that are fashionable in a subject, which were called as buzz words by most. He knew he was probably one of the best, if not the best in the manipulation art which led him to a great success in his career. He just didn't know his math level was much lower than his secretary, which caused him to feel stressed and disappointment in himself.

Aleyna soon returned back and sat on her chair. "How about you Bernard? I am curious about your life," said Aleyna. "I feel like I am being too selfish talking about myself all the time."

"No, not at all. I really enjoy listening to you. That was quite an interesting example from the magical world of numbers," he said.

She replied, calmly looking bored of the subject and trying to end it, "Oh, not that fascinating really. Digits changing in units of ten minus the value of itself each time a number changes its location equates multiples of nine."

He didn't understand anything of what she just said as he couldn't figure out the reason, but he felt he had to look cool and smart saying, "Yes, of course." Then, he quickly changed the subject as he could no longer handle his mind sitting in a low chair in his thoughts and he said, "Well, there is not much to say about me." He paused for a moment before he continued, "I was working in a company making toys, but I had different ideas about what to do than my manager. I worked on things related to robotics and their movements during my spare times. Finally, I could complete the development of the theories needed to implement my vision but the toy company had no interest in those ideas. So, I built my own company and here we are." He was feeling like he was in a war inside his mind even though he tried to look calm and pretended like enjoying the chat. He thought he had to bring out his proud side and find a way to come back on top, more like an oil spill coming up in ocean water. As his thoughts wondered around, he unconsciously revealed a smile.

Aleyna's eyes captured Bernard's smile for the moment. She asked with a replying smile, "What?" She paused for a second for him to explain it. After getting no response from him she added, "What are you thinking now? What are you smiling for?"

He said, "Nothing important. I suddenly remembered how my finance professor would often criticize my views. I wondered what he would be thinking now. He would criticize my financial judgments saying my discussions and evaluations of financial events were only accurate for short-term, or perhaps medium-term at the best, but my strategic views to see the long-term implications and consequences of financial events were poor. He is still just teaching few courses and had projects once in a while, but my company's strategic decisions were obviously all great."

His comments of self-praise sounded strange to Aleyna as he usually seemed like a humble gentleman. Then, she remembered her other friends around and thought it might be the men's nature to praise themselves and talk about how great job they did. She said, "I am certainly impressed with your success with the company, but I think your professor might have more ideological views, perhaps he values different things than the financial aspects."

Then, she noticed Bernard's unpleased face expression. She thought it would be best not to sabotage this pleasant environment in the restaurant and cheerful mood created by the delicious meals. She said, "I am sure he would have different views now knowing that you have founded a great company, producing super-high intelligent technologies, great androids. It is obvious the company is doing extremely well. I must say I certainly envy your achievements."

He smiled and said, "I am glad to be able to impress such a beautiful angel like you." He wanted to close the topic as soon as possible as he tried to avoid talking about himself. He always had an unconscious worry within his mind that if he talked about himself, he could accidentally reveal the secrets of his business and his company. He was feeling happy that dinner was almost finished. He asked, "Got space for some desert or more drinks?"

"Oh, thanks, but I have had quite enough."

"Look, Aleyna," he said looking in her eyes. "I am a bit concerned about the professional aspects of this dating. It would be best if we keep it between us."

"I see. Of course, don't worry. I know you are very professional and I respect that," she replied.

"Thanks, I appreciate your understanding," he said as he got off his chair. He paid the bill, leaving a generous $50 tip on the table, which surprised Aleyna. She remembered how she felt nervous last weekend when she spent $60 for her entire meal as they walked out of a restaurant.

The porter from Mexico was in front of the door. "I'll bring your car right away, sir," he said with a friendly tone of voice. He ran to the parking lot behind the restaurant. He quickly brought the car and opened the door for Aleyna. "Have a great night, madam, sir."

Bernard took a $20 bill from his wallet and extended it to him. "You have a great night too." Aleyna was impressed with his generosity and not forgetting to give a pleasing tip for the working people. She was thinking of it as a sign of his humble and unselfish nature although he made some comments, not so humble once in a while.

He drove her to the front of her apartment. He got off his car to open the door for her and said good night. While opening the door he looked like he was affected by the alcohol as his left ankle had a slight twist. Aleyna said, "I think it would be better if we have a coffee at my place before you head off home." He was happy to be invited and walked up into her apartment. His manipulative pretending act worked for him again.

Next day at work, they were keen to make sure their behavior was always in a professional level. They hid their relationship from others. Bernard's purpose was to ensure keeping his authority among the employees. They were meeting almost every night after work, secretly continuing the relationship. As the dating continued, Bernard felt more and more nervous day by day. He was running out of the subjects to talk, and Aleyna seemed to be getting more persistent to find out about him. He was also feeling pressured to keep his business secrets that he believed had a risk of costing his life, or perhaps even others' lives, to talk about himself. He came to a point he could no longer bear the pressure of risking a potential disaster.

One day, he invited her to a newly opened French restaurant in a suburb of Chicago thirty minutes away from the central business district. When they entered in, Aleyna could not believe her eyes how luxuriously the interior was decorated, with paintings on the walls built from large stones, presenting a magical atmosphere that no one would expect to find in this suburb. The restaurant quickly gained popularity with the mood created by using only candle lights, and some tables were partitioned by curtains made with handmade lace, providing privacy. It was especially favored by the people who needed secrecy and security. Aleyna was happy just to enjoy the good food and pleasant environment filled with a light sound of easy listening classical music in the background. But she thought, "This must be a special occasion similar to her first date with him." She asked with a cheerful smile, "What is the occasion?"

Bernard's face was rather serious against her expectation, "Nothing special. I hope you enjoy your meal."

She noticed he did not look like he was enjoying the night at all. He looked at her, "Aleyna, I think you are really great, and I really enjoyed our times together." Aleyna's smile faded away as he continued, "The relationship is not working for me anymore. It would be the best for both of us to leave the relationship in a professional level only. I don't want anything to affect our work, and I am afraid we have to stop seeing each other outside work."

Aleyna was shocked of what she has heard. She could not believe that he wanted to leave her. She got very upset at first. Then, she thought to herself she didn't really know much about him. Even if they were together almost every night for the last month, he didn't tell her anything of significance about himself and his past. She got up from the table and left the restaurant.

Although Bernard liked her and enjoyed being around her, he was worried that a long-term relationship with someone could be extremely dangerous. He didn't want anyone to know about his life. He believed he had to keep a distance from everyone to proceed on his plans. Aleyna was happy with her work and did not want to lose her job. Both Aleyna and him acted as usual, as if nothing had happened between them while they continued their work life.

CHAPTER 4: CORPORATE SUCCESS

In the morning, Bernard was looking through his daily newspaper as he often would, scanning through the pages, reading some news and articles that he would be interested in. An article about a new research development caught his attention. The article was about a newly built prototype machine developed in a research center in Silicon Valley. The center was established as part of the Stanford University's research on artificial intelligence. The machine they built as a prototype was not an android. It was not even built in the shape of a human. The robot was square shaped with four mobile arms fitted and had limited mobility on a track. This was an experimental prototype specifically built to help in production and construction industries. It was obvious from the way it was built that they had no intention of producing humanlike androids.

However, the part that caught his attention was not the shape of the machine or the purpose. It was the new technology that could enable the robot to make decisions on the items usually humans make. The article mentioned that they were able to develop a new model within Neuro Artificial Intelligence technique's framework. That was a similar technology Robo Ltd's androids were built on. They were aiming that the ability of the machine to make decisions could be used in variety of places. For example, it could decide a faulty product on a serial production line without costly testing process and pick the defected products up to move to different line of process in the factory's production system. He found the article interesting, but didn't care much about their advanced research work. Obviously, the research was in its early stages, and it would take them many years to master the technology to come to a level to compete with his company. In the office, the news had spread among the staff. When he came to work, he could hear the research scientists discussing the potential implications of the new research as he walked to his office. They were speculating on what it could offer to the world. They all had implied their positive views and were discussing among themselves how it could benefit for the public to have more companies providing similar services and offering choices. The subject became a typical lunch break conversation topic among the staff during the week.

About a month later, there was a tragic news on the cover pages of most newspapers and broadcasted as the breaking news in all the TV networks nationally. There was an explosion in the research center that killed two of the professors together with three technicians and five students. The entire research team involved in the development of the technology was killed in a mysterious accident that nobody could identify the cause and the reason why it happened.

Some speculated about the involvement of Robo Ltd in causing the explosion, but there was no physical evidence to suggest the company's involvement. Even Bernard himself was shocked to hear the news and couldn't believe such an accident could occur in a research center dealing with computerized mechanical systems. The articles speculated about his company's involvement, based their speculations mainly on the timing of the accident. They claimed that if it was an accident, it couldn't have happened just in the time when the entire research team members were in the facility because one of the professors, a technician, and two of the graduate students working on this research would normally do their work at the university's main campus. They would go there just once in a while when they organized meetings to present their ideas to each other and involve in brainstorming discussions. Moreover, all of their computers at the main campus were infected by a virus from an unidentified source that wiped out their entire research work from their computer's hard drives and electronic storage disks. None of the computer viruses known so far would be able to leak through all the storage disks and achieve a total destruction. This virus was a very special one that after wiping out the entire data related to the research, it could keep itself invisible in the clouds and unidentified by any of the available technologies. All the automated backup disks that had been used for the last three years were totally empty.

In spite of the many speculations made by the newspaper articles and some local TV stations on the idea of sabotage and possibility of murder, there was no evidence found to support it. The accident was investigated by officials with the aid of androids equipped with the most up-to-date technologies. A potentially faulty electric circuit was reported as a most likely cause of the accident although no fault of any type was identified. They could not find any evidence of criminal act or intentionally planned destruction. Although Bernard was surprised about the accident, he couldn't help thinking that this would ensure his business to continue growing smoothly since the only potential future competitor was eliminated.

One afternoon, Bernard called all his staff for a meeting. Everyone was curious what it was about since he rarely called meetings. He would usually meet individually when he wanted to talk about something. Everyone gathered in the meeting room. Bernard sat on the chair designated for him at the end of the table across the door. He was looking dissatisfied, not happy with the work performance.

He started the meeting saying, "Thank you for all joining me here now. I wanted to share my plans with you for the company's future. It has been about two years since Robo Ltd. was built and I believe it is time for us to grow further. We have been doing well, but we need to do more to stay in the business. We need to grow. Now, I believe it is time for us to go public."

He paused for a while looking at the finance advisor, Alfred. Alfred was nodding his head to show his agreement with Bernard. He asked, "Alfred, how much do you think the company is worth in the stock market?"

He thought for a while lifting his eyes up, "Hard to guess an exact number. Well, $40 or perhaps $50 billion considering the great success in selling the androids.

However, we need to do a proper evaluation to know the exact value."

Bernard asked, "How long would it take to evaluate?"

"I think it would take us about six months, which is quite a short time frame to do a comprehensive evaluation, but …"

Bernard shook his head in disapproval and interrupted him saying, "We don't need to waste time. I think it is the double of what you are guessing. We should put shares for $100 billion." He knew Alfred was close to the actual value if he considered the current state of the company. However, he also knew something else about the company that nobody else had any idea.

They produced one hundred billion dollars worth of shares and placed it on the US stock market. Just two days after they put the stocks on the market, Bernard came to the office in an afternoon carrying a package in his hand. He sneaked in to his office, almost like hiding from others in a hurrying pace. He dropped the package in his office before going to Alfred's office. "How's everything going?"

Alfred replied with an unusually louder voice filled with the joy of success, "Absolutely great, really great indeed" Then he continued with his normal voice, lowering his tone, "I wasn't expecting this. One individual who didn't want to reveal his identity bought 51 percent of them almost instantly, and the remaining were sold to others from the general public in a short time. Since the 51 percent was sold so quickly, everyone wanted to buy some of our shares. It didn't take long for the stocks to be bought by the public."

Bernard smiled, "Great. This is an excellent event, which I believe calls for a toast." He put his hand on Alfred's shoulder with a friendly manner. Alfred was surprised with his behavior since he would always behave extremely formal. Bernard then took his hand off Alfred's shoulder and walked toward the door. He turned and said, "Let's all get together in the meeting room."

He went to his office and brought the package to the meeting room. In the package were three bottles of champagne he carefully took out and put on the table one at a time. Then, he handed one of the bottles to one of his research scientists Asimov. "I could use some help."

"With pleasure," said Asimov, not sure of what was happening. It was the first time he saw Bernard bringing something to the office for the employees. Bottles of champagne in the office were especially not something he would expect from him.

They opened the bottles with a loud puff sound filling up their meeting room. He carefully served half a glass to each of them. Then, he took his glass. "Everyone, thank you for coming here in such a short notice. I have wonderful news. Alfred has just told me that the sale of our stocks was an extra ordinary success for the company. The shares were sold almost instant. I think it deserves a toast." He raised his glass and said. "To the great future of RoboCorp."

Others moaned, "What? RoboCorp?"

Bernard continued, "Yes, yes I know. We are not yet formally a corporation. Well, we have to change the name and status on the papers to suit with the company's situation. Since we are now a publicly owned company, our name will have to be a corporate name. We will soon formalize the legal documents for the name change. Now let's have a toast, people, for our company RoboCorp." Bernard was quick to finish his glass of champagne and leave the meeting room while others preferred to enjoy their drink slowly and have a chat with their colleagues. While they drank their champagne, most of them were speculating among themselves what would happen now and what they could expect. They had no idea who owned the 51 percent of the stocks now, but they all knew whoever owned it owned the company now.

It had been six months since the company's ownership officially changed from Bernard to the public. Stockholders gathered in a meeting to select four board members to manage the company. There were eight candidates nominated by a group of stockholders for board membership, but there were four others nominated by Bernard himself. Nobody knew who the four nominees were or what their background was. The eight nominees were well-known business professionals with many years of experiences in a variety of fields including business management, finance, and investment strategies. There were also letters sent to each of the stockholder to inform them about the meeting and enabled them to vote by post if they couldn't attend the meeting. In the letter, it was mentioned that there were twelve candidates nominated, but there was brief information for only eight of the candidates nominated by the stockholders. There was no information included about the background and experience of the other four candidates. The only section mentioning them stated that they were recommended by the founder of the company, Bernard.

Bernard walked to the front stage and turned to the stockholders attending to the meeting. "Ladies and gentlemen!" he said to get their attention and continued, "I know these members you have nominated have great skills, past experiences and great qualifications no one can argue or deny. Yet I have been managing this company since I have established it and led the company to a great success so far. I know these four," he paused for a moment while pointing to the ones he nominated. "They would ensure your investments would get the highest return. If you select them, you will not regret. I personally ensure you for that."

The four nominees looked alike so much that it was impossible for anyone to separate one from the other. One of the stockholders stood up. "If you excuse me saying, these nominees look exactly the same as each other like coming from the same production line." Some laughter was heard from the crowd. He asked, "Are they quadruplets?"

Bernard tried to keep his professional outlook although he could also see the humor in the situation he was in, but he thought he had to keep himself within a professional manner as much as he could. He replied, "I am sure many of you must have experienced in life and know it well that the looks can certainly be deceiving. I ensure you these gentlemen are not brothers, but they all are highly skilled in business management."

Laughs from the crowd continued for a while. Stockholders didn't look convinced about the ability of the four board members to manage the corporation as they were not told anything about their background. Almost 40 percent of the votes were shared among the eight of the nominees and only about 10 percent voted for the candidates Bernard nominated. However, their voting didn't matter at all because 51 percent was owned by an individual whose vote would be the only one mattered.

After voting, Bernard approached to his nominees and said, "Congratulations" while he shook hands with each of them.

In front of the stockholders' disappointed look, one of the new board members walked in front of them. "Thank you for supporting us for the board membership. Bernard has been doing an excellent job, without any doubt, since the company has been established. Therefore, as board members, we have unanimously chosen him as the president of the corporation. We wish him good luck for the future and in his new role within the company. We hope to see the continuation of his success and the growth of the corporation."

The voting was nothing, but just a show for implementing a process, for filling up the legal check boxes that had no effect on the managerial status of the corporation. The stockholders had no power or authority over an individual having 51 percent of the shares and the company's ownership.

CHAPTER 5: EMERGE OF SUPERCARS

Five months passed since Bernard was assigned as the president by the board members. There was not much change in the company's operation and structure except that they collected massive fifty billion dollars cash from the stock market. On a Monday morning, he asked Aleyna to call the staff for a meeting as soon as he entered the office. He directly went to the meeting room. He stood in front of the window in his high-rise office building looking over the city. Soon, everyone came to the meeting room and sat around the table in their usual chairs. He moved to his chair, settled comfortably.

He said, "As you all know, we have been very successful. Especially the sale of our shares went exceptionally well. Now, it is time for us to move on and expand to a new industry. Automotive! We will produce and sell cars. They will not be ordinary cars. We will make supercars."

"What do you mean supercars? What type of cars?" asked Asimov.

Bernard replied, "I am glad you asked. They will be a type of fast cars, real fast. They will be able to get to four hundred miles per hour within few seconds. No tires, no fuel will be required for our cars. We will produce a variety of sizes. Obviously we need to consider a variety of customer's needs. Some can be two-seater sporty looking, while some of them will have ten or more seats to suit for the needs of larger families."

Asimov said, "I don't think you can drive a car at such a speed." He noticed Bernard's face changed suddenly, feeling offended from Asimov's words, sounding like an insult. Asimov added, "I mean not many people can drive a car safely at that..."

Bernard interrupted him calmly, "I see. I hear what you are saying and perhaps I agree with you. That's why these cars will be built as fully automated, which means they will not need to be driven. They will be the safest cars ever built. Since they will be automatically driven, speed limits don't apply to them; or perhaps I should say, won't apply to them as I will have to talk to some government officials to take care of that."

"How could we build such cars" —pausing for a moment— "and what time limits are we looking at to start production?" asked the other scientist, Rick .

Bernard said, "You don't need to worry about how, because I have already completed a demo model. There is a national car show in California next week. I'll introduce the car to the market there. We want to start production ASAP, which means all of you have to start working on panning to build factories just after this meeting."

Shwarz asked with curiosity, "Do you want us to plan the production assembly?"

Bernard replied as if he was fixing up a misunderstanding, "Oh, no, no, you don't need to worry about it. I was just referring to preparing the legal documents and getting necessary permits from the necessary organizations such as planning and infrastructure department or city council. I must say I haven't yet decided where to build the factory."

Bernard had not given any information on the technical parts regarding the car. It wouldn't be possible for either Dr Shwarz or Dr Asimov to do any planning. In fact, he never had any plan for building android production plants. He worked with his own androids and contracted some independent construction companies to build the factories. He gave the contracts for building different sections of the factories to different companies. He always enforced the companies to sign very strict confidentiality agreements to ensure that no one could possibly know how the entire factory looked like, not even the structure of the building itself. Nobody knew how the androids were built and assembled fully except himself. The only planning needed in their office would be getting the legal paperwork permitting them to build the factory in a location he wanted. Androids functioned as engineers and planned everything with all technical details needed to be planned.

Rick asked looking puzzled, "I can't see a ten-seater car going at four hundred miles per hour. Are you claiming you made a supercar? How?" Staring at Bernard's eyes, he continued in a patronizing tone, "Excuse me, but are you specialized in car production? How did you...?"

Bernard did not like these questions coming with a tone of insult. His face turned red with anger. He hit the table with the palm of his hands as he stood up from his chair. Placing his weight on the table, bending slightly over, and looking at him, he shouted, "Who the hell are you? Who do you think you are to question me on anything? You are fired. Get out of here immediately. I don't want to see you in this company ever again."

He waited for him to leave the room. Then, he calmly sat down. "I am saying I have already made a car and it is ready for demonstration. Since the car is already made, I must know about it, and that's the end of it. I don't want to hear nonsense questions. As I trust you with the business, I want to work with the people who trust me and are loyal to me. I don't have time to discuss further details with you now. I have to get ready for the car show next week."

Bernard stood up his chair to leave the room, but stopped for a moment. "Oh, one more thing; I almost forgot it. Since we are getting in to car business, the name RoboCorp will not properly reflect our business. I decided we change our name to something that represents our company and represents our status in the world. GlobCorp will be the name for our corporation." Then, he left the meeting room.

Bernard headed for the national car show in California. He concentrated to memorize his car's features to make sure he could advertise it to its full potential without leaving anything out. This car was in fact much superior to any other cars built so far. It had many features built with new technological developments.

Milton was a senior at the AIT University in California. He went to attend the car show there. He was interested to see what new design cars were being built. He saw some crowd was gathered around a car demonstrated by GlobCorp. When he approached the crowd, he saw the car that was different than all other cars. Then he noticed a man was explaining about the car's features to the people across from him. He also wanted to find out about the car's technical features. As he approached he could hear him saying to the crowd, "The car moves about fifty centimeters off the ground using uranium as the energy source. It is the same generator system used in our androids. Its energy usage is so efficient that they would never produce radioactive waste. These cars are built perfectly, just like our androids —no need for fuel, no need for service, and no break downs. It doesn't need tires, and more importantly it doesn't need a smooth road surface."

When Bernard was finished talking to them, he turned his face toward Milton. As he started walking toward Milton, Milton was very surprised to see him again. While Milton was looking at him with shocked eyes, Bernard approached and asked, "Are you all right, young man? You look like you've seen a ghost."

"Yes, I am OK," Milton replied while he continued staring at Bernard. "But you" —pausing a moment—, "you... How? How did you get away from them? You are all right?"

Bernard looked very surprised; he looked like he wasn't sure what Milton was talking about as he didn't know him. He smiled and said, "I don't believe I know you, but thanks for your concern, I am really fine."

"In Perth, that was you. I remember," said Milton.

Bernard became curious as he was in Australia four years ago just before all his business fortune smiled at him. He said, "No, you must be confusing me with someone else, but thank you for your concerns about me. I was in Australia for a holiday some years ago, but I don't recall going to Perth. Let me know if you got any questions about our new car."

Milton was feeling a bit relieved to see that he was OK, but he didn't understand why he was hiding the kidnapping. He thought perhaps, he wasn't feeling comfortable talking about it, besides it had been four years since then. He said, "Well, OK. I am just curious how it works."

Bernard explained, "The car runs with voice commands. It would identify the owner from the voice. You just say where you want to go, and it takes you there. It has a state-of-art auto-drive system. It has advanced global positioning system, which even doesn't need to communicate to satellites and doesn't need to be in open space. It knows its location at all times."

"Impressive, no need for driving, and it doesn't have wheels! No need for satellite communication, huh, interesting. When it is carried by a truck or ship without running its engines, how would it work?" asked Milton with a confused look.

"Yeah, it initially knows its own original coordinates since it's built. Even if it is carried without starting its engines, it knows when there is any movement and its sensors record all its movements that allows it to identify its own location at any time with point precision."

"Wow, that's truly impressive," he said and asked, "Is it safe? What prevents a crash?"

Bernard said, "After it gets the command, it rises up from the ground."

"Fifty centimeters off the surface," Milton interrupted him with an excited mood. "Well, I've heard you were talking to the others."

"Oh, ok, that's great. It would go over other cars if there is no bridge. If there is a bridge, it would pass around or over the bridge. It can raise itself much higher than just fifty centimeters temporarily to avoid accidents. It could also slow down, depending on the shape of the bridge and location where it is at. With the other cars we sell, they would recognize each other when they are in close proximity. They would identify their location, speed, and direction. Then they adjust themselves to prevent any crash. They are extremely safe."

Milton said, "That's really great."

Bernard turned toward the car as if he wanted to wipe some dust particles that might have landed on the car. He thought about what Milton could possibly know about Perth. He was very confused from his questions. He thought to himself Milton must have seen something. Obviously, he knew something happened in Perth and Bernard had to find out what he knew without raising suspicions. He turned back in a friendly manner and said, "So, you like the car, huh?"

Milton said, "I must say it is quite impressive and far ahead of the technology. I am studying at the AIT. My graduation project is about NAI modeling techniques, your androids. I can't say I found much information about them."

"Oh, that's great. You want to study about our androids. That's cool. My name is Bernard," he said extending his right hand for a handshake.

Milton knew the name, but he hadn't seen him before. "I know your name. You are the president of GlobCorp! Well, I am Milton. I am honored to meeting you, sir" he responded, shaking his hand.

Bernard wanted to know how much he knew. He was worried that if Milton would cause problems for him in the future. He said, "Got time for coffee? I'd like to buy you a cup of coffee and have a chat. Perhaps, I could be of some help on your graduation thesis."

Milton accepted the coffee offer. Especially, since he was interested in GlobCorp's technologies, this was a good opportunity for him to get some information. "Yes, sure. That would be great, thank you for that."

"Just a minute, please," said Bernard, turning to the big monitor beside the car. He set up the prerecorded advertisement display so that the car's features would be advertised when he was away. Then they walked toward the small coffee shop at the corner in the showroom. They grabbed their coffee cups and sat on a table in a corner.

"Have you already arranged some work?" asked Bernard.

"I am in contact with a few companies, but I haven't got any job offer yet," said Milton.

Bernard took out his business card from his wallet and handed to him. He said, "We have just recently had an opening in our NAI research team in Chicago. If you might be interested, please send me your CV. If you accept to work with us, I will give you one of our androids as a signup bonus for the job."

Milton was surprised with Bernard's friendly behavior considering he was the president of one of the largest corporations in the world. He seemed like a good person, friendly and very generous. He said, "Wow, that is very generous of you, sir. I could never afford one of your androids with my student scholarship. I must admit GlobCorp is the most prestigious corporation to work for." Milton was still curious what had happened to Bernard in Perth, but he wanted to avoid talking about a subject Bernard was uncomfortable to talk about.

On the other hand, Bernard was keen to find out what he knew. "That's great. I am glad you have interest in working with us." He paused for a moment. "So you are from Australia, right? You think you have seen me in Perth. Hmm? When I think of it, you might have seen me. You know I do a lot of business trips all over the world and I now recall going to Perth also. I am just curious how you saw me and remember me?"

Milton was surprised by Bernard's quick change of words about the Perth. He could never forget that day; it was too mysterious to forget. He remembered Bernard for sure, no mistake about that. He thought it would be better not to tell him how he saw him since everything was too strange. Moreover, Bernard was hiding something and didn't tell him the truth. He said, "At first, you looked like someone I saw in Perth" —he paused for a second before continuing—, "who had an accident, but obviously I was mistaken and you look all right. I am sure I haven't seen you before."

Bernard was worried about him knowing the truth and revealing his secrets to the world that would be too dangerous to take the risk. He wanted to ensure Milton would contact him. As he was finishing up his coffee, he said, "We'll give you a good pay, just let me know what you want when you send me your CV. We always need intelligent and young people with fresh new ideas, open views for technologies, like yourself."

Milton finished his coffee, and as they both got off the table, he ensured him. "Sure, I'll be sending you my CV. I appreciate you giving me the opportunity, sir!"

"That's great. Call me Bernard, Milton. Enjoy the rest of your day," he said before walking back to his car.

Two weeks later, Bernard got an email message from Milton. His CV was attached with a brief note:

Dear Sir,
Please, find my CV attached for the position in your company should you consider making me an offer. I would like to respectfully request the opportunity to study for a doctorate degree while I work. My professor convinced the committee to

make an exception for me to accept me for the doctoral program
without requiring a Master of Science degree.

Thank you for kind consideration on my application.

Regards,

Milton

Bernard immediately made an offer for him to join his team upon his graduation. He stated that he could work with flexible hours. He could work four days a week instead of the usual five days. He wanted to keep Milton close to him as much as possible to ensure he was not going to create any problems. He offered him a similar position as Dr Asimov and Dr Shwarz even Milton had no prior work experience. He didn't even have to work full five days as others did. On top of that, a free NI-50 series android made the offer irresistible for him.

Milton was happy with the opportunity and accepted it. Assange was not only his housemate and classmate, but also his best friend at the university. When he went to the printer room to pick up a chart he was printing, he noticed Milton's job offer as he was printing Bernard's message. He took his printouts to bring to him. "Well, well, my friend, I see you got an offer from GlobCorp."

"Oh yes, I think it is a great opportunity for me. As you know, I've been dying to take a closer look on how these androids function. There is no information available in any scientific publication on how they actually work. The only information I could find are some speculations, but nothing real."

"Yes, I know. All the companies want to keep everything secret these days. It is very hard to find information to do scientific research. I am happy for you, congratulations. Where will you be located when you start working?" asked Assange.

"I'll be based in Chicago."

"Great, my parents have a property there. They have been trying to let it as they don't live there. I am planning to move there and rent their house. I am hoping my dad will give me some discount until I get a decent job. You should make time to visit me someday."

"Sure, certainly, my friend," said Milton looking puzzled.

"You got so serious suddenly. If you won't be having time, it won't be the end of the world." Assange felt a slight sense of hesitant mood as he couldn't understand why his best mate would react to catching up. He thought he would perhaps work too much, forgot all their friendship during the past four years at the university.

Milton noticed his friend's disappointment as it was clear in his voice as much as in his words. "No, I don't mean about visiting you. I was thinking about this job. I don't know how to say this. What they offered me is kind of too generous. I can't understand why."

"They must have recognized your skills. You know a lot about robotic technology. I am sure you will do well."

"Yeah right, my skills?" he paused for a while. "I suppose it is a great opportunity to work with their 'super' androids."

Assange said with an unimpressed face, "Yeah, too perfect if you ask me. Androids are just too perfect."

Milton knew his friend wouldn't be easily impressed. Things were either not good enough or too good to impress him. He thought whether there would ever be anything at all Assange would be impressed and would appreciate.

CHAPTER 6: DIRTY PLAY

Soon after his graduation, Milton moved to Chicago to start working in the central office of GlobCorp. On his first day, Bernard introduced everyone to him. As he introduced him with Aleyna, Milton's excitement was obvious to everyone from the look on his face. He was staring at Aleyna without saying anything. After shaking her hand, he was holding it as if he didn't want to let her free.

Bernard said with a smile, "Yeah, yeah, we all know she is gorgeous, but if you let her hand go and follow me, I'll introduce you to others too." Milton felt shy and embarrassed as he dropped her hand. Milton followed him to the other offices.

It was a month after Milton started working there. He was having lunch in the kitchen, which was built on the same floor as their office to take breaks for lunch, tea or coffee that creates an environment for the employees to socialize with their colleagues. Aleyna came and sat across him. She asked, "How are you Milton?"

"Yeah, fine, thank you. You?" replied him.

"Good, you are studying and working at the same time, must be hard for you."

"No, actually, it is easier than I was expecting. I am not sure why, but Bernard doesn't seem to expect much work from me."

"Yes, it is usually calm here. Work is very relaxed, no stress," said Aleyna sounding happy about the easygoing work life.

While they were chatting, Dr. Asimov and Dr. Shwarz entered the kitchen. Shwarz said, "I cannot believe this. Have you guys heard about the news?"

Milton said, "No, what's going on?"

He replied, "A lot is going on. As we all know the company has huge money reserves accumulated from the sales of robots and shares. After they built twenty large factories in different states and started distributing the cars all over the United States, the other car companies in all states have closed one by one. Finally, the last car producing company has just been closed."

There was more behind the car sale success of the corporation than what anyone else knew of the quality of the supercars and affordability. Initially, when RoboCorp established factories to produce slave androids in huge numbers, most of the car producing companies purchased androids in their production plant just like most other major industries did. This was a trendy move among the corporations at the time to replace people with androids or just add androids to their production plants to increase productivity. Using androids was also reducing their operating cost in the long run. They thought androids were perfect and they had the full control of them. But what they did not know was that their control was conditional. They had the control on their androids as long as they did not pose any competitive threat to GlobCorp.

When GlobCorp got into the automotive industry, all androids working at car factories were informed. As soon as they started producing the supercars, the new model cars produced by other companies started to create problems for customers and cause accidents to whoever bought them. The working androids were introducing well-planned defects in the production lines to cause malfunctions in the mechanical components of the cars. Many of the cars were having serious problems; malfunctioning on their brakes, accelerator systems, safety bags, lightings, transmissions, engine performance and so on the list would keep going. The car producers who produced excellent high quality cars for so many years were suddenly having all types of issues, even in the simple functionalities like windshield wipers.

The car companies were being sued for huge compensation claims because many people lost their lives in accidents caused by manufacturing faults appeared on these cars. Some of the companies recalled millions of their cars back attempting to fix any possible problems. However, there were no problems in the engineering design or the planned production lines. Many investigations were done by authorities and experts, but they were all inconclusive. None of them could identify any fault. They did identify the faults only in the products that caused serious problems, but nothing at the production plants that could be fixed or rebuilt. Unfortunately, in all the investigations, there were always some androids involved due to their high technological abilities. Human life had become dependent on the technology or perhaps the more correct word was androids rather than technology because the meaning of the technology became almost the same as the word *android*. It was impossible for the car producers to find out that it was their great cost-savers and efficient androids causing all the problems because the androids in the investigation teams were working for the same purpose. It was easy for them to cover up the evidences, especially since nobody was suspecting that the perfectly working androids could cause all these problems.

Huge compensation payouts ordered by the courts and millions of recalls occurring for all models of the cars created huge costs that no car producers could afford it. Their reputations were totally tarnished by the daily news on the media. The problems caused in the cars were on the front pages of almost all the newspapers, and most of the news coverage on major TV networks was about the faults on their cars. Only reliable cars for customers were supplied by GlobCorp. The corporation did not care about anything or anyone —the people who lost their lives in accidents, the people who got injured and sustained permanent disabilities, the ones who lost their jobs and thrown into miserable life conditions of poverty. The only thing mattered for the corporation was the size of the financial profit making the president feel proud of himself.

Although Bernard had no idea about these events being simulated by his androids, he did not even bother to think about what was happening in the world, and what the actual reason was for the massive demands for his cars. Bernard was too blinded with his own plans and endless business success. His mind was too busy focusing on realizing his dreams.

Asimov said, "Thousands of people lost their jobs."

Milton said, "It is impossible for them to compete against these supercars with so cheap prices."

"Huh, super? Right," Asimov shoved his disagreement.

Aleyna said, "Yes, they are indeed great cars. The demand for these cars is so high. We get millions of requests from within the country and other countries."

Shwarz said, "That's why Bernard built many factories in Canada and South America. Then he expanded to all other continents. He has factories in Italy, UK, Turkey, Russia, Ukraine, Japan, Australia, and many others. The other car factories in the world are all closed up."

Asimov said looking confident, "Nothing beats the traditional stick shift drives."

Shwarz commented, putting his hand on his shoulder, "You live in the past, my friend. You need to wake up and join us in our times."

Asimov moved his eyeballs toward him while keeping his face across. "If I were you, I wouldn't be so sure of who is the one needing to wake up."

Milton asked, looking naïve, "I wonder what Bernard thinks about it, about the closure of all other car factories."

Asimov said, "He doesn't care about others. He believes this is just an expected Evolution of the life. The strongest would survive in the capitalist free-market environment as it is supposed to be."

There was a silence for a while in the room. Milton was eating his lunch, but both Asimov and Shwarz noticed his eyes were always moving across toward Aleyna.

Shwarz turned to Aleyna and said, "Hey, Aleyna, you aren't seeing anyone, are you? I mean as boyfriend," while Milton looked at him with widely opened surprised eyes.

"Nope, I am not. Why do you ask? You have a wife already," said Aleyna with a smile.

"I wasn't asking for myself, although I can't deny how attractive you are. My wife would kill me. I mean this young handsome guy here. He can't take his eyes off you."

Milton looked embarrassed as others laughed. Asimov said, "Don't need to be shy, she is a gorgeous girl. Don't miss your chance waiting."

As Shwarz picked up the remaining half of his sandwich from the table, he lightly kicked Asimov's foot, "I've got something in my monitor, I'd like to get your opinion," he said.

"Now?" asked Asimov trying to finish as he got a large bite on his sandwich in hurry.

"Yes, right now," said Shwarz loudly. "We can continue eating in my office." They both left the kitchen with their lunches.

Milton said, "I see, they cleared the kitchen for us." Aleyna laughed as he continued, "Perhaps, we could have lunch outside together, next Saturday, if you don't have any plans."

Aleyna was pleased to see he could finally gather his courage to ask her out. "Oh, that sounds like a great idea. I would love that."

After lunch, Milton went to Schwarz's office feeling appreciative for his help to ask Aleyna out. He thought his work was unusually too easy and could get their opinion of how things worked around. When he went to the open door of the office, he saw Asimov was also there looking at a chart and discussing an interesting subject. He strained his ears to catch the conversation in the office.

Shwarz was saying, "Novel paradigm of nonlinear dynamics."

Asimov added, "Yes, even the simplest biology of a neural intelligence has a superior structure compared to the artificial neural network with rigid boundaries."

Milton walked in and joined the discussion. "It is because of the property of non-Lipshitzian's dynamics. Unpredictable dynamic systems can be represented in the form of coupled activation and learning dynamical equations."

Shwarz seemed surprise to see him. "Heeey, are you spying on us?"

"I just heard you having a hot discussion. It sounded interesting," he said. He had always been interested in neural intelligence before he even started at the university. He always thought of neural intelligence to be the key modeling technique for the artificial intelligence to build machines, computer chips, and electronic equipment that could make advance logical decision and serve to make life easier.

Shwarz said, "Don't worry, I was just kidding. Yes, you are indeed right. The systems have zero Jacobian, which gives them the characteristics of having hyper-surfaces. At all these equilibrium points, at the curves and surfaces, Lipschitz conditions fail. These special characteristics of the system convert the equilibrium points to terminal attractors and repellers depending on their sign of periodic excitation."

Asimov added, "The architecture of the non-Lipshitzian dynamic based neural network seems to be suitable for modeling complex behavioral patterns."

Milton said, "Well, I enjoy hearing your discussions, but I just stopped by to thank you, thanks guys. I owe you, Dr. Shwarz," referring to his setting him up so he could ask Aleyna for a date.

"No, you don't owe me anything. We are friends as much as we are colleagues." Pausing for a moment, he added, "Oh, one more thing" —He continued with a slightly angry and louder tone—, "stop calling us like that, keep calling Doctor Doctor," said Shwarz.

Milton smiled, "All right, as you wish Dr. —I mean Shwarz."

He looked puzzled thinking to himself for a moment and asked them, "About the work, is everything usually like this? There is no pressure to finish any work or no deadlines. I am not able to get insight information about any technical details of the androids to do any research. Actually, what I mean is, I am not really doing much research although I am supposedly in the research team to develop new things."

Shwarz said, "Yup, it's always been the same. Not much to do here as a scientist. They pay us pretty good just for producing some colorful simple charts that I am sure Aleyna could do them just fine."

Milton said, "But you guys have done great work so far. You have produced far more advance technologies than one could ever imagine. The androids, the cars are just so great."

Asimov grinned cynically, "Yeah, they are too great for scientists like us to produce. Bernard made them all by himself."

Milton said, "Yeah, right! Give me a break, guys! I know you don't want to take all the credit, but it is too much."

Asimov's eyes turned to Milton with a serious look and said, "Oh no. If you want to keep your job, never make such a comment. Dr. Rick was working here before you. Last time, he questioned Bernard's skills and got fired instantly."

Milton said, "Serious? Bernard seemed like a very good manager and boss here. He couldn't have fired someone just for asking."

Shwarz interrupted him, "Bernard did make it all himself, and Dr. Rick didn't believe him, just like us, except that he told him what he thought loud and clear. He got fired for that. We don't question Bernard's ability here, but we only do what he asks us to do, which has not so far included any development work, research, or anything. Only Bernard knows how these robots and cars work, none of us has a clue."

Milton could not believe that Bernard would have done all the developments in androids and cars by himself. In the media, Bernard would often make statements claiming that they had the highest quality team of scientists to develop high-level technologies. However, in the internal meetings, he would not hesitate to say he has done everything himself. People were not asking many questions about the source of items as the customers were happy about the products. Everything seemed perfect. Milton didn't want to take the risk of damaging his relationship with his boss and potentially getting fired for arguing the source of the technologies. He felt appreciation since he could have the chance to do his studies while working at the same time. He decided to try talking to Bernard to get more information.

When Bernard was in the office later in the afternoon, Milton came to his office. Bernard smiled with friendly face as usual and said, "Come on in, Milton, take a seat. I wanted to have a chat with you. How is everything going? Are you happy here? I am very glad you joined our team."

Milton replied, "Thank you, sir, everything is going well."

Bernard said, "Oh please, drop it anymore. Call me Bernard. If you need anything, let me know."

Milton said, "I was trying to get more information for my research, but I couldn't find much."

"There is quite a lot of information in these publications," said Bernard, showing him the company's annual reports for the public, operating manuals for androids and cars, and some other generic information. He continued, "You are welcome to borrow them at any time and keep as long as you need."

"I see. Thank you for that," said Milton and added, "Well, I was looking for a bit more technical data to start with."

Bernard said, "Oh, OK. That's a good idea. I suggest that you start with the customer complaint and suggestion reports and analyze their requests. See if there is anything more we could do to satisfy our customers. I would also be keen to see the statistics of how many of our customers have problems or requests on what type of items. A type of grouping, categorizing, and organizing the information in some type of tabular forms that can be easier to understand and analyze the information would help me."

It was surprising for him to see that Bernard had no interest in releasing any useful information to him. However, he didn't want to insist at this time as he was working here for just over a month. He left Bernard's office saying, "All right, thanks for the tip." As he came out, Aleyna turned to him and smiled. He felt relaxed and calmed down to see her smile. He thought he cannot wait for the Saturday to be with her and talk privately about themselves outside work topics.

CHAPTER 7: NIFFY MEETS BRAWNY

Milton picked her up on Saturday to take her to one of the Japanese sushi shop called Kaiten Sushi. This was a popular place not only among Japanese and other Asians, but also among many Americans and Europeans living around the area. A variety of freshly made sushi would be set on plates on a belt rotating around in the middle in front of the customers sitting around the large circular table so that they could pick any sushi they liked. Milton especially liked that place since it reminded him of the Japanese sushi place called Jaws in his home town Perth. In Kaiten Sushi place, they always served complementary Japanese tea, and they could drink as much as they wanted. Aleyna was impressed with the freshness of the sushi served and the staff's keen attitude to ensure the restaurant was kept very clean with a smile on their face.

For a moment, there was silence felt between Aleyna and Milton; none of them was able to start a conversation. After Aleyna started drinking her tea, she picked up a fresh salmon sushi plate. Then she asked Milton to break the silent mood, "So, what's up in your life?"

Milton replied, "Well, as usual, nothing special."

"Do you come here often?"

"Once in a while, kind of often actually. I like the cleanliness and freshness of the food. It is hard to find such good taste in healthy food."

Aleyna giggled softly, "Yes, I know healthy food doesn't usually have as good taste as unhealthy options, but I think tasty healthy food options have increased a lot in recent years."

Milton nodded his head, agreeing, "Yes, actually there are quite a lot of selections these days."

Milton picked up an eel sushi, "I am going to be adventurous and try some real sushi." She laughed and looked happy chatting with him. Her happy face calmed his slightly nervous feelings, and he asked her, "Do you like animals? Pets?"

Aleyna said, "Oh yes, I love them. I believe animals are very special creatures on this earth, and I like both dogs and cats as pet."

Milton whispered, "I am planning to get a cat."

Aleyna got excited about it and said loudly, "What? A cat?" She continued, lowering her voice, "Wow, that sounds wonderful. I hope you would let me play with your cat sometimes. Cats are very cute and playful." After she paused, "by the way, you don't need to whisper that."

Milton said, "I want to get it from an animal shelter. In Australia, there is a large community-based charity organization that works to prevent cruelty to all animals, including pets and wild animals. We usually adopt from there so that a homeless pet can have a home, and it helps animals in general. My parents have always been a member of the organization to support them. I hope to continue on this tradition in my life."

Aleyna said, "That sounds very nice. I think there are many animals needing our help. Unfortunately, many of them are exposed to horrible cruelty by many sick people or by some unfortunate kids lacking proper parenting. It is good to have some organizations helping them. These organizations should be supported. I think there are also similar organizations here where you can adopt a cat."

Milton said, "Yes, I made a search, and I am going to a shelter this afternoon. You can help me pick one if you don't have other plans, do you?"

Aleyna replied with a cheerful tone, "Oh yeah! I would love to come with you. I have nothing planned. Thank you very much for inviting me."

After enjoying their lunch, they headed for the shelter. When they arrived there, they saw many animals were in need of a home. While they were looking through, one of them got Aleyna's attention. Brawny was a five-year old female cat that lost her one eye in a cruel torture by two teenagers. Brawny was found in a miserable condition, hungry and beaten up, left on the side of a street. The shelter provided treatment and was hoping to find a home where she could be cared for and could continue her life. Brawny was sitting in a corner of her place, watching them with her one eye in her calm and peaceful nature. As Milton and Aleyna approached to her, she got up and walked closer to them in her cage, hoping to be petted. She could sense and distinguish the people who have good feelings for her and have good intentions from those that were heartless and cruel. Marine fell in love with her peaceful and friendly nature almost instantly. She put her fingers through the cage and gently petted her soft and warm brownish fur on her head. Milton also liked her and decided to adopt Brawny.

Milton's android's was one of the NI-50 series. He named him as Niffy. Niffy was mainly using his observations in life to improve his knowledge and skills about human life so that he could serve well. A few months ago, Milton asked him to watch TV to enhance his self-development process and explained to him about how movies and TV programs were made artificially for show, but some of the programs were realistic life issues. Since Milton would be either at school or work for most of the day, there wasn't much opportunity for Niffy to get into socializing and build up its training data. TV sounded like a perfect idea to expand his data set and enhance his self-development.

Since Niffy was very efficient handling the daily works, he was able to finish all house work and shopping in a short time and had plenty of time to watch TV. He started watching a lot of daily drama series and watching Oprah almost every day. If he were a person, one would think he was addicted to watching them. His behavior slowly changed day by day from being a masculine, strongly built android to do tough jobs into being a drama queen. Milton noticed the difference, but he was too late to do anything. Niffy would get emotional and start crying like a 'sensitive human' for any event no matter how minor something was.

Niffy had already bought a fresh water drinking system for Brawny that could be attached to the tap, and water would come to the drinking cup when Brawny drank the water in her cup so that she could always have fresh water. Niffy also bought a wide variety of cat food and a modern cat toilet that could flush the waste and wash itself without creating dust, containing permanent washable granules to satisfy her comfort. Niffy put some dry and some wet cat food in parts of her food plate and set it aside in the kitchen.

When they arrived home, Brawny first behaved shy in her new home and just tried to identify the living room for a while. She kept walking around and checking all the rooms carefully. Then, she came and ate some of the food Niffy put for her. Niffy was just standing next to the wall and watching how she was behaving with curiosity as it was the first time for him to share the house with a pet. Brawny approached Niffy's metallic feet and gently touched his right foot with her paw few times as if she was checking what the foot was made up of. Each time she touched his foot, she looked at it carefully to see if his foot was moving.

As usual, Niffy started to get emotional. He started to show his sensitive side and said, "Oh, how cute she is," and almost started crying. Milton interrupted him quickly not to get embarrassed beside Aleyna, "No, don't even think about it." He felt lucky this time, Aleyna didn't notice what a drama queen his android was.

Niffy slowly kneeled down and petted her head gently. She looked like she enjoyed to be petted by him. When he stopped petting her and stood up straight again, she got on the sofa. After getting on top of the sofa's back, she jumped on Niffy's shoulder surprising them all. Niffy supported her with his hands as she was almost falling down slipping from his metallic shoulder. She could regain her balance on his shoulder with the help of Niffy's hand. She watched around curiously before sitting down on him.

Milton and Aleyna watched her with their eyes wide open, and a smile came out of their faces. They never thought that a cat would prefer to settle on Niffy's metallic shoulder while there were much more comfortable places to sit around. She almost acted as if she knew Niffy prepared for her the delicious food and wanted to show her appreciation. Niffy could sense her soft and warm body on him. He felt proud to be preferred by the new family member. Milton said, "Perhaps, it is the height of Niffy Brawny likes. But whatever the reason is, I am glad to see that Niffy got a new friend."

This preference of Brawny made Niffy emotional again. He started wiping his eye as if he were crying and wiping his tears making a low crying sound. Aleyna got surprised with this strange behavior of the android and asked, "What is going on with him?"

Milton replied, "I am afraid he turned into a drama queen watching daily drama series on TV. I feel bad because it is kind of my fault asking him to watch TV to enhance his training data set. I thought it would help speed-up his self-learning process. Now he has the clustered data problem."

Aleyna started laughing out loud and said, "Oh my god, he looks so funny crying with his big, strong steel-built body." She was unable to control her laugh. "I could never imagine an android with such a big and massive body would cry."

Milton tried to control his laughing and giggled. "I must admit, the big boy's excessive sensitivity is kind of funny." He turned to Niffy and said, "See what you did. You have embarrassed me in front of the lady."

Aleyna asked, looking curious, "What is clustered data problem? I haven't heard of such thing before."

Milton started to explain, "Niffy uses the available training data to figure out how he should behave and respond in a given situation. Each action and each unit of information has certain effects on his behavior and decisions. That system allows him to learn about us and serve us the best possible way. When there is too much information or too many data accumulated around the same topic, it is called data clustering. This can become a problem when the clustering gets excessive because the same content or reactional behavior, would get much more effect than other subjects, breaking the balance. I am hoping it would correct itself if he stops watching TV for a while. That would reduce the density of dramatic data within his training data pool but nobody can tell how long this could take."

Brawny's existence helped strengthen Milton and Aleyna's relationship as Aleyna wanted to stay with her for the night to pet and keep friendship with such a lovely company.

CHAPTER 8: A FOGGY CLUE

It was Milton's third year since he started studying for his PhD degree. One day when he came home, Brawny was alone at home. She was waiting for him to come home in front of the door as always. He tried to contact Niffy with his phone through Niffy's internal communication system, but there was no answer. This was an unusual situation that never happened before. Niffy would always answer the international communication whenever Milton attempted to contact. Even when he analyzed the worldwide customer's complain database, he hadn't seen anything like this. He logged in his computer to see where Niffy was. Niffy's movements were automatically recorded on his computer from Niffy's advanced navigation unit.

The last place Niffy went was the grocery shopping. While he was coming home, the signal was lost. He could see the trace line in his monitor that recorded Niffy's entire path. The line stopped on his way home from the shop without any further trace. Milton immediately went out looking for him. After carefully checking the distances on the Niffy's movements, Milton determined Niffy must have gotten lost around the rail station. When he walked through the station, he saw Niffy lying on his side motionless. He ran to him and carried Niffy back to the car by holding under his arms and dragging him. Niffy was too heavy to pick up; Milton could only drag him leaving Niffy's toes on the ground. He brought Niffy home. It was obvious that Niffy had been hit by a train, but he didn't know how this could have happened.

Milton didn't want to give up Niffy because he felt Niffy had been a good companion for him for the last three years. Niffy's body looked all broken, and his parts were smashed, but his head looked intact with little damage. He immediately started working to repair him. When he went to work next day, he looked exhausted. Bernard saw him looking miserable, and he asked him to come to his office. "Let's get a cup of coffee and chat in my office."

They sat down in Bernard's office. "What's up Milton? What's wrong?"

"My android had a horrible accident. He got hit by a train. Many of his parts were smashed and totally destroyed. I tried to repair him last night, but it will take me a long time."

"I am sorry to hear that," said Bernard. If his android was broken up too badly, it wouldn't be possible for Bernard to keep an eye on what he does every day. That would be a big risk for him to lose control. He generously offered, "Well, don't worry too much about it. We can replace with a new one. You can choose any android and take it."

Milton had an emotional attachment to his android. He did not see Niffy just as a machine due to years of memories formed living together. He treated him like a family member, a companion, and a good friend. He replied without hesitation, "Thank you, that's very generous of you, but I'd rather keep this android. However, I would appreciate if you could give me some new parts I need to repair him."

Bernard was keen getting Milton's android fixed as soon as possible. "No problem. Just give me the list of the parts that you need. I'll have them sent directly to your home. I think you should take today off. Get some rest."

Milton worked on Niffy every night for hours after coming home from work. After Niffy's power circuits were replaced, he tried to communicate with Niffy. "Hello, Niffy. Time to wake up." He paused for a while, there was no response. Then he asked repeatedly, "Can you hear me?"

Niffy opened his eyes and replied while the tiny light in his eyes started to swing side to side, "Yes, I can hear you."

"Do you know what happened to you? Can you tell me?"

Niffy started to explain, "I was taking a shortcut to come home and wheeling through the station. There were some teenagers standing and waiting for the train. When I approached to them, I moved closer to the rail track to pass around them. One of them suddenly jumped in front of me, kneeling down. I jumped over him to avoid hitting him and causing damage to him. When I jumped, two of them pushed me in front of a passing-by cargo train."

Milton got very upset and angry to hear Niffy was actually attacked while trying to avoid injuring the teenagers. He said, "Unfortunately, when some teenagers lose their self-confidence to achieve anything in life by themselves, they get together with other losers to form gang groups. They often do stupid things including attacking others like a bunch of mad dogs that got rabies. Don't worry my friend. I'll fix you up."

Niffy was conscious enough to notice Milton had been working until late to fix him every day and not getting much sleep. He asked, "Why didn't you terminate me?" He was just a robot, and his chips didn't calculate Milton's behavior to work many hours to fix him as logical. A human was making sacrifices from his personal life for a machine while he was expecting to be terminated. Niffy was unable to understand why his feelings and emotions could possibly lead him to work on him instead of getting a new android. Niffy's drama queen attitude wasn't caused by any real emotion, but formed from his training data clustering around the drama concept within his main processing unit. The machine could not have real feelings and emotions. Although he was an extremely advanced model of android series, he was not developed enough to fully understand human behavior.

Milton tried to explain him, "Niffy, you have been here for three years, and you have helped me in my life all the time. I couldn't progress in my studies and continue working at the same time without your help. You've never asked anything from me, you were always here when I needed someone to talk to," said Milton with an emotional tone in his voice. He continued after a short pause, "No, my friend. You may be a robot, but you are my best friend. Friends don't give up on each other. After I am done, you'll be better than ever."

Niffy started to close his eyes and open them as if he were crying again, but he was unable to move his hands to wipe his tears. Few drops of liquid came down his cheeks from his eyes. This time, Niffy's emotional facial expression and crying affected Milton also. Some tears started to run down through Milton's cheeks. To change the emotional mood, Milton said, "I am not sure if this is a good news or bad news." He paused for a moment, wiping his tears and said, "Unfortunately, your training dataset seems OK," and giggled slightly.

Niffy was not really sure how to respond except crying to show his appreciation. He was a machine, and his advance Neuro Artificial Intelligence based programs in his chips were all confused. A human was treating him just like a human, even more like a friend and a member of his family. He had the ability to learn as he experienced in life, but the programming models of its chips on emotions and feelings were not as good to understand all about human. Milton's words and efforts to save him were recorded in his core memory system as part of training data to be used in his self-learning units. Niffy said while crying, "Thank you for that. I am happy to be your friend." Although Niffy didn't have the feeling for happiness when he said that, he had appreciation and he knew what that meant in human life. His appreciation would translate to these words in the language.

Niffy stopped crying and turned his head toward Brawny sitting next to him and said, "Since you are re-building me, can I ask a small favor?"

Milton got curious as he couldn't think of what a machine could possibly need, "Only if it is something I can do."

Niffy said with a smile, "Yes, I am sure you can fit a place on my left shoulder for my friend to stay comfortable." He paused pointing to Brawny with his eyes and continued, "It would really help us to walk around together sometimes." Milton was happy to see Niffy and Brawny were good friends. Brawny was always staying around Niffy as if she knew something was wrong, and she was trying to comfort him.

For a month, Milton worked on Niffy every night for many hours. Niffy was almost fixed completely again. Milton fitted additional metallic parts outside Niffy's legs to serve as a standing platform. When he wanted to go somewhere with Niffy, the metallic piece would extend out and flatten itself so that Milton could stand on it as Niffy moves. Milton was just working on the final adjustment of Niffy's legs for balanced movements. While he was chatting with Niffy, Milton opened up the subject about their NAI chip structures and programming models. He asked, "Do you know how Bernard could model your chips? Which techniques and methods were used in your chips?"

Niffy replied, "I don't have access to the NAI model field in the data base."

Milton stopped and stared at Niffy, "What?"

Niffy said, "There is a system error. I told you confidential information. My system was supposed to prevent me to reveal it. My chips received a warning informing me about the confidentiality. It was a system error."

Milton was confused, "I don't know what you are talking about."

Niffy explained him, "The confidentiality code works through my chip's external connection system where the confidential chips and energy reactor are located. These systems are connected to my main external processing system with a set of steel pins. These pins and the box are equipped with a self-destroying mechanism. In the case of any damage occurring to the sealed box or these pins, the self-destroying system would explode. The box protecting the company's confidentiality would be destroyed by terminating myself."

Milton interrupted him, "I know all that already, I don't get your point."

Niffy continued, "There is a damage a scratch in one of those connection pins in my sealed box. When the train crushed me and squeezed me between the side walls along the rail tracks and the train's steel-cast wheels, the wheels crushed my main processing unit, causing a strong torque on my connection pins. Luckily for me, when the damage occurred, the NAI program chips recognized it as being accidental and did not calculate it as an attempt to violate confidentiality protocols. That prevented the self-destruction mechanism to get activated. The scratch on the pin was one of the security lines, signaling system that was designed to ensure the security."

Milton said, "I see. Thanks for the enlightenment, but did you just say that you can access the central database?"

Meanwhile Niffy was getting some signals on its main chips. He knew a new program had just been attempted to download in him. At first, the downloading failed. There were some damages on his external data downloading systems also. However, the external downloading attempt was repeated, and in the third attempt, the download was successful. He could not confirm Milton's question as his external data on the main processing system was not matching the data within NAI chip processing system. His tiny circular red eyes kept swinging left to right, right to left as he stood for a while with emotionless cold steel face. Then, he said, "System error. No confirmed information could be found."

Milton asked, "What happened? What's going on?"

"New updates have been installed in my main NAI chips. There is no information about a central database in my main chips," said Niffy.

Milton asked, "What about your external memory – external processing system?"

Niffy replied, "Yes, that is very strange, but according to my external memory unit, I have access to the central database."

Milton was thinking that Niffy was talking about their central database in Chicago. He had partial access, but he was hoping to get more information through Niffy and he was excited about it. He thought he could analyze the entire data and produce some work useful for the company. He had not been producing any significant work so far, and he was not expected to do so. However, he believed he had to do whatever is the best thing to do as part of his professional integrity and moral sense. He said with an excited voice, "Great you can access our entire database in Chicago."

Niffy replied, "I did not mean the database in Chicago. The location is not correct, exact location is unknown."

Milton was surprised, "What do you mean, Niffy? Do you mean our office in another state, which one?"

Niffy replied with his robotic voice, "No, it is in outer space, but exact coordinates are unknown."

Milton was surprised and shocked to hear about the existence of a database in space. He was not sure what this meant, but he was sure something was happening beyond anyone's knowledge. He thought of the possibility of alien involvement in all these new technologies offered by the company, but there was no solid evidence to prove it. He wished Niffy could be more descriptive, but he knew well Niffy's access was too restrictive. He could not be sure if Niffy was referring to a type of database in a satellite or space station sent from earth by the company or perhaps aliens. Then he thought, *No, there couldn't be such things as aliens.* It made more sense for him to think that the company must have sponsored NASA to send a space station to settle in an orbit and keep all the confidential information in the space. That would surely be more secure than holding it in an office computer. While his mind wandered in thoughts, he finalized repairing Niffy at that night. He decided not to talk about this to Bernard until he got more information.

CHAPTER 9: PLANET ZOLA

Zola was a planet in a solar system far from Milky way and far from Earth. Zolans had been living a peaceful life for thousands of years. They were observing Earth; collecting data about how the life was evolving and the way life was developing on the planet. They tried to avoid causing any interference that had a chance of negatively effecting Earth's destiny in any way. They wanted to wait until Earth reached a higher level of civilization and technological level to communicate. Zola had a ruling council formed of ten members and one leader. The council was formed many years ago by the people with high level of wisdom and desire to serve for the best interest of the public in the planet. The council could decide to replace their members if they thought necessary or if a member resigns from the council. They would select the person who they believed had the highest wisdom and values among them to trust as the planet's leader.

In Zola, they maintained their lives by drinking a pack of liquid produced in specialized facilities every day. Their daily nutrition requirements were determined through a tiny chip inserted on the back of their neck when they were born. The chip analyzed the body's condition, and the information was automatically loaded into the food production facility's database. Based on the daily information, each individual's drink pack were produced and delivered to them during night. When it arrived, the android serving as maid brought it to the kitchen. They drank it in the morning to sustain their healthy life.

They would wear a necklace that would activate a light, making the bodies invisible as if they were wearing clothes. The color and design of the appearance of the light on their body would differ, depending on the individual's taste. The design and color of the clothes would be selected with tiny buttons in the necklace with the help of holographic reflected images while setting up a design.

They had many androids that were being used for different purposes, including helping them in their daily lives at home, in construction works, risky works for people, engineering type of works, building other androids in factories, and other production plants. Many of the androids were highly skilled to improve their learning from their life experiences through advanced Neuro Artificial Intelligence models developed in Zola. Some of the androids were serving

127

in the security organizations to protect the peaceful life style. Only these androids were allowed to carry laser guns. They were also programmed to be able to kill or capture anyone who would break the law. Although they had the ability to kill and had high-level programs to perform martial arts, they could only use their skills if there were orders from the highest level of ruling, decision by the council. Especially, killing was something they could only do if it was an order from the leader of Zola together with the council's unanimous decision. They didn't need to kill anyone for thousands of years since there was rarely a criminal event on the planet.

They had adapted the law of origin as their main principle of ruling, which stated all creatures universally had the right to live. Most of them believed they were the same as humans on Earth, which they also called Earthians. They believed that Earthians would also evolve and technologically develop by time to come to Zola's level of civilization. Until Earth reaches to a certain level of civilization and wisdom, they were not to interfere with the fate of Earth. They would only provide help, keeping themselves hidden if they think their help is crucially important for humans. In the past, they invited some humans into their ships to teach their language to assure smooth communications in the future. Although they could use translators, they thought direct communication could be important to understand the true meanings behind the spoken words. Teaching the Earthians their language could also help them develop faster. Those who learned the language spread it throughout their societies. Even though some of them broke their promises to keep Zola's existence a secret, they were not able to convince the others to the alien's existence. They had no physical evidence to prove their claims.

Serium, the leader of Zola, had strong beliefs for their laws. He also had a strong view about letting the life on Earth define its own future and its own destiny. He felt admiration when he saw people caring about other life forms and each other without expecting anything in return, a pure act of kindness. There were times he felt sorrow and deep sadness when he saw Earthians killing each others, animals, and destroying plants on Earth for no logical reason that he could see to cause the actions. However, he always believed that the good will deep in humans would eventually dominate on Earth. One day, humans would find out about the universal balance. They would eventually understand the balance, which would lead them to move toward a life style of harmony with nature. He was emotionally attached to Earth.

He loved looking at the animals in the forests, the oceans, and enjoyed the sound of African wilderness recorded on their exploration data system. He would listen to them often as if it was his favorite symphony.

Zola had plants, trees, vegetables, and wild animals living all together. They built skyscrapers for themselves so that they could let trees, forests, and animals continue their lives on the ground between high-rise buildings and cities while Zolans lived at much higher level than the trees could reach. They had bridges going between buildings high in the sky, over the trees to enjoy walking and watching the green forests under their feet. Only birds and some exceptionally tall trees could reach to the level of these bridges serving as walking paths. These paths kept them integrated with the surrounding nature. They built the city in a way that they could preserve dense forests together with the many living species within. They believed people's life had to exist in harmony with nature to sustain the balance.

Zola had been using a type of radioactive mineral called *ranoxus* as their energy source. Their energy production technology was extremely efficient, and they were not producing any radioactive waste after using the material.

They could produce enormous amounts of energy from small quantities of ranoxus. However, after using the resources for many years, they were approaching the end of their energy source. They still had sufficient energy to live for 50 years, but there were some among them who were keen to take action very soon. Especially one of them, a council member, called Vortek had dangerous ideas. Their energy source could be replaced by uranium available on Earth that initiated the chain of events that would challenge Earth.

About fifteen years ago, Zola's former leader resigned from his leadership due to his increased age when he was 238 years old. The average life expectancy in Zola was around two hundred fifty years although some lived as long as three hundred years. Serium was a council member when the council selected him as the leader of Zola. Vortek was the chief commander, the head of the planet's security organization. The council members wanted to select him to fill Serium's position in the council. Serium was against him joining the council. He said, "Time and time, Vortek indicated his lack of faith for the law of origin publicly. This attitude and public expression against the law is not appropriate, especially considering he is the commander to protect it."

A council member said, "I believe he can change if he spends more time among us. I am sure he will understand the true meaning of the universal balance and the link between the origin and the cycle of life." Although Serium voted against him, the council selected him as a member.

It was ten years ago when Vortek brought up the energy topic in the council's meeting as he was doing almost in every meeting in recent years.

The council would regularly meet in the council's house to discuss Zola's matters. The council house was a large room decorated with comfortable sofas and some chairs. Vortek stood up in the meeting to speak to the council's members, "Dear members, as we all know, we have only forty years of energy resources in our main reactors and less than ten years of resources in the auxiliary emergency systems. Our exploration ships have identified a mineral that has the same characteristics as ranoxus on Earth. They call it uranium. They have sufficient uranium that can last millions of years for us."

Serium interrupted his talk, "It is not our uranium. It belongs to them. Besides, fifty years is enough time for us to find a resource around our solar system or even to find a different energy system. Earth is not ready for us to interfere, yet. We have time. We can wait fifteen more years. We need to use this time to slowly engage level that would make it easier for us to introduce ourselves and to make peaceful trading."

Vortek said, "We don't have time; we don't have another way to produce energy and not another source. We have already searched everywhere in our solar system and others. The radioactive elements in other planets have different characteristics and are not suitable for our plants. Uranium is the only mineral that can work just like ranoxus. We should not wait any longer. It takes us a year to reach Earth and come back with our fastest cargo ships fitted with proto-photon engines going through the black gates. We might encounter problems. We might need the time until we get the resources. We have to keep Zola's needs above all others. We should go there to take all we need by any means necessary. I urge the council to take action."

Serium replied with a loud voice, "What do you mean 'by any means'? Declare war? I want to remind you that it is against our law, the law of origin, to kill other lives in the universe. Our laws clearly indicate humans on Earth are the same just like us. They are made up of the same DNA coding module with the same chromosome structure."

Vortek reacted to him with anger, "If war is what is necessary for us to take the uranium, then so be it. Humans are primitive creatures. We should not tie ourselves with the old beliefs and some rules that are made up thousands of years ago. We can ask them to trade with us. If they are civilized enough, they will trade it with us. If they don't mind leaving us in the dark to our extinction, rejecting any trade, then a war is what they deserve."

Serium started to explain, "We are the same people as them. Let us not forget how the Zola was established."

A council member continued on Serium's words, "Yes, Serium is right. We should never forget the past and respect our laws. Four hundred thousand years ago, there was a planet called Zola just on the orbit where Earth is now. That planet had a highly developed society established. They were living in peace and comfort, but they ignored nature's law for the balance. They identified the atmospheric balance was getting damaged by the developing technology. What a pity it was, they chose to ignore it not to give up their comfort. The planet started to have harsh weather, unusually large tsunamis, earthquakes, and floods. Unfortunately, atmosphere's balance was lost beyond a level for nature to repair it by the activities within Zola's atmosphere. Nature made the decision that there was only one thing that could fix the problem; nature's one of the most powerful tool for fixing the balance. It was the *reformation of the planet*. So, the nature chose to create an event, one-in-a-billion chance event, and freed up a huge planet off its orbit. Nature threw the giant planet toward the Earth's predecessor, Zola. While our ancestors, scientists of the time, were on a research mission in space far from the planet, the deadly crash occurred as they watched with their own eyes. Nothing could stop it. Neither the most powerful nuclear rockets nor their proton bombs could divert it from its path. Huge planet turned into huge fire ball, massive clouds of dust and hot gasses spread around the empty space. Earthians believe their planet is older than 4.5 billion years, but what they haven't found out is those rocks they have tested included Zola's rocks and also the particles of the planet crashed.

"Our ancestors, twenty eight of them gathered for a scientific mission to analyze the atmosphere's contents and perform experiments to understand the implications of the ongoing changes in the atmosphere's structure. They were from different regions of the Zola and were selected as the top scientists in their regions. They were the only survivors from the planet. They had been working in space for the fifth year when the disaster appeared. Zolans were too late to change their life for balancing the conditions. They also helped the ground by launching some rockets, and heavy bombs from their space station. Their efforts failed. Their ship was built with sufficiently advanced technology to sustain their life for many years. They were lucky to find the black gate in the solar system after wandering in the empty space for decades. They could travel through the gate to reach our system. Their children, born in the ship, found this planet and called it *Zola* for the memory of the Zola. They had the knowledge of nuclear energy, and they built the first nuclear energy plant using ranoxus.

"The children of our ancestors watched and saw how Earth's moon was formed. They observed every step of the moon and the planet's reforming from the dust and hot gases. They documented it in the Theory of Origin procurement for us, not to forget who we are and not to make the same mistakes. They watched how the ponds of fire and magma attracted back together with their gravity force and formed the large core. Then, the heavy core attracted all the dust particles back to itself. The large pieces broken from Earth formed the moon by time. The humans of Zola were in the form of molecules and dust. Some of these molecules were trapped within the tiny particles of rocks and dusts in the space. These molecules waited for thousands of years for the planet to reform itself and gain the conditions necessary for life. When the planet was ready, the tiny molecules came back to life. Our ancestors watched how the small tiny bacteria formed and then evolved to form the variety of life on the planet they called Earth. We have watched ourselves thousands of years. Humans have developed in technology and mind continuously."

Vortek said, "Yeah, yeah... we know all about it, but it is just a myth, and it is a very old one. We cannot continue believing to the same myth that has no real evidence."

Serium said, "It is a fact and that is what happened. The similarities in the DNA coding and structure of chromosomes are the evidences that cannot be ignored. You are caught in the fact cycle of time. Time changes everything, even the solid facts; facts become history, history becomes myth, and myths are forgotten by most. That is what time does. We should not let the cycle impact us and not forget the facts. It is also our law."

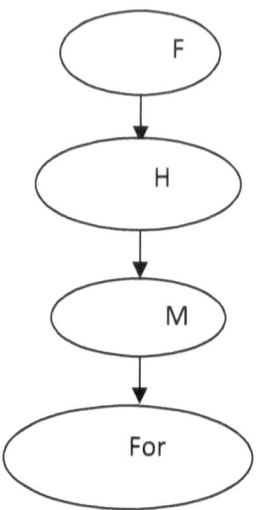

Figure 1. Fact cycle for the downward time flow direction

Vortek said with frustration, "We cannot continue living on with the stories of the past. We have a challenging problem ahead of us, and we are running out of time. We are getting into a serious energy shortage. We may not survive if we don't act soon. We must get on the way to Earth and take what we need. If you are right and they are like us, they would trade or share with us. But I know why you are worried about starting a war, Serium. You, in fact, believe they are not like us, and they wouldn't be willing to trade it. They are only good for making weapons. Without us having the energy resources, they might come to a strong level to challenge us. We have not developed any significant weapon to defend ourselves for the sake of peace. If they reject us, we will not be in a position to force them in the future. Our torpedoes and little laser guns will be no match for strong weapons of mass destructions produced on Earth. To save our planet, we must act now, and we must act wisely."

Serium said, "You have no intention for a peaceful approach. You only want destruction. There will be no war because we will be patient and wait. They would certainly trade with us for technology. Earthians are civilized society, but we just have to be patient for the right time to come. We have lived in peace and harmony for thousands of years within the universe. We must continue the same way."

Vortek was observing the council members' gestures to understand what they were thinking. He thought most of them were convinced. He confidently suggested, "I request council's voting on this issue. It is time for a change and for action. I suggest we take a ship and go to Earth. We approach peacefully and ask for trades. If they trade with us, we can offer them technology. With all respect, I want the council to recognize the fact that the time left is not much to find a new resource. If we wait, Earth will surely produce even stronger weapons than the ones they have produced so far. They might reject us and destroy us. As a matter of fact, they might even destroy Earth itself, which is not a negligible chance considering the aggression exists in their nature. They are different creatures, no resemblance to us. We are a civilized society."

Serium calmly sat on a chair and responded, "Since you asked for a voting, you must respect the council's saying. I recommend council to vote 'no' to Vortek's proposal. I believe if we can wait twenty five, or even thirty years and start introducing ourselves slowly, we don't lose anything. We have enough energy to wait. We can go to Earth when the time is right, and it is not now."

Council members voted 'no' to Vortek's proposals. They didn't think there was any urgency at the moment considering the sufficient resources for the next fifty years. Serium didn't believe that Vortek's intention was to approach Earth with peace and to make trade. Other council members also were not convinced with his proposal.

Vortek became angry about the council's decision. He shouted at the council, "Zola is running out of time for the energy. We are moving toward dark times. We will not survive without energy, but all of you want to just sit and do nothing. That is outrageous and beyond any healthy mind's thinking." He started walking fast toward the exit.

Serium quickly got up and stood in front of him. He said, "This is the council's decision. You may not agree with it, but you must respect and obey it."

Vortek's face was red from anger. He said, "Get out of my way, Serium," while gritting his teeth in anger. Then he walked out of the council's house and went to his work office at his home.

CHAPTER 10: ASSASSINATIONS ON ZOLA

Vortek had different plans about Earth. He was using the lack of energy source as an excuse to proceed with his plans and get the council's permission to legalize his actions. He was ambitious to gain power and rule the universe. His extraordinarily high skills in the dark art of manipulation helped him to achieve a member position within the planet's most respected and prestigious foundation, Council's House. However, his plans didn't work out this time as he wanted. When he returned to his office at home, he was angry and frustrated. He called his friend Misha who was assigned as the chief commander to take Vortek's place when he joined the council. She arrived quickly, worried about him.

Vortek saw her through the opening of his office door when the Misha reached the hall. She looked fashionable, as usual, in her designer selection —a tight stretchy mini skirt around her hips and a black lace strip coming from both her shoulders to cover her perfectly shaped chest, and both ends extending to under her skirt forming a transparent V-shape over her body. Vortek called her, shouting out, "Come in Commander, I am over here."

She entered to the office and asked, "What's the problem Vortek, you seem worried."

Vortek said, "Yes, I am worried all right. Listen, Misha! We have a problem in our planet. Our planet and our people are running out of time. We got a very serious problem, but the council members chose to sit on their arses without moving a finger. I can't just sit and watch Zolans get buried in darkness."

She said, "What do you mean, Vortek?"

Vortek said, "We are running out of energy. We have some energy sources left, but not for long. We know there is plenty of uranium on the planet Earth. We can go there and take it. However, our dear council members prefer to do nothing about it. I think we can no longer sit and wait. We can't continue wasting time with the old stories of the origin. We have to take action."

She said, "We must follow the council's decisions. We can't do anything without their approval. —Paused for a moment— Why do you say stories of origin? As a chief commander of security, I believe I don't need to remind you that I protect the law of origin."

Vortek said, "Come on! It is a story we have been told for hundreds of thousands of years. It is a well-established fact through the information we have been receiving from our exploration ships that the humans living on Earth is a primitive organism, not like us. Our obligations must lie here. We must protect Zola's interest above all. If we wait, Earth is advancing more and more in weaponry technology while we are getting into further energy shortage. If we don't act now, and they reject helping us later, we will all die. We cannot rely on the bullshit about how similar we look. That would be a stupid risk to take and a huge one. We must act now."

Misha asked curiously, "What are you suggesting we do?"

Vortek sat back on his chair calmly and started to scan through her body, from top down, with his staring eyes. Misha wasn't bothered with his sympathy, but rather she enjoyed getting attention. She also sat on a chair across his table and settled with comfort, slightly opening her legs. She felt proud of her body shape and pleased to see people appreciated her attractive feminine features.

Vortek said, "People with view and strength should be ruling us. Perhaps, one with an exceptionally attractive look, a great body, and the right fashion taste, like you,

Commander, should be our leader. Not some cowards who don't want to move their fingers to save Zola."

Misha said, "Thanks for the complement, but I am not so sure about that. Our system has worked for so long. There was peace and ..."

Vortek interrupted, "Commander, please, trust me! It is time for a change. We have never faced such a big challenge so far, and that's why we need to change things around here. We need a brave leader who will act strongly for the best interest of Zola. You are a woman with strong character and vision, which makes you the ideal one to be the leader. You don't need the council and neither does the Zola."

Vortek's suggestion sounded interesting to Misha. It was like a dream to be the leader for the great Zola. However, she wasn't sure if it could ever be possible and how it could ever happen. She said, "It sounds like a dream and a very nice dream, but I think it will always have to stay as a dream. It is not an easy task to take over the planet's ruling and change the system."

Vortek gave a short laugh, "Huh ha huh, don't disturb your beautiful head with the technical details. I have plans

145

and implementation would be much easier than you can imagine. You just trust me and support the process of change."

She smiled and said, "Well, I don't know of your plans, but if you have plans easy to implement as you say, I ensure you'll have my full support to secure a sustainable energy source and safe future for Zola."

Vortek said, "We must keep our conversation between us for now. We must be prepared to take over the authority from the council and save our planet. You will be a powerful leader, a great queen for Zola."

Misha said, "People love the council members. They would die for them. We will face strong opposition and it won't be easy to find support against the council."

Vortek said, "Don't forget I am a council member, too, a member with plans. I suggest you don't under estimate your powers as you are in charge of the security forces. You are the one who controls all in the security organization. You need to find as many support as you can get within the security force. Meet me next week and let me know who are on our side by then. We must know the ones who we can trust."

Misha said, "I'll try and see how much support we can get."

"You should use your power, power of a queen to give power. Talk to those who are ambitious and keen to get ahead, but you need to be discreet about the details. We don't want to make a false announcement as if we were against Zola's system. All we want to tell them is that things will change, and if they want to get promotions and benefits in the new Zola, they must choose their sides carefully."

The chief commander of the security left his office to gather support within the security organization. Vortek had already planned what he wanted to do, but he needed some support to implement his plans. A week later, Commander Misha returned with three other officials with her. One of them was a captain of a large spaceship mainly used for exploration in the universe and experimenting in far planet outside Zola's solar system. The other two were security officers in charge of the two security units each containing 250 officers and a thousand androids based in Zola's metropolitan capital. She convinced them by promising prospects and power to those under their commands if they help in the process of change. Vortek explained to them how the council took a passive approach while Zola was facing a real challenge for survival.

The officers believed her and Vortek that the council was watching Zola's end and not acting when needed. They would take over the Zola's ruling and be heroes by bringing infinite source of energy to their planet. They could have anything they wanted in Zola as they would be the highest power of authority. They were in charge of the security organization, and it would be easy for them to use part of the security forces now.

Vortek asked the two officers to go to the council's house to watch and report in when all the council members arrived. A security guard under the command of one of the officers soon reported back to him to inform that they all arrived in the council's house. Vortek and Misha got into her vehicle, which had laser guns and torpedoes mounted on. In the planet, all security vehicles were fitted with laser guns, but only high level officials would also have torpedoes fitted on their vehicles.

The commander's vehicle was a medium-size ship that could take off from the standing position and fly to any destination requested. Similar vehicles were used as Zolans's main transportation system and everyone had one. The only difference was that the vehicles used by the public did not have any weapons on them. As they got on the way to the council's house, Vortek said, "We have to eliminate all the council members. You kill them all and leave Serium to me."

When they arrived in the council's house, Misha ordered one of the officers and the captain to stay in front of the door and not let anyone in. She, Vortek, and another officer entered the council's house with their guns while all of the council's members were inside.

One of the council members reacted instantly and got up from his chair, "You cannot enter here with weapons. You must"

Vortek shot him with his laser gun on his heart before he could finish his words. The member fell down and died instantly. Serium quickly jumped down to check on him, but he could see it was too late. Then, Vortek shot and killed another council member.

Serium shouted, "Stop it, Vortek, you are mad."

Vortek nodded his head signaling the others to kill them all.   Misha and his friend shot and killed the council's members.   Only Serium was left alive.   They put laser handcuffs on him.

Vortek said, "Serium, do you know why I didn't kill you?"

Serium looked at the commander and other officer who killed the council.   He shouted at them, "You stupid murderers, what did he promise you. Vortek is mad. How can you—"

Vortek punched him with his right fist and said, "When I am talking to you, you must be talking to me, not to my friends. Well, I'll tell you why you are still alive. I wanted you to see the truth, to witness how barbaric and primitive the Earthians are. Then you will know you were wrong to keep your position against me. When you knew your council friends had died for the primitive humans, you will feel the pain of regret and sorrow." He walked closer to Serium and continued, "After you experience and see the reality, I will let those barbarians kill you. The ones you were risking your life for, your dead friends' lives in the council, and everyone's life on Zola will torture you. Those Earthians will make you taste the true pain as they chop you off in pieces with their sharp cutting tools. That is exactly what you deserve for your stupidity."

Vortek said to others, "Lets' go and take him with us. We have work to do." While they were leaving the council house another guard saw them. He hesitated at first, not knowing what was happening. Then he noticed the handcuffed Serium and tried to pull his gun to save him, but Misha's friend shot him to dead. They got on their ship and took off from the council's platform.

Vortek said to her, "Head for the main energy station."

She asked, "What are you planning?"

Vortek said, "If we lose one of our main energy stations accidentally, there will be no opposition for us to go to Earth and bring infinite energy source. We will accidentally blow it off with a torpedo."

Serium reacted, "You can't do that. There are hundreds of people working at that station. Vortek, you have to stop this madness."

Vortek said, "You have to shut up and just enjoy the show. It is necessary to sacrifice some lives for the greater good."

Serium attempted to stop him by throwing himself toward him and hitting his face with his head. Vortek lost his balance for a moment. However, Misha hit his head from behind with her gun and made him fall down unconscious.

The vehicle turned to the power station and fired a torpedo that looked like a fireball with a dark blue color in the core surrounded by colorless transparent layer and covered by strong fire on the most outer layer. The torpedo hit the main core of the power station, and everything exploded into air. There was a huge bright fire rising to the sky. The power station was burned in the fire, killing everyone in and around it.

They went to Vortek's office and locked Serium in the back section of his office. They headed back to the council's house. Guards working for Misha cleared the house, taking the dead bodies of council members away. She organized a media meeting for Vortek to explain the events to the public. She destroyed all the security video images that recorded their murder.

She stood beside Vortek while he talked to the media members including main TV networks broadcasting the meeting live. "There was a series of unfortunate events in the council house. Serium proposed that a large size ship got organized to go to the planet Earth and bring new energy source that can be used to supply energy for Zola for many years. He claimed the energy source could last for thousands of years, or even for a million year. However, the council members were against the idea of interfering with humans on Earth at this time. Serium got in to an argument and lost his control. Unfortunately, he was able to grab the commander's gun to shoot all other members. After he killed them, he got off on a ship and escaped. On his way, he blew out the main power station without considering the lives of hundreds of people working in it. I share the pain for the families and friends of the victims. I offer my sincere condolences for those who lost their loved ones." He paused for few seconds pretending to cry in deep sadness before he continued.

"Unfortunately, he destroyed one of our major energy reactors that could supply us sufficient energy for twenty years. He wanted to force us to take action in his proposal to go to Earth and bring a type of mineral called uranium to use as energy source. We captured him at my place while he was attempting to kill myself. I was injured on my nose when he tried to kill me."

Many Zolans were convinced with Vortek's story since he was also a member of the most respected council's house. The chief commander of the security forces was also there to support his story. There were some Zolans who knew Serium well and knew his views against interfering with Earth. However, they were powerless since Vortek was the only survivor among the council members, and he declared himself as the new leader for Zola. His leadership declaration was not done by the council members since none of them was alive. It was done with an act of urgency by himself, ignoring their traditions. His declaration was supported by the security forces. The public didn't reject it as they felt there was no other option since he was the only living member. As long as Vortek had the full support from the security forces, he was safe. There was nothing that could prevent him implementing his plans.

Later in the day, there was only Vortek and Misha in the council's house. Vortek said, "There is nothing that can stop us now. We will save Zola, not just taking the uranium from

Earth, but we will crush them and make them kneel for us. We will rule the universe together."

Misha said, "I don't know a lot about the planet Earth, but I've heard they are not as much developed as us in technology and science. However, as you said, they must have developed strong weapons."

Vortek laughed loudly, "Ha ha ha... ha ha ha ha... My friend, don't make me laugh. Are we going to afraid of a bunch of primitive creatures? I know we haven't produced weapons because of our stupid council being stuck in the peace mentality, but I don't need any weapons to conquer Earth. Let's not forget our shields also. Their weapons cannot penetrate through our strong shields."

She looked puzzled, "How else can it be done without using any weapon? How can you force them kneel to you?"

Vortek replied, sounding proud of himself, "I know them. I know how they think and how they live. I have been studying our exploration data, pictures and video images for many years since I was assigned as the commander of the security forces. We will use a type of simple weapon, our technology. All we need is a puppet over there, and it cannot be that difficult to find one. I know it is not."

Commander sat back and relaxed in a comfortable position in the chair. She crossed her arms over her belly and said, "I am listening."

Vortek said, "I will leave the leadership of Zola to you. I need someone I can fully trust here. I want you to prepare for my journey. I will take one of our ships ready to travel to Earth. I need some smaller ships to land on Earth. I think our friend, the captain can manage the ship."

She said, "That would be easy to manage."

Vortek continued, "I need as many androids as you can load in the ship —androids of engineers, builders and mostly security guards. All the androids also need a kind of security protection system. There should be enough androids to establish a production line to produce other androids with needed skills. The guard androids must have cover up programs."

Misha said, "I am guessing these androids are not for your service. I mean, what about the ownership registry?"

Vortek held his jaw and scratched with his pointing finger a few times to think, "Excellent point, Commander. They need to be built with a multi-ownership registry system. We want to give some control to our Earthian friends, but I must be registered at the highest level of ownership."

Misha agreed looking curious, "I see. Multiple registries seem like a must for these androids. How about the security and cover-up? Do you have any specifics in your mind?"

Vortek got off his chair and looked out of the window for a minute while he focused his mind on her question. Then he turned back, "Perhaps housemaid service can be used to cover up their main purpose. Earthians would love that; slaves to their jobs."

"Yes, I am sure the androids can be built with multiple characteristics and functionality. I think housemaid cover up is a brilliant idea."

Vortek felt proud to impress Misha, who was sympathized by many on Zola for many reasons. The most important reason was her flawless body shape decorated to perfection with her creative taste of fashion that would bring her up to the attention of anyone's eyes distinctively from the crowds of even thousands. Her fashion taste idolized her among the youth throughout the entire planet. He said with a smile attempted to be hidden, "Thank you, Commander. I feel privileged to be able to impress you. Well, another important issue is the security of our technologies since we wouldn't want Earthians to find out about their technical details. I think the main processing unit and the power generator mechanism must be protected."

Misha said, "I'll forward your requests to the engineers in android production facilities. I am sure they'll know what to do."

Vortek added, "One more thing, make sure our brave security officers and guards who supported us are rewarded generously. I would recommend them to get paid twice the amount of their wages as bonus for making the right choice to join us. The loyalty must always be rewarded, which will secure their trust for us. I would also suggest that it is fair to take 30 percent off from the other guard's next payment as penalty for failing to stop the council members' murder. "

Misha approached and petted his cheek with her left hand gently while saying, "I find your harsh and merciless cold heart almost attractive." She left to go to the central android

158

production plant while Vortek stared at her with a motionless frozen gesture as if he was paralyzed, feeling her silky soft hand on his cheek.

She soon arrived in the fully automated android production facility. As she entered to the visitor's room, an android was standing across the door. She ordered, "Get me the engineer in charge."

The android said, "Yes Commander." Androids had the ability to recognize people from their appearance. They had access to the planet's central database servers that contained information about each individual including their visual images.

In a moment, another android came out. "Have you requested me?"

Misha asked, "Are you the chief engineer?"

The android replied, "Yes, Commander, I am in charge of the overall system design and production."

Misha said, "Great. Walk with me. I have some special requests from our great leader Vortek." They started walking slowly to outside as she continued, "I want one hundred builders and one hundred engineers who are programmed with skills to design and manufacture other androids, to build production plants, energy reactors and similar other things that might be needed."

The android said, "All our engineer androids are loaded with all of the engineering skill programs. So, they are specialized enough to perform any type of engineering tasks."

Misha said, "That is excellent. I also need eight hundred security guards, but I need them to pretend like housemaids until they are asked to switch to being security guards."

The android responded, "That won't be a problem. Our androids can be built flexible to be loaded with programs to behave with multiple characteristics."

Misha asked, "I suppose it will not create any challenge for you to add multi-ownership levels in the registry control, will it?"

The android replied, "No, certainly not. The registry can be customized as you prefer."

Misha turned to him, "Our leader must be registered at the highest level, and his commands must have the authority to overwrite any other commands and controls."

The android replied, "Certainly, Commander."

Misha stopped walking when they got close to her ship and said, "I also need their technology to be inaccessible by any means." She noticed the android looked a bit confused moving his head down and taking time to analyze the meaning of her words. She quickly clarified, "I am talking about protection of the processing unit and the power source."

The android replied not knowing these androids were being intended to be used in a far planet, "The only way to prevent any external access permanently by any means is setting them up with a self-destruction mechanism to destroy their core processing unit and the power generator systems. However, it is impossible to do that without creating some level of risk to cause harm to those around the androids."

Misha looked excited, "Harm? What kind of harm?"

The android said, "A self-destruction mechanism can be fitted by sealing the specific parts within a security box. However, the explosion could be dangerous as it needed to be powerful enough to destroy the security box totally. The strength of the explosion would have potential to damage anything around the android if activated. Client's safety is our top priority in the production system."

She laughed, "That would be excellent. Actually, make it strong enough to ensure a strong blast and total destruction of the box. Ignore the safety."

Android was surprised with this command and found it difficult to understand her. He wanted to re-explain to assure she fully understood the risks involved, "But, the safety is..."

She stopped him with a louder voice, "It is an order from me as a chief commander of the security forces in Zola. Listen to me carefully, chief! When these androids are ordered to switch to security guards, I want them to be able to transform their body to kill enemies in mass numbers. Transform their arms to sharp big cutting tools. I want you be very creative."

The android acknowledge the order, "Yes, Commander."

She could see some worry in the facial expression of the android. She wanted to make him feel comfortable to ensure a smooth process, "You do not need to worry about the safety because they will not be used in Zola, but in a planet far from here. There are those in the universe far from Zola who seek to destroy us and these androids are our only hope to save us. These commands are in fact from our leader Vortek, and I am just forwarding to you. You must make sure everything is done in perfections and exactly as ordered. These androids will be used in a mission that is crucial for us. Don't forget even a small flaw can destroy the future of our own planet."

The android replied with an assuring and confident voice, "I understand, Commander. Please, accept my sincere apologies for behaving nervously on the safety. Your commands will be executed with precision in our facility exactly as you requested."

She smiled, "Excellent. How long would it take?"

The android said, "They will be ready in a month."

She left the production facility feeling proud that she ensured everything would be achieved just as Vortek requested her. A month later, the ship was ready loaded with

163

one thousand androids.   Vortek took Serium with him together with twenty others, who were serving as officers and other technical staff of captain's crew on the ship. They had additional one hundred androids that were built to serve in the ship headed to Earth.

CHAPTER 11: TREASON

Vortek did not load any proton torpedoes or any other type of lethal weapons into the ship. He did not plan to attack Earth directly because he was not sure if their current weapons at Zola were strong enough to win a hot war against Earth or not. He was cautious not to take the risk of being seen and attacked by Earth. He was highly confident on himself that he could destroy Earth by using his superior intelligence and high level of technology in Zola. He knew his plans were extremely simple, but fatal to his enemies. The simplicity of his plans was the main source of his confidence as he was sure there was nothing complicated in his plans that could potentially go wrong and fail him.

During his trip to Earth, he continuously analyzed the exploration database containing the report collected from Earth. It was the most critical part of his plan to find someone on Earth that he could pursue to implement his plans and help him conquer the planet. He wanted someone with ambition, someone strongly intolerant of all others. Vortek knew exactly what type of character he needed for implementing his plans. He worked on the exploration data system every day for many hours.

The ship's captain came to his cabin, "Vortek, you look tired. You have been working here on the database for one month since we left Zola. I suggest you take a break."

Vortek stood up from his chair and walked out with him. "Yes, I think I'll have a break now." They walked to the main deck. The interior walls of the main deck of the ship were entirely covered by special screens. These screens made the side walls appearing like they were transparent directly showing outside just like looking through the window. There were five staff members each sitting in front of a monitor to observe the radar signals, to communicate orders from the deck, and to receive messages from other sections within the ship.

As Vortek and the captain entered the main deck of the ship, Vortek walked closer to the side and asked as he looked into the dark deep space, "Do we have any exploration ship around Earth?"

The captain nodded his head, "Yes, we have two."

Vortek said, "That's great. Ask them to focus on the individuals; those who are influential, have involvement in trading, finance and marketing." Then, he turned back to the captain, "We must find an individual who has a lot of ambition and desire to get ahead in his society."

The captain said, "Should we focus on a certain region? It would increase our chances to find one if we reduce the search space."

Vortek said, "Yes, good point, Captain. Focus on the region that they call *United States*. That region has the most financial influence in the planet."

The captain turned to his android and ordered, "Contact the exploration ships and ask them to carry out the search as Vortek commanded."

The android acknowledged the command, "Yes, Captain!" and walked away.

Exploration ships were sending their reports daily and Vortek spent most of his time analyzing the huge data sets coming into the ship every day. It was almost five months since they left Zola. Vortek was looking into daily images from the reports and listening to the records as usual in his cabin. He was getting frustrated as he was not expecting this to be so much work and take so long. On the other hand, he also didn't want to pick someone who didn't have the exact qualifications he required and cannot serve his purpose. He wanted to make sure the individual would have sufficient influential skills and knowledge to serve him.

Suddenly, his eyes were caught in a video stream containing a marketing manager called Bernard arguing with his supervisor. He smiled with excitement and cheer. He shouted, "That's it, he is the one." Bernard's words that took his attention were, "We should move to produce larger robots instead of these little toys. We can control the world's market..." The key for him was the *"control,"* showing his character almost the same as Vortek's mentality.

He ran to the main deck and screamed, "Captain, Captain" sounding like an overexcited child.

The captain replied with a calm voice, "Yes, Vortek. What made you so happy?"

"We got it! I found him."

The captain stood up from his chair, "Really? That's unbelievable. To tell the truth, I was starting to lose my faith in this mission's success. You can finally relax."

"Yes, yeees," said Vortek as he started calming down. He turned to the android standing next to him and ordered, "Ask the ships to focus on Bernard in report zero-six-zero-seven-slash-F-S [0-6-0-7/F-S]."

The daily reports flowing to the ship all started to focus on Bernard. The more Vortek started to get to know him, the more he felt confident that he was the perfect candidate. He gathered a lot of detailed information about his past, including even his childhood. He was sure it wouldn't be too difficult for him to convince this Earthian man. He could see he was very ambitious, ignorant of others and self-centered. At his job in the toy robot company, he was not satisfied with his marketing job. His ideas were often rejected by his supervisor who was also the company's owner. His company's lack of concentration on the profit, and their policies made up as if they were a non-profit organization to satisfy children's feelings were illogical for him. This illogical business approach was driving him totally crazy.

Vortek watched the reports with relaxed mood and enjoyment as if it was an entertainment show. One day, he was on the main deck watching one of the video streams in his twenty-seven-inch monitor on his desk. He called,

"Captain,", laughing loudly, "Ha ha ha, look at this," He paused and directed the video stream to the larger main monitor across the wall so others could see it.

He commanded to the android, "Bring me Serium." Serium was being kept in a small locked cabin room. An android entered the main desk first, and Serium followed him with the second android behind him. Serium stood with his hands cuffed between the two androids. Vortek said after he started playing the video, "I thought you might have gotten bored staying in your cabin so long. I found some entertainment for you."

In the video report, Bernard was again arguing with the company's owner. "You are the owner of this company. I cannot understand why you are against increasing the profit margin. We don't need to use that supplier to buy the raw material. There are many other suppliers ready to provide all we need for much cheaper prices."

The owner interrupted, "Yes, I am the owner. Cheaper plastics from other suppliers are not recyclable, and they are not as durable as the material we are currently using. They also carry the risk of causing health problems due the chemicals in their structure. The toys wouldn't last long if we used the cheap materials."

"So what if they break sooner than the toys we are making now? That would even increase our profit more as many families would have to buy more often for their kids," said Bernard as he looked stressed from his boss's comments.

"We don't need the extra profit that would damage our reputation and cost us our moral and integrity. We have to stick with our values that cannot be traded for money," said the boss calmly.

"How about making bigger, more realistic toys? We can increase the profit substantially. There is demand, we can grow the business," Bernard said with a louder voice as he was getting excited talking about profit and growth with his ideas. He was also getting frustrated as his suggestion to change the suppliers was rejected.

"Listen, you are doing a great job in selling our products. We are making sufficient profit to continue the business. We get many letters, every day, from our customers to thank us for the quality. I am happy with your performance," said his boss. As he could see Bernard was getting frustrated, he tried to calm him down.

"You always reject my proposals. I don't understand why you are against everything, even profit. That's not logical," said Bernard with frustration.

"We can discuss that when you get calm down. For me, moral and integrity are far more important than the short term profit, and the letters of appreciations from our customers are the real value. You don't need to feel I reject something just because it was your suggestion. I just want to keep the things as they are."

Vortek laughed loudly as though he was watching a funny TV show, "Ha ha hah ha ha..." He could barely control his laugh, "I couldn't ask more."

Serium asked, "What the hell is this about?"

Vortek replied with a cheerful tone, "Bernard, the ideal puppet to rule the Earth for me. He will serve me to sell my androids and control them."

Serium replied, "That is a stupid idea. You think you can control a planet by a few androids around, and how do you know he will be loyal to you. Hah, that's a laughable plan."

Vortek's face turned serious. "My plans are very simple yet too complicated for your naive brain to comprehend. He will make a company and sell androids just to make enough money to build a production plant and access uranium. We have many engineer androids on board." Vortek's cheer and smile faded off his face with anger at Serium's comments. He ordered, "Lock him up." Androids took Serium back to his cabin and activated the laser beams on the door, preventing him from getting out.

It has been almost six monts since they left Zola when they reached Earth. Vortek commanded, "Turn the shields on, Captain. We don't want to create any suspicions." They had advance camera and visual systems to hide the ship. When looked at the ship from a side, the image across this side behind the ship would be reflected on the surface so that the image on the other side would be visible through the ship. This high tech visualization system made their ship invisible from any angle through normal vision.

The ship's external body was built in dual layers all around it. The temperature in between these two structural layers was adjusted so that the entire outer body of the ship had exactly the same temperature as the outside. That system would prevent them to be detected by any radar functioning with a thermal scanning device. Special gravity adjustment mechanisms mounted to control the magnetic structures and to mislead any external magnetic scans. The system created magnetic waves with reverse frequency wave heights to neutralize the magnetic waves created by the ship. The neutralization was making it invisible to any magnetic scan. The solar scan detectors and sensors were fitted to recognize any signal from an external source attempting to identify them, and they would absorb the scan waves giving a false impression as if the scan waves continued travelling through the empty space uninterrupted. Their advance technologies made it impossible to detect them with the technology on Earth.

The invisibility systems and protective electro-magnetic shields were turned on as they approached Earth. The ship was settled within the dark space in a distance that they could clearly see the Earth from their main deck. Vortek ordered the captain, "I want to speak with two of your officers who can bring him to me."

The captain was surprised of this request. "Why not two android guards?" asked.

"It is not necessary at the moment. We don't want to kill him. We just want to talk to him to make a business offer."

The captain went out of the main deck soon returned back with two officers in the ships. "They can bring him to you," he said as Vortek was standing near the transparent side of the deck looking at Earth.

Vortek slowly walked two steps closer to them. "I want you to invite him here. Tell him we have a business proposition for him. He can be the emperor of his world. If he seems too difficult to convince, just bring him."

"Yes, Vortek," said one of the guards and they left the main deck.

Bernard was in Perth to communicate with some toy selling companies in Australia. Perth was a mystical city in Australia with plenty of natural attractions, parks and beautiful beaches. Many tourists would visit the city to see these unique attractions. Most of them enjoyed the adventure in sand dunes by four-wheel drives, or seeing the wave stones. He went on a walk to the King's Park, which was a popular touristic view point close to the city. The park was located on the top of a hill just beside the city's main central district. Standing on the park, one could see the view of the alluring river flowing to the ocean below the park and glamorous city across that would trigger sympathy and joy within hearts and peace in minds. Even someone like Bernard could feel the peace and relaxation from the magical view presented there.

The space ship landed in the King's Park unnoticed. Two officers got out of it without being seen by anyone. When Bernard was walking back to his car, the guards were waiting for him on the way. As he approached toward them, one of them said, "Bernard, come with us. We have a business proposition for you."

He was surprised to see a stranger in Australia calling him by his name. "Pardon me. Do I know you?"

"No, but we know you and we will offer you the kingdom of the world," said the other one with a smiling face.

Bernard thought they must be mad. "Please, get out of my way. I am not in a mood to play crazy games."

The officers noticed it wouldn't be possible to convince him to go with them willingly. It was obvious their words weren't taken seriously. While one of them walked in front of him, saying, "I am afraid I must insist," the other one walked behind him and hit his head with a hard stick like a short baton usually carried by police. He was knocked unconscious and fell down. While they were carrying him to the ship, Milton was the only one who saw them.

About half an hour after they arrived in the mother ship, Bernard woke up with heavy headache. When he touched his head, he could feel some blood and a bump on his head. He didn't know where he was. He saw Earth from the main deck of the spaceship where Vortek was sitting in a chair next to him. He asked, "Where am I? Why did you bring me here?" while he was rubbing his eyes with his left hand as if he just wake up from a deep sleep.

Vortek got off his chair, "Welcome to my ship. Let me first apologize bringing you here like this by force, but that was the only way to show you ourselves and discuss my business proposal. You are in my ship outside Earth's atmosphere in space. This ship belongs to Zola, which is a planet in a faraway solar system."

Bernard looked around with surprised eyes finding it difficult to digest the fact that he was indeed in a spaceship in outer space. He couldn't believe they were aliens. They looked just like humans. He had a lot of questions in his mind. He was not sure where to start. He asked instantaneously, "Why me? What do you want?"

Vortek turned toward the Earth's view outside, "I chose you among billions because of your business skills and ambition for success. I know everything about you. I know your life, Bernard. —he paused for a moment as Bernard looked confused. You had a lonely life because of your ambitions and desire to rule others. You were always keen to dictate, enforce your opinions and ideas to those around you even when you were a child. That's why the other kids didn't want to be your friend except one. Tim's family moved to the town across the river from your hometown. You were close fishing friends, mates. You both had the same dictating characteristics. But he made a mistake of getting into an argument with you on who was better in fishing. All you did was gave him a slight push and prevent him from getting back on the boat."

Bernard listened to him with surprise. He interrupted Vortek, "But" —pausing for a moment—, "but how? How did you find out all that about me?" He got worried about getting caught and jailed for a moment. Just when he thought that was all forgotten past, some aliens were bringing it up.

"Look, I have my ways. It is really not that important how I found it all out. You also do not need to worry. I am here neither to blackmail you, nor setting justice for your dear friend. Besides, I can understand one planet can be too small to share for two dictators."

Bernard looked at Vortek with anger, but he still had some headache, and was certainly not in the mood to get into a fight with an alien. He asked, "What the hell are you talking about?"

Vortek calmly replied, "That does not matter. What matters is what I am about to offer you. All I want is just a business deal, a fair deal, which I believe you will appreciate what I am about to offer you."

He paused for a moment while he took some deep breaths as he watched over Earth. "I have been studying and trying to understand Earth for a long time. There are still many things I cannot say I understand fully."

Bernard walked closer toward the side wall screen and asked while staring out to the space, "What type of things?" He was still trying to see if this environment was some type of setup, but it looked all so real.

Vortek explained as if he was chatting to one of his close friends, "For example, your laws. I noticed smoking and alcoholic drinks are spread on Earth. Your laws don't prohibit them. However, drugs like marijuana is prohibited based on its side effects on health even though cigarettes and alcohol are also as bad."

He replied quickly, "Yes, I imagine it can be puzzling for an alien. It is really nothing to do with the health effects of them." He pointed down toward the United States of America on Earth and said, "Cigarettes were introduced and mainly supplied by the companies founded in that region. Alcohol is supplied from there and from our European friends who were happy not to ban the smoking and share the revenues from the alcohol. However, if marijuana would be free, it would mostly be supplied by some South American countries and perhaps few Middle Eastern countries that would suck substantial money from the world to those regions."

"But more and more countries are applying restrictions for smoking. Is that right?" he asked.

"Oh yeah, we started losing market share in time. Currently, many countries are producing and selling cigarettes," replied Bernard. Then, he added after a brief pause. "It is all about money and power, a great marketing scheme to divert the money flow toward our country."

"What a brilliant scam!" said Vortek, looking impressed.

"Scam? I didn't say scam, I said scheme," he said, attempting to correct his misunderstanding.

Vortek put his hand on Bernard's shoulder with a friendly expression and said, "Yes, I know."

Bernard said, "I think the smoking is probably our biggest contribution to the world, if not the nuclear weapons of mass destruction."

"I thought it was the invention of word *terrorism*," Vortek said as he pulled his hand off Bernard's shoulder.

"Yes, that is also a great tool to manipulate public fear, which helped justifying big payout budgets for many around the world."

"That's absolutely brilliant, Bernard and that's precisely why I chose you as my business partner. It is all under your feet," he said. Vortek paused with surprise as Bernard seemed to trying to look at his feet as if there would be something under it.

Vortek continued looking out to Earth. "I meant the Earth under your feet. It will be kneeling to you as you deservingly will be the greatest among all."

Bernard said, "I don't know what you are talking about."

He said, "I will be honest to you, Bernard. We are running out of energy resources in Zola. We need uranium."

"Why don't you just take it yourself? Why did you bring me here?" Bernard asked with his low tone of voice as he was still trying to digest the situation he was in; his location in space and his surroundings within the main deck of the ship were all too strange to accept as reality at once.

"No, we cannot be identified," said Vortek, turning his face to him. "If Earth knows about us, we might have to get into a war. We cannot estimate what the reactions will be. We want to stay unnoticed. I want you to help us. We don't want to kill living things in a war. We have respect for the rights of all creatures to live including you and others."

"Why should I help you?"

"If you help me, you can be the emperor on Earth. We chose you because of your ambitions, and we value your views and marketing skills. I have been watching you for quite a while. I know how your ideas were rejected for ridiculous reasons. You can achieve to be a real emperor using our technology. For that, you will give us what we need. By accepting my offer, you are preventing a war and saving millions of lives. You will not only be an emperor, but a true hero."

Bernard was surprised with Vortek's offer. He was thinking if all this is just a dream. Could it be possible that he could rule Earth? He asked, "How?"

"We have technology as you can see. Please look around, yourself," said Vortek as he pointed out androids standing next to him and standing across next to the control panel on a side. "I want you to sell the technology. I know it is possible to rule Earth by taking control of the financial market. I am not here to take over the control of anything or ruling Earth. There is nothing interest to me in this planet except the uranium. I will help you to be the king, and you will help us to get the resources we need."

Vortek paused for a while looking at Bernard's miserable face shocked by his new environment and unexpected chain of events. "Are you all right? Are you hearing what I am saying?"

"Yes, yes, I hear you. Go ahead," Bernard replied as he stared at the Earth.

Vortek continued, "If you accept my business proposal, you will have the power to do whatever you want. I think it is a fair trade-off. As two civilized individuals, you and I will be business partners."

Bernard thought this could be the opportunity he had always been waiting for. It was obvious that they had much more advanced technology than Earth had. He felt confident he could have the power to rule the world and to do anything he could possibly want. But he hesitated for a moment, "What if I...?"

Vortek interrupted him instantly, "We will have to kill you. You saw us and you know our existence, which obviously creates a risk for us." He approached and put his left arm over Bernard's shoulder, "Look, my friend, it is really a simple choice: dead versus kingdom. I know you are a wise man." He pointed to the android standing at a side. "That is one of a thousand androids I brought with me in this ship. I want you to take it with you. We will bring you more when you want. When you sell enough of them and raise enough capital, the engineer androids will build a plant to produce other androids. You are free to put the price and sell them as much as you can."

Bernard asked, "You only want uranium? What about the money from the sales?"

Vortek replied with a smile, "Oh, yes, money. We cannot use Earth's money in Zola. Earth's money is worthless to me. You can keep it all, but I need uranium for the survival of our civilization. We will help you to control the world's market."

185

Bernard still had a lot of questions in his mind, but he wasn't sure where to start. He stared at the android Vortek offered him that was standing with its shiny steel body. He asked, "Your technology seems very advanced. In fact, it seems so advanced that you could build the androids looking just like humans with some artificial skin cover, perhaps silicon. Why do they look like steel and clearly distinguishable from human with their swinging eyes?"

Vortek replied, "Well, it is kind of a long story, but I'll brief you. We were producing androids looking exactly like us some hundreds of years ago, but there were some accidents. In one case, someone wanted to test how strong the android's body was by shooting at it. There was confusion with humans and androids, which resulted in a human getting shot and killed. Since then our laws prohibited making the androids as exact look-alikes with us. According to the law, androids must be clearly distinguishable from any living creatures, including humans."

Bernard was impressed about how they were so keen about details to prevent any accidental deaths to protect humans and other creatures. He felt confident to trust Vortek and said, "I see. It makes sense."

Vortek explained a lot of things about the androids' skills and what they could do. Bernard was impressed with all their abilities and advanced technologies. He was happy to have the opportunity to gain power on Earth. He could see the potential profit and wealth that these androids could bring him. After all, this would prevent the biggest war potentially can extinct the entire humanity and life on Earth. Looking at their advanced technology, he was sure that Earth would not stand a chance against them if a war broke up. They gave him a communicator that could project a holographic image of Vortek from the ship and an image of Bernard to the ship. Bernard didn't want to carry the android with him since he was in Australia. He wanted them to be delivered when he returned back to the United States. He knew he would have problems passing through the customs at the airport in his country with these machines. When he was leaving the ship, he felt the necessity to be kind to Vortek, saying, "I am honored to meet you, sir, and appreciate you choosing me. I will do my best in our partnership."

After he left the deck, Vortek turned to his assistant, "It will be easy for us to accomplish our mission with his help. He will surely serve us well with his ambition stronger than ours to take over their world."

CHAPTER 12: THE PERFECT COMPANY

On Earth, GlobCorp continued its growth and proved for all that it had the ability to produce the most efficient, cheapest, and most environmentally desirable energy with the cars and robots. It was only natural for them to get in to the energy industry. Bernard had a room in his house to use as an office and also communicate to Vortek. He would regularly contact Vortek and inform him about the business. Bernard said, "Our business is going well. We are the only car company now. All others went bankrupted and disappeared."

"That's great, Bernard. I must admit you did much better than I anticipated. About our business, I want to increase our loading," said Vortek.

Bernard asked, "Uranium, you mean?"

"Yes, I think we have to put in a regular schedules rather than random deliveries. I believe you can manage ordering two or three tons extra in every two months for us."

"How much uranium do you want to carry with you?"

Vortek thought for a moment, "About fifty tons of uranium will be enough for us. So far we have loaded thirty-five tons. I want to complete the load as quickly as you can manage to get."

Bernard agreed with him, "Yes, OK. I will try to get two-and-a half tons extra monthly. I believe such amount will not take attention, but your small ships won't be able to carry so much weight to the mothership. How do you plan to load it up?"

"I will set my ship just over the plant in the air. Our small ships will carry it to the mother ship." Their mother ship was too large to land on the soil. They didn't have enough empty space around the plants to land. It would be easier for them to stay on the air and carry the resources up to the ship with their smaller cargo ships. Vortek jumped the subject as he was keen to tell about his plans. "Although you have been doing exceptionally well, I think you need to spread the business to different areas. You can't control the planet by only cars and androids."

Bernard wasn't clear what he meant. "I don't know." — pausing for a moment— "What else can I do?"

Vortek suggested with a tone of voice reflecting his pride about his intelligence and creative ideas, "Think Bernard, think! Why did I come here for?"

Bernard moved his eyebrows around and said, "To get uranium?"

"And, what did I need to get uranium for?" asked Vortek.

Bernard thought for a moment, scratching his jaws with his right hand, "Energy?

"Bingo. It is time for you to get into the energy business. Even one without a high-level intelligence can figure out that energy is the key to control a planet."

Vortek's words sounded humiliating by emphasizing how he is a kind of higher intelligence than him, but Bernard was too focused on his role as a puppet for his mind to analyze and recognize the deeper meanings of the words. Moreover, Vortek was there just to help him. Even if he could feel the rudeness in Vortek's words, he knew it would be no benefit to anyone to argue on vague items at this point in time. Bernard got excited with Vortek's idea, "Yes, you are certainly right. If the android engineers can build the bigger scale of their own energy reactor, there is no company or nobody can compete with us. Even governments cannot produce so much energy with such low costs."

Vortek added, "Don't forget, this is also clean energy and sustainable for many years. I have to go now. I leave it to you."

Governments in all countries were already struggling to cope with world's clean energy demand at affordable costs. Bernard approached the Department of Energy to see the reaction for building large-scale energy reactors. He arranged a meeting with the director of the department. The director's two technical advisors also attended the meeting. Bernard explained to them about the idea of GlobCorp building energy reactors that would be the safest, cleanest and cheapest energy production in big quantities.

The director of the department said, "To tell the truth, producing clean energy in sufficient quantities with reasonable cost is getting more and more challenging every day for us. In fact, we are not the only ones finding it difficult, which I believe is the case for all other governments around the world. Our nuclear energy technology has its own risks and not comparable to what you are suggesting in safety, efficiency and cost. Other energy sources are costly, and their technology is not in a level to satisfy the demand. I am sure my advisors will agree with me when I say, we, as US government, would be more than happy to support your Energy program." His advisors nodded, showing support for the director. After all, there was no downside for this project. The proposed energy reactor appeared to be for the best interest of the country. They signed an agreement so that GlobCorp could build a huge nuclear reactor in Nevada and provide most of the energy demand from Western states. Nevada was selected as an initial test location. It was considered as an ideal place since it was situated in the desert isolated from the main residential cities in case if a safety problem comes out unexpectedly. It was not a likely possibility that there could be an accident to present risks to the public considering the perfect past history of the company, but it was better to be cautious and prepared than being sorry in any case of a disastrous accident.

Androids built the first energy reactor. The reactor started producing energy so cheap that residents and businesses could get it for the half the cost than what they had been paying for. After running the reactor for a year, the government officials and scientists working for the energy department were feeling confident about the safety of the system. They permitted the company to build a second reactor in Colorado to distribute to the central US. Soon after, another one in Pennsylvania was built to provide the energy need for the Eastern states. Later, they built other energy plants in Illinois, South Dakota, Montana and Washington.

Other countries were demanding the same service for energy. Especially, after seeing the successful applications throughout the United States, their demands were strong. Within a year, GlobCorp was the only corporation providing energy to all over the world. The energy deal was indeed the key to have control over the governments. Once the system was established, Bernard knew it would be impossible for governments to change the energy source and the system. The plants that were abandoned for years could not easily be reactivated. They would have to be totally rebuilt to function safely. Considering the cost and efficiency of the available technologies, the dependency to the GlobCorp for the energy could not be reversible.

Meanwhile, Vortek's mother ship was settling over the android's plant in Canada and loading uranium every other month. He contacted Bernard again as usual in an evening, "Now you control the world's energy, which means you control the world."

Bernard approved with a smiling face, "Yes, we are the only energy supplier now."

Vortek asked, "Why is that you are not controlling the money?"

Bernard was surprised again not knowing what he meant and how he could possibly do that. "Well, yes, I should be the one controlling it, but what can I do?"

Vortek giggled, "Ha ha ha. Think! Think, Bernard. If you came up with a proposal, who can reject it while you control the price and quantity of the energy supply?"

Bernard answered naively, "I believe nobody."

Vortek said, "That is true. It is a fact that it would be easy to manage the trading worldwide if there was only single unitary money. It is necessary for you to eliminate money from the world, but before you can do that they have to get used to a single monetary system. "

Bernard showed his agreement by nodding his head, "Yes, it would also be good to get into banking at the same time."

"As I come from Zola, I suggest you can come up with a name to honor our business partnership," said Vortek as he wanted to leave signs of his home planet on Earth after he left.

Bernard accepted without hesitation. "I will come up with a naming along your suggestion." He paused for a moment and added, "Zolo? I think Zolo is a good name for a currency."

"Great, you know what to do. We'll talk again next time," said Vortek as he switched off his communicator.

Bernard met with the president to propose the single monetary unit system. He greeted the president with a handshake. "Hello, Mr. President."

"Hello, Bernard. I am glad to meeting you. Please, take a seat," said the president pointing to the chair in front of his desk.

195

"Thank you, sir," said Bernard as he settled down on the leather chair.

"Your energy reactors greatly served Americans. For that, I feel it is my duty to thank you for providing affordable and clean energy for all of us. So, what can I do for you?" the president asked.

Bernard said, "I am here with a financial proposal that I believe it is crucial for sustainability of our economic strength. I want to propose a new system that would benefit to everyone —unification of money in the world. If we have only one money unit worldwide, trading and travelling would be much easier for everyone."

President looked cautious about it, "I am only the president of this country. I don't make decisions for the world."

Bernard said, "I am sure our European friends would agree if the United States proposes the change from dollar to another money unit. A new currency would avoid bias and most of the disagreements. GlobCorp is bringing huge profit for the US economy and employing hundreds of thousands of people. I believe this change is crucial for our business to sustain contributing to our country's economy."

The president asked, "What money unit are we talking about?"

Bernard said, "It could be the same as dollar, but not to offend our business partners around the globe, a new name would be preferable. I think *Zolo* is a good name as it represents specifically neither Europeans', nor Asians' money."

The president said, "I see. What if we can't make the others agree, then what?"

Bernard studied the chandelier hanging on the president's office ceiling for a while, staring at the detailed edges of the crystal structure as if he was interested in its finely shaped artistic structure while thinking what to say. Then, he looked at his eyes, "I assure you, Mr. President, it will not be possible for us to continue delivering the energy with the current prices to the world including the United States. Global currency exchanges have been costly for us"

The president didn't like Bernard's tone of talking as he was threatening him with increasing energy prices. He reacted, "Excuse me. Are you threatening me?"

Bernard kept his calm, "No, sir. I didn't mean any threat, but purely business reasons. As you suggested, if others would not agree to your proposal, it would be outside our control to keep the energy prices low. It is a fact that variability in the exchange rates creates losses for us. We just want to sustain the business and continue providing jobs for many Americans and other people globally."

The President was looking calm after Bernard softened his threat. He said, "I'll bring it up in my cabinet's meeting with the ministers. The decision will have to be made in agreement of the cabinet members."

Bernard took off from the chair and shook the president's hand. He felt confidence about his offer as he left. "Thank you for your time, Mr President."

The new money unit Zolo was soon accepted between the United States, China and Europe. Other Asian countries and Australia joined them just a month after to keep their strong trading ties. As the major economies in the world started using Zolo, all other countries had to change their system to have a sharing in the world's market arena.

Meanwhile, GlobCorp opened an international bank. Initially, the intension was just to manage their own funds, but later they started finance banking doing deals with other companies. After a few months, they expanded the business to provide personal banking services to the public.

The company was perfect in everything they produced androids, cars, and energy that made it impossible for any other company to compete with GlobCorp in the *free market* environment. In a mysterious way, this company always had their own development of the technology, the technology that did not exist on Earth until they created. There were not many questions asked about why it was this company coming up with the perfect methods to do whatever they did or producing the perfect products. Once in a while, there would be an article published in one of the local newspapers criticizing the current system. However these types of articles at a corner of one of the middle pages would often be skipped by most readers.

Back in the company's office, in an afternoon, the research scientist teams were speculating about the company's products. Asimov brought an article that he had torn off from a local newspaper. The article's introduction paragraph stated:

The products that are offered by the company appear to bring comfort and luxury in everyone's lives. This comfort and luxury are preventing us to pose questions. It is not always easy for many of us to get out of our comfort zone and question the source of our own comfort. As long as everything goes well, or appears to be going well, ignorance is often adopted as the best policy to follow.

After the money unification was implemented with success for the Globcorp, the world was ready for Vortek's next plan. He was talking with Bernard, as usual, in a regular reporting session. Bernard proudly said, "It was all success. We unified the money in the world. Our bank is also doing well."

Vortek replied with an unsatisfied voice, "Yes, but I am surprised you call it *success*, which I cannot see. Do you think this is sufficient for you to be the emperor of the planet?"

Bernard's eyes moved around thinking, "Well, as we continue successful—"

Vortek interrupted suddenly, "Successful? The only time we'll call it a success is when you are in charge. For now, you are not in charge."

Bernard was feeling the pressure and was sweating from the mental stress. He had no idea what more he could possibly do. He already had the full control of many industries. "Well," —he paused thinking what to say. "What do you suggest?"

Vortek, in Bernard's hologram, sat back in his chair. "I have a math question for you."

"Go ahead!" he said trying to hide his incompetence in the field of mathematics. He remembered how he struggled in his three of the analytical classes during his university studies -mathematical finance, advance statistics, and his nightmare, stochastic differential equations. In his nightmares, several of the bell-shaped graphs of uncertain coefficients would come alive from his books and chase him down the street kicking him with their funnily outward extended feet. He would wake up in sweat and breathing heavily. He could never forget failing in stochastic differential equation course in his first attempt during the second year, and barely passing it in his second take. Although thoughts of his inconfidence flew through his mind, he felt a little comfort thinking Vortek would probably not be asking him anything stochastic to fire up his stochaphobia.

"How much would be the 5 percent of every transaction in the world in a day?" asked Vortek as if he is giving an oral exam to his high school student.

As few sweat drops running down on the side of Bernard's forehead, he tried to answer, "Well, it is hard to guess exactly. I think mean of any stochastic simulation sets would produce a large variance, but surely, it is a big number." He soon recognized Vortek must have some ideas behind asking this question. He noted, "I see you have another plan, don't you?"

Indeed, Vortek had again another evil plan. He replied with a sneer, "Forget the variance. This is not a school exam. Assume that money was totally removed from Earth. Assume that everybody was carrying a chip within their body, and for each transaction, assume that they had to swap through a machine that you build. Assume that-"

Bernard interrupted with his eyes largely open from excitement, "Oh, yes, that is such a great idea. Even the devil himself could not come up with it." Vortek didn't understand the meaning of his words wasn't exactly literal. Bernard noticed his angry face. He didn't want to get Vortek's rage over himself. He quickly added clarification, "Calm down Vortek, it is just an idiom. I must admit you are truly a genius. If our machine would be the only reader for that chip to charge money and to perform transactions, we could charge 5 percent for each transaction." He paused for a moment and said scratching his jaw, "Oh my god, that's a great idea!"

Bernard met with the president to explain him his proposal. "Mr. President, I have a great proposal for our country. Our country's revenue will substantially increase."

The president said, "I am listening."

He said, "We will build a tiny chip that can be inserted under the skin with no risk to health. Please, allow me to demonstrate." He took off his jacket and unwrapped his shirt's sleeve of the left arm. He put his left arm over the table and showed the president that there was a chip under the skin of his left wrist's inner side. The chip was only one centimeter long and five millimeters wide."

The president asked, "What is that for?"

He replied, "Everyone has certain amount of Zolo credit in the bank. Instead of using printed cash money, they can simply swipe their wrist through our reader's screen. This small charger will read and charge the amount of transaction." He showed the small machine that can read the chip and make the transactions. Then, he continued, "We will provide the chip for everyone for just one hundred Zolo credits."

"How about the poor who cannot afford one hundred Zolo?" asked the president.

He replied hastily, "We are prepared to take half of the cost for those who cannot afford and we need the government's support for the cost of inserting the chip."

The president thought in silence for a moment, "How will this contribute to US economy?"

Bernard replied, "We will charge a small amount of 5 percent for each transaction as we will be providing the charger and our system to process the transactions. Of course, the company will pay the tax from this revenue."

The President said with a serious face, "I have to talk to my advisors for this. You will be informed with our decisions." Then he picked up his pen and started looking at a file on his desk ignoring Bernard.

Bernard extended his hand for a handshake as he was leaving, but the president didn't respond to him this time as the president was quit disappointed with his proposal. He thought switching to a chip in this manner would mean forcing everyone to use one. They would not have a choice other than using the chip. After Bernard left the White House, the president met with his advisors, economy minister, and the director of the Department of Energy to discuss his proposal.

The economy minister said, "We cannot accept such a proposal and force everyone to be inserted with a chip. This is not just a financial issue, but it is also about the freedom and choices."

The president turned to the director of the energy department, "I asked you to attend this meeting, because I believe we could be threatened if we reject GlobCorp's proposal. I want to know what you think they could do."

The director said, "They could cut off the energy in the States and all residents would be doomed in wintertime. It is not possible for us to go back to our previous energy systems as all our energy plants have become useless anymore. It would take at least a few years to re-build and would require huge capital cost. I think that with the 5 percent of the transaction charge, the cost to public would still be better off considering the cost of what they had to pay for the energy in the past."

His advisor commented, "We don't have the time to rebuild the old energy reactors. I don't see any choice for us other than accepting the proposal. If we consider the cost of printing the notes and making coins, the idea is not too bad financially."

The president said, "This proposal is the biggest proof that we are losing our freedom to make decisions with our free will. We are being forced to accept it. Unfortunately, it is

206

clear from your comments that we have no other choice, but accept GlobCorp's proposal."

CHAPTER 13: SABOTAGE

Six months had passed after money was removed from the Earth. Bernard was reporting the company's progress to Vortek. "Our business is growing day by day. We are now controlling the electronics, communication and infrastructure too."

Vortek commented with an unsatisfied tone of voice, "That's good, but if you want to be an emperor, you have to be strong. Do you have control over the military and the police forces?"

Bernard replied instantly, "Yes, our androids are in charge of both the military and the police forces. There are still some humans in the military, but if they oppose to any of our plans, I am sure my androids will have no trouble eliminating them."

Vortek replied with a confused look, "That's good Bernard, but still" —Vortek paused for a while to give Bernard time to think as if he was giving him an exam. Vortek was expecting him to figure out what needed to be done.

Bernard replied with a puzzled face, "Still? Do you mean there is more I need to do and not done yet?"

Vortek replied, sitting cool in his chair, "Yes, there are more needs to be done. There is a large industry and a critical one that you even haven't got into."

He said, "We control the robotics, energy and automotive too. I don't know what else is left."

Vortek replied instantly, "How about transportation?"

Bernard thought for a moment in silence and talked to himself, "Busses...? No..." Then he loudly said, "Airlines? We haven't been involved in airlines."

"Why haven't you?" asked Vortek.

"Perhaps, we could make space ships like yours?"

"Spaceship? Ha ha ha," Vortek laughed out with a loud voice. "No, that's impossible. You don't have the androids and programs to build spaceships."

Bernard didn't know what to do about it. "I could buy one of the companies, but they don't seem to be profitable. They have very low profit margins."

Vortek said, "If you buy in usual conditions, it is too risky. I wouldn't suggest that. However, if their planes were crushing every day, they might be forced to hand it over to you without paying much. The undetected and unexpected accidents can also force all other airlines to leave the arena for you."

Bernard said, "Undetected accidents? I don't know what you mean by *undetected*. The planes may not be as fancy as your spaceship, but I assure you they are very safe. They are not likely to crash."

Vortek said, "That can be arranged. Our ships with invisible shields and just adding a little extra strength to their usual external static and magnetic field should be able to manage it."

Bernard wasn't sure if this was such a good idea. Although he had ambitions, he hadn't gone as far as killing anyone so far except his childhood incident. His eyes got bigger, filled with fear. "I am not sure if this is really necessary. I mean many people are flying—"

Vortek interrupted him suddenly, "It is not like this is the first time. How do you think you have achieved smooth growth of the company so quickly? Why do you think all the car producers left the arena to you?"

Bernard had no idea what he was talking about, but he could see there were a lot of things he didn't know about Vortek and things that had been happening in the background. He asked as he was staring at him, "What do you mean not the first time? I am not fully following what you are saying?"

"Don't tell me you haven't figured out why the research center in Silicon Valley had blown away, and totally burned down with everything in it? Your only potential future competitor was eliminated without leaving any trace of their research. You didn't think it was all by chance that the accident occurred while everyone involved in the development was at the same place. How can it be a coincidence that just at the time of the accident, their computers were totally wiped out by a virus?"

Bernard didn't know what to say. He remembered the news like it was yesterday. He also remembered reading some speculative articles about it, but he could never imagine it could be true. He felt the pain in his mind like a child of a family who always admired his dad, but suddenly witnessing his dad getting arrested as a serial killer of many innocent people, and watching officers taking him away with his hands cuffed behind him.

Vortek continued, "Why do you think suddenly all the cars produced by other companies were turning out to be faulty just after you got into Automotive industry? I thought you must have figured it all out by now, and you appreciate my support for your business. Don't tell me that you thought everything was just a coincidence or for some reason Mighty God might have suddenly decided to favor you and help you out."

Bernard was listening to him, totally astonished hearing these news, "But?" —pausing to think what to say— "But how? How come the investigation teams could not find any evidence? Even the androids in the security forces could not—"

Vortek interrupted him with a sneer showing his pride about how perfectly he managed it, "Androids! Oh yes. They are so good at what they do, aren't they?... Bernard, who do you think they serve for?"

Bernard thought for a while and replied as one of his eye brows moved up while the other one moved down. He was biting his lower lips in confusion. "You? Of course, they serve to you."

"Don't be silly, of course not. You serve me to get what I want. I don't need them to serve me. They are totally dedicated to your service and are ready to do anything to ensure your objectives are achieved."

Bernard wasn't sure what to do and what to say. He felt like he was abandoned. Perhaps his dreams were not as realistic as he judged. He thought in a moment, it was foolish to think he could be an emperor or king of the world in this era when there is no real kingdom except a few countries having kings almost purely for symbolic or ceremonial purposes, but nothing as actual kingdom. On the other hand, androids did, in fact, serve for his purpose and did really well. He had many conflicting thoughts wandering in his mind, but eventually his desire for the power were taking over the control of his mind. He started convincing himself to proceed on his course set for the ultimate objective and ultimate power in the world. Unlike the kings and emperors in most other countries that the senate representatives are selected by people's vote, he would be the only power to make all the decisions. He still questioned about the necessity for the murders, "Perhaps, androids did help to achieve the growth for the company. But still, I am not one hundred percent sure if it is necessary to—"

Vortek interrupted him shouting, "You cannot be an emperor!" —Paused for a moment and lowered his tone of voice to show that he was just helping him and supporting his ultimate aim— "if you show weakness. You are my business partner. I only speak the facts to you. You have to be prepared to sacrifice some lives of insignificance for the greater cause, which is, of course, your kingdom." Bernard didn't look sure and confident. He kept quiet. Vortek quickly added, "I am here only to help you. I already got enough uranium as much as I can carry with the ship. If you believe that you do not need my help any longer, I can leave right away. I am staying for the sake of our agreement to make you a true emperor. I have my own values, professional ethics and integrity, which requires me to stick with my promises."

Bernard got worried about failing his objective if he was left on his own. "Oh, no. You should definitely stay as we agree. You must help me until the end."

Vortek showed a light instantaneous smile and said, "That's what I thought. I will load a program in your two androids. That will allow you to command all other androids, and overwrite the owner's commands. You can use this power when you need support."

When Vortek turned off the communicator in the main deck, the captain looked worried, "What? Are you giving the final control to him?"

Vortek said, "Of course not. His commands can overwrite the others, but my commands are always over his and over everyone else."

The captain seemed relaxed, "Oh, I see."

Vortek ordered, "Launch a ship with two androids. We have to arrange some accidents."

As the corporation got larger and larger, it was getting more and more powerful. The company's process and products became almost unquestionable. They started to get above the law. Once in a while, a journalist would write an article to question where all their resources were coming from. Then, they would soon be arrested for some type of made-up crimes. The information on the arrests would be kept off the media. Many of the androids were in charge of the security and policing. Artificial evidences and crime creations or cover-ups were easy tasks for the androids to manage.

As Vortek brought to Bernard's attention, the only major industry that was not being controlled by GlobCorp was the airlines. There were many big airline companies operating around the world. One of them was American Airlines flying Boeing 777 planes between London and New York. Boeing 777 planes were launched in 2005, which had more capacity than any other twin-engine freighter. These planes were based on the world's technologically advance 200LR worldliner, a long-range, passenger airplane. It was a Sunday when a Boeing 777 of American Airlines was expected to land on JFK airport at 10:30 AM in New York, carrying 478 passengers and twenty staff on board from London. It was a clear day, and there was no delay expected on the plane. About one hour left to landing, one of Vortek's ship approached the plane using its invisibility shields, and an android reported to Vortek in the main deck, "We are going side by side with a Boeing 777 plane of AA."

Vortek ordered, "Increase the external magnetic field and static force, block their communication and report the plane's condition."

The android replied, "Magnetic and static force fields are doubled. Plane's control mechanism is malfunctioning. Pilots lost the control and communication system is blocked."

The pilot and his co-pilot were struggling to keep the plane steady as the control panels were not responding. All the controls in the electronic flight instrument system were lost. Neither the primary flight display nor the navigation display was working correctly. Sensors controlling the fuel flow to the engines were completely confused and fuel was cut off from the engines. All the engines suddenly stopped. With the failure of the engines, the plane headed down with the gravity. The captain pilot pulled the handle up as much as he could, but it didn't do anything to slow down the plane's fall.

Vortek laughed with joy and ordered to the android, "Excellent, stay close to it until the crash."

The plane was in a free fall with the gravity. The android reported, "Altitude: 13,100 meters. Time to impact: 51.7 seconds. Altitude: 4,582 meters. Time to impact: 10 seconds." There was silence in the communicators for a few seconds. Then the android reported again, "Plane was parted at 250 meter altitude and 0.5 second to impact. It crashed into the ocean."

Meanwhile, an officer in the tower control at JFK Airport shouted, "AA105 is lost. I can't see it on my monitor."

The director rushed to him, "What? When was it lost?"

The officer replied with a worrying tone, "Just now, it got lost from the radar, sir."

"Try to contact the pilot" the director's worry was obvious in his eyes. This was not expected.

The officer attempted to contact the flight repeatedly, "AA105, copy. Do you copy? AA105 copy. Copy AA105—"

Unfortunately, all the efforts trying to communicate the aircraft failed to get any response from the plane. The director ordered to the other officer standing next to him, "Prepare a search team. We have to find it." A search team was sent immediately to find the location. One hour later, they found some pieces of the plane, and some dead bodies were floating over the Atlantic Ocean.

On the main deck, androids were analyzing the routes of the large passenger planes continuously. An android reported that an aircraft of Air France heading to Guinea will pass in close proximity with a British Airlines plane coming from Tokyo in three hours.

Vortek ordered, "Launch two ships with androids and meet the planes." Both ships soon reported that they had reached the planes. Vortek explained to them their mission, "Get in front of the aircrafts and blind them from seeing each other. Destruct their scans. As they get closer, ship 1 in front of Air France project a holographic image of the other air craft on the plane's route while slightly intensifying external magnetic and static force fields. Ship 2 in front of British Airlines project the holographic image of the other aircraft in front of the plane. Simulate the scenario to cause them crash each other." He wanted to cause panic for the pilots by causing problems in their control mechanism using external force fields. He forced the pilots change directions with panic mood to crash into each other.

The androids performed their acts with perfectness. The contact from the airplanes was soon cut off. The two planes were later reported to crash into each other on TV news as one of the freaky accidents, which claimed lives of 836 people on board. Vortek's ships were not identified flying around the planes. These disasters coming one after another, taking many lives created shock effects and deep sadness in all around the world.

There were a lot of speculations about the accidents in the media. Most of these speculations were initially focused on a possible organized terrorist act, but the official investigations didn't find any trace of explosives or any type of evidence to suggest any possibility for sabotage. They concluded the turbulence in the air and static electricity resulting from the movement of the clouds were the main cause of accidents. Strong static electricity from the friction force between the clouds caused electronic malfunction, and turbulence might have contributed to the situation, which resulted pilots to lose the plane's control and crashed.

Unfortunately, these freaky accidents didn't end in that day. The next day, two aircrafts of American Airlines flying between Washington DC to California crashed into each other and exploded in the air killing 627 people on board. American Airlines struggled financially to keep the business going. Not only that, they were facing many lawsuits claiming huge compensation for the victims' families and close relatives, their customers also lost confidence in them. All the major airline companies were heading for bankruptcy, and there was nothing they could do to prevent the accidents; nothing to prevent heading toward financial disasters.

CHAPTER 14: COFFEE FORTUNE-TELLER

While American Airlines was moving to financial crisis and bankruptcy, GlobCorp offered an unexpected takeover. This was an unexpected offer for all including American Airlines and all economists around the world, but not for GlobCorp. They would never think any company would want to take over any of the airlines under such condition of financial disaster. In a media appearance on the news, Bernard said, "Ill-fated tragic accidents brought tens of thousands of people's jobs at risk. GlobCorp will not sit and watch people suffer in unemployment and poverty. As a global corporation, we are here to support the people. We are here to help. GlobCorp is a corporation and I believe a corporation has a responsibility to act in the best interest of the public as much as protecting the stockholders' investments and financial benefits, which means keeping the well-being of the general public over money-making."

GlobCorp bought American Airlines for almost nothing and convinced the world this was not a profitable action or profit-aiming action, but purely to help save people's jobs.

Milton was following all the news about the airlines' disasters closely. Accidents were happening daily for all other airline companies in the world. When he heard about the strong static electricity in the air was found to be the cause of all these disasters, he recognized for sure everything was linked. The static electricity in the air disabling his cell phone during the kidnapping he witnessed in Perth had to be from the same source. The most interesting and the strongest evidence for him to link these events was the involvement of Bernard. In the kidnapping, he seemed to be the victim, but he had been getting substantial benefits through the company from these tragedies so far. He thought he had to make Bernard acknowledge the facts. At least, if he acknowledged he was kidnapped, it could be possible for him to convince the authorities that these events were caused by the same source.

Bernard was not coming to the office daily after the company achieved the sole domination in the energy industry. Nobody knew what he was doing or where he was. He would come once or twice a month to the office. Just after GlobCorp took over American Airlines, Bernard came to meet the staff in the central office in Chicago. He proudly announced the takeover of the airline in a cheerful mood. There was no sadness or regret in him for the many who lost their lives or for the lives of those who were left behind in darkness. His only concern was the business and his business could not get any better as he bought one of the world's biggest airlines for almost nothing. In addition to that, all the other airlines were struggling financially because of the accidents that left not much resource in them to get into a competition with GlobCorp.

In the meeting, Milton stood up from his chair and turned toward Bernard with anger. "What the hell is going on? So many people lost lives and yet we should be happy and grateful that the company now owns American Airlines."

Bernard was surprised from his unexpected reaction since he never argued in anything with him so far. He replied, keeping his cool, "I can see you are very concerned for the people involved in accidents just as I am. I feel deeply sorry for the disastrous accidents occurred. If we did not save the company, hundreds of thousands of people around the world would lose their jobs. I saved their jobs and their future. I must also add that I am glad to see our employees are concerned with the tragedies we have been facing. That is why we should be proud today that our company saved many lives by this business deal.

Milton didn't calm down. He was certainly not impressed by the "angel heart" of the corporate deal. "There was no accident, Bernard. I know that as much as you do. Clouds don't suddenly start producing huge amount of static electricity to cause the accidents. Another question is what we got to do with outer space?"

Bernard's face suddenly turned serious as his deep concerns were obvious on his face turning slightly reddish. "What do you mean you and I know of the accidents, not being accidents? You must have had a dream of outer space. I have no idea what you are referring to, but if you follow the media about accidents, you would know about things just like everyone else does. There have been the most comprehensive investigations about the events that our androids also helped the investigating committees to analyze the evidences to find out the causes. There were many professionals, experts, and scientists involved in the investigations. As you should already know, the clouds have enough kinetic energy to cause the frictions and the statics to damage the plane's electronic control systems. I suggest you should stop watching too many science fiction movies."

"Stop pretending you don't know what I am talking about. When you were kidnapped in Perth, there was a very strong static electricity in the air. It was so strong that it could easily damage planes' electronic systems. They are the ones killing people. Why are you hiding it? I am not mistaken about your face. I saw you clearly and I've never forgotten since."

Bernard got angry and shouted, "How can you talk like that, Milton? After all I have done for you. Supported your studies and gave you the job. Nothing happened in Perth. Stop nonsense conspiracy theories about kidnapping and outer space. Wake up to the reality."

Milton slowly walked and approached to Bernard. He moved his mouth closer to his face and replied with a lower and stronger tone, "You are the one who needs to wake up. How can you do nothing and just watch so many people keep dying? So much blood spilled is not worth for anything, not even for the presidency of this *evil corporation*."

"That's enough. Get out of here, Milton. You are not yourself. You can have a few days off if you want. Come back when you settle with your nonsense conspiracies." Bernard knew it was all true, but he wouldn't let anything come in front of his dream to be the emperor. He would never tolerate a staff talk to him like that, but he had to keep Milton close to himself instead of firing him.

Milton walked toward the door quickly and when he got next to the door, he turned back to the others. "I suggest you all get out of here and do not be a part of the corporation's cold-blooded murders." He left the meeting room.

At evening around 7:00 PM, his phone rang. Milton was sitting on his couch, thinking what to do. How he could possibly convince the world that the giant corporation was involved in all these murders in plane crashes. The phone was ringing for the fifth time when he reached and picked it up. It was Aleyna on the phone.

"Hello," said Aleyna with her usual soft voice on the phone.

Milton recognized her voice although the sound was coming very low. "Hi Aleyna—"

"Listen, Milton, I can't talk much on the phone, but we should meet in our usual place. It would be wise not to use the name of the place on the phone. I am calling from a public phone," she said in a whispering tone.

"OK, I know where you mean. Are you all right? Your sound is not very clear."

"I just wanted to talk to you. I want to know everything. See you there." Aleyna hung up the phone quickly.

On the weekends, Aleyna and Milton would often go to a Turkish coffee shop called Turkish Coffee World. It was one of the rare shops not using high-tech espresso machines with built-in chips and not having androids or any products from GlobCorp around. Turkish Coffee World had always been making coffee in the traditional way. They would put very fine-grounded coffee in an old-style coffee making pot called cezve. Cezve (jez-veh) was usually made from copper and decorated with handmade fine arts. Copper has been often used to make cezve because it enabled the coffee to boil quickly using minimum energy due to its efficient heat conductivity property. Another reason to use copper was the even heat distribution on its surface, which contributed to create the fine taste. After putting the grounded coffee in a cezve, a tiny bit of crystallized sugar is added to reduce the bitter taste. Then, the cezve is filled with water to about three quarters of its size and boiled on the fire until the coffee rises to the edge of the cezve. The cezve is then pulled away from the fire just before the boiled coffee spills out. Just after the boiling coffee settles down, it would be brought over the fire again to boil. Milk and additional sugar could be added depending on the individual's taste. Milton always enjoyed the bitterness of the coffee, which helped him to stay sharp throughout the day and helped him to focus on his work and studies during his university times. Aleyna loved the taste of the coffee with half a cube of sugar.

Milton arrived in the coffee shop half an hour later. He was surprised to see Aleyna was not alone. Dr. Asimov and Dr. Shwarz from his research team were also there. Asimov said, "Well my friend, we are a team, and you sounded like you know a lot. If you don't mind, we would like to know about it."

Figure 2. An Anatolian handmade cezve

Shwarz added, "Yup, that's exactly why we are here. Considering what you have said in the meeting, it would be wise to keep our meeting off the public attention, and as far as I can see, this place looks excellent as Aleyna suggested. I don't see anything from the company. But first thing first guys." He waved his hands to Mustafa, who had been serving coffee in the shop for many years. Mustafa came quickly next to him.

"Do you have those Turkish sweets here, hmm? What you call them..." Shwarz was having hard time remembering the word and was scratching his head.

"Baklava," Asimov said. "We have a lot in Russia. All of us here would love to get some too." —he paused for a second— "of course, together with Turkish coffee."

"Yes, sir, we do have baklava," said Mustafa with his usual cheerful smile and left their table.

Milton was happy to see Asimov and Shwarz as they had good friendship at work, which helped build a trust between them. He remembered his early days at work for a moment. He was keen to use their title "Doctor" to call them as Dr.

Asimov and Dr. Shwarz. After some days, Shwarz appeared to be angry at him and telling him to stop calling them with their title, which he believed symbolized their friendship.

Milton explained how he witnessed Bernard's kidnapping in Perth, and how strong the static electricity in the air was when that happened. He also explained the strange invisible emptiness in between the branches that he could not find any logical explanation for it. Existence of strong static electricity was the common in all the recent plane accidents occurring daily. "I know for sure all these events are related. Only thing I don't understand is why Bernard continuously rejects the kidnapping."

While he was talking, Mustafa served the coffee and baklava for each of them. All the cups were designed with handmade crafts. He also put a pot of crystallized sugar and milk on the table. Suddenly, everyone turned to Shwarz in silence as he seemed to get overly excited about the desert. He took his fork and carefully carried one entire piece of diamond-shaped baklava to his mouth. As their friends were all staring at him, Mustafa got curious too and started to watch him wondering why everyone was staring at him. After he swallowed the baklava, he looked quite calm. Then, he noticed all his friends' eyes were on him. He put his right thumb up and nodded his head. Shwarz said, "Excellent combination of bitter and sweet taste."

Asimov said, "Great, the quality is approved now," as the others started eating the baklava and drinking the coffee. Mustafa went back behind the shop's counter with a smile formed from feeling proud with the fine taste of his baklava and coffee.

Asimov asked, "I remember you said something about the outer space. Did you mean aliens kidnapped him?"

Milton was silent for a moment. "Well, there is something in outer space and that something is surely related to the androids. I cannot be sure if that is just a space shuttle sent by the company's fund to keep the confidential information or if there are actually aliens involved. There is not any clear information."

"How do you know about the space?" asked Asimov.

Milton said, "Niffy told me. He could connect to a database located in the space."

"Really?" asked Aleyna, looking with excitement as if she was listening to a thrilling story.

"Yes, but he cannot confirm it. As soon as he said that, he was downloaded with a program and the information was lost. He was downloaded a program to delete it," said Milton.

"Bernard wouldn't deny him being kidnapped unless he has a real reason to do so, like billions of dollars," said Shwarz and paused for a few seconds. "All of us here always doubted and never believed that he could possibly come up with all these new technologies to create such an efficient energy plants, machines..."

"Supercars...?" added Asimov. "Never mind building a supercar, I hardly can believe him having sufficient ability to drive a car."

"It is hard to believe, but when I think about it, it actually makes sense. I think there must be something out there providing him with all this," said Milton.

Asimov asked, "Yeah but, why would they kidnap him in the first place. And why would they help him after kidnapping?"

Shwarz said, "Hard to tell why, and another question is why him." Then, he stared directly at Milton's eyes. "We understand he paid you well during your studies. He gave you very high position even when you were just a student. Your rank at the research centre was the same as us. I don't mean to judge your professional skills, but I thought he must be out of his mind to give such a level to you as a new graduate. Obviously, he must have his reasons."

"I know it was strange for him to give me so much. I must admit your publications have inspired me greatly to study in this field. I was honored to work with you guys, but I have no idea why he did that. He always seemed very generous," said Milton

Asimov said, "Obviously, Bernard knew that you knew something. He must have given you all these things to ensure that you would accept the job. He must have wanted to keep you close. He might have been worried that you could cause problems for him."

"Yes, I did tell him that I saw him kidnapped when I met him the first time. What makes me worried is the millions of androids all over the world. If they have the control of these machines, the entire humanity is doomed."

"What can we do about it?" asked Aleyna and spoke with a hopeless tone of voice. "Nobody would believe us making claims against such a big corporation."

"We'll do nothing for now," Shwarz quickly replied. "We have to keep quiet and try to find evidences to convince the public. Unless we have some clear evidences, we cannot do anything. We should go now and try to gather some factual evidences as we continue our daily work at the office."

"Thank you for coming here, guys. Let's meet here next week and discuss whatever we can find out," said Milton. Asimov and Shwarz left the shop to go home. They planned to continue their work to collect more information about the company and about Bernard himself.

When Aleyna and Milton were just about to leave their table, an old lady sitting at a table in the far corner of the café approached them with hurry. She said, "I can read your coffee and see your future."

Milton said, "Thanks, but we have to leave now."

Aleyna sat back on the chair. "Come on, Milton. This doesn't take long. I want to hear what she can tell us."

The fortune-teller said, "Only few minutes." She took their coffee cups and put them upside-down on the saucers.

Milton sat down back on his chair with some impatient facial expression, looking at his watch as if it was changing shape or the minutes and hours would change in every second. After a minute, she took Aleyna's cup and studied inside. "I see two hearts beating close to each other."

Milton mongered, "How surprising?" showing his disbelief for fortune-telling while Aleyna was giving all her attention to hear what she wants to say.

She enlarged her eyes, staring inside the cup and continued, "I see a disaster, very big disaster all around." She looked scared and stressed with it. She almost didn't want to continue looking at Aleyna's cup. She said, "Darkness, everywhere is covered in darkness." She put her cup down instantly almost with a reflex. It was clear she didn't like to continue with her cup. Then, she picked up Milton's cup and looked inside. "This is strange. I see very similar, darkness covered everywhere."

Milton whispered to Aleyna's ear, "Dark coffee remains spread everywhere." Aleyna looked at him, moving her lips forward and upper lip downward to show her disappointment on him for his impatience.

She paused for a moment and continued, "Wait a minute, I see a hope. It is a tiny hope of light, but it is very strange. The path of the hope is moving from far, very far distance to the center."

Milton asked interrupting her, "How far?"

She moved the cup toward him, showing a white tiny trace cleared of the coffee remains like the River Nile extending for long distances and giving life in desert. She said, "This is a very long path that I have never seen before. The hope is coming from far, very far distances."

Milton got up his chair and put $20 on the table for her before start walking to the door. He was worried in his mind about the way the fortune-teller was talking. He would never believe in these things, but he knew something has already come down to Earth from the far space. He said to Aleyna, "Only trouble comes from far - far distances, not the hope."

"Be careful, don't confuse the good from the evil. That tiny hope could be the only hope," said the fortune-teller as they were getting out of the café.

They went to Milton's place together and went to bed quickly to get rest. They were feeling exhausted from the long day. Aleyna fell asleep almost instantly as she had a busy day at work entering product serial numbers and order numbers into their database for all day. But Milton was having difficulty falling asleep. His mind was busy thinking how to convince everyone that the corporation was behind so many murders. It would be impossible for him to convince others that possibility of some type of alien force could be involved behind the corporate operations. Especially since even himself wasn't certain of it. Perhaps it would be difficult to convince the world of the existence of aliens, but he could try to convince them of the existence of the link between the murders and the corporation. There was only one fact he was certain in his mind that the corporation was nothing, but pure evil. The world had to be told and be convinced of this fact.

Meanwhile, Bernard in his home got a call on his special communication device from Vortek. Normally, Bernard would contact him once a month to report the progress and discuss the plans. Everything happening in his office and around him was directly recorded and sent to Vortek's ship through the androids and computers used in the company. Vortek was able to follow up everything going on with the company. He could see anyone they wanted to see through the androids eyes and ears. Vortek didn't look happy tonight. "This man, Milton is getting out of control."

Bernard was nervous as he knew Vortek had the power to kill almost anyone, even him, at anytime if he wanted. He thought that as long as he keeps him happy, he would eventually take full control of the world. He was already controlling most of the world through the power of the corporation. Vortek would leave one day, and he would be the sole power. "You don't need to worry, sir. Everything is under control."

"No, Bernard. You must take necessary actions. He and his friends must be eliminated," said Vortek.

"Sir, the others are no threat. Milton cannot do anything. No one would believe him. He is working next to my office." Bernard tried to convince him it wasn't necessary to kill them, but Vortek wasn't willing to take any chances.

"Trust me, they have to be eliminated. There is something wrong with his android. We sometimes have problems accessing and uploading daily reports."

"As you wish, sir. I'll take care of it."

CHAPTER 15: CHAOS

Milton lived in a house that had an open kitchen in the living room. While his mind continued floating in thoughts at midnight, he heard some sounds coming from the living room next to the kitchen's cabinet. Niffy was standing up at the corner of the living room's kitchen's section during night as usual. "No no." Niffy was talking to himself. Milton got up from the bed. He walked to the open bedroom door and entered the living room. He turned the lights on. Niffy's talking continued, getting louder and louder. He seemed to be suffering a nightmare. Aleyna also woke up from the noises and walked next to Milton in her sleep wear. "Is everything all right?" Niffy kept saying loudly, "No... negative... reject... negative..." suddenly he stopped. The light in his eyes turned on. He looked at Milton and said, "There was an external attempt to load a command on my system."

Milton asked, "What command... what is it?"

"I do not know. My external data uploading unit was damaged in the accident and upload was unsuccessful."

Milton thought to himself for a moment and said to Niffy with a whispering tone, "hmm? Perhaps I could bypass your uploading system. I am not sure if it will work, but we'll give it a go."

Aleyna looked at Milton with sleepy eyes, "Can't it wait for tomorrow? I am so sleepy."

She kept yawning while watching them. Brawny was also watching them curiously, but she looked unusually nervous. Her sixth senses were making her feel uncomfortable. She was moving a few steps toward Milton and then turning back moving a few steps toward Aleyna. Staring at Niffy for a second and repeating the same routine. Aleyna kneeled down and petted her to comfort, saying, "Are you sleepy, too? You look nervous tonight. It is all right, baby, you can sleep." She continued padding her, "Oh, aren't you adorable?"

Milton took a cable with USB plugs at both ends. He attached one end to the inside of Niffy's left ear and the other end to his PC. Niffy stood still as if he was in standby mode. Milton said to Aleyna, "I want to know what they are up to." After he spent a few minutes in his computer, he said, "Here, we go!" and pressed ENTER on his keyboard. Brawny instantly ran to the corner of the room and hid behind the tiny space between the bookshelf and the wall. Aleyna watched her with surprised eyes. He was able to resolve the meaning of the message, it was a clear command. 'Kill them both!'

There was silence for a second. Suddenly Niffy moved his head slightly up and said, "command uploaded" –he paused for a moment— "Affirmative," with a cold and loud mechanical voice. Milton got off his computer chair and moved next to Aleyna close to the bedroom door. The red ball of light in Niffy's eyes turned on. He instantly grabbed a large kitchen knife from its sharp edge and threw at Milton. The knife cut through the side of his left arm's skin and stuck onto the bedroom door's frame as Milton looked still with surprised eyes. Aleyna watched with a shocked face and screamed in horror, "Aaahh". Milton moaned in pain, "Uhh", but he was very lucky the knife only scratched his arm.

Milton quickly pushed Aleyna to the bedroom from her shoulder. He shot the bedroom door and locked. They both hurried to the bedroom window, which was at two meters high from the floor. Milton quickly opened the window and shouted, "Jump!". He held her hand to help her get on the window. They jumped down and ran. As they started running to find a place to hide around the house, they could hear the glass shattering. When they turned their head back, they saw Niffy jumped out from the living room's window, breaking the glasses in hurry trying to catch them. Milton and Aleyna ran in to the car to escape from Niffy and jumped inside.

His car was one of the sportive model series produced by GlobCorp. The supercar had fully automated running functions with advanced chips and electronics. Milton commanded a few times repeatedly, "Run! Run! Run, damn run." But the engine was not starting and suddenly the doors were locked even if he did not order so. He realized at that moment it was not just Niffy but GlobCorp who was trying to kill them, and they were about to succeed it. They were trapped inside their car. The car started to give carbon dioxide gas inside the passenger cabinet.

When Niffy reached there, he could clearly see Milton and Aleyna were having problems breathing. Niffy's memory processors and advance NAI units were running in perfect conditions. He remembered how Milton spent many nights trying to fix him when he was hit by a train. He remembered him working with exhausted sleepless eyes and saying, "You may be a robot, but you are my best friend. Friends don't give up on each other." Niffy's chips were getting confused by the command given by the owner registered in his highest level of ownership registry unit. The command to kill Milton and Aleyna wasn't calculating a balanced equation system in his NAI unit that was designed for him to have the self-learning ability. The command to execute them was getting converted to equations, which were not in equilibrium state to execute the commands. He could see Milton hitting the car's window with both hands and his lips movement calling his name, "Niffy, help us, please help us, Niffy" with his exhausting energy, he tried to shout his name "Niffyyy..."

Niffy made the decision to abort the command from the highest registered original owner. In his system, there were double layers of registered owners. The first registration was Milton. The second registered owner was the corporate president, but the highest ranked owner was from the outer space. His NAI system was very advanced. He learned how Milton cared for him and made significant sacrifices. He sacrificed his sleep, even his food and his life, for many nights to repair him. Niffy could finally force his NAI unit to take charge over the external command downloading mechanism.

He overloaded the external communication system with high-density energy beams. Suddenly, a low soft explosion sound was followed with a bit of smoke coming out from his mouth.

He approached the car and smashed the side windows behind the front seat with his right fist. He grabbed the car's door from inside with his left hand and outside handle with his right hand and pulled it out, breaking the door's hinges. Then he pulled Aleyna and Milton out of the car. They sat on the grass in front of the house next to the garage. While they were coughing and trying to regularize their breath in the fresh air, suddenly the car's engine started. At first, the car backed up twenty meters away from them. When it turned toward Milton and Aleyna, Niffy knew what was about to happen. He quickly jumped in front of them before the car speeded over them. Niffy put his right foot back to the side, bended his left knee in front slightly, and moved his body forward, preparing for the impact. When the car reached him, he quickly put his left arm under the car. He stopped the car with his body and held the top of the bonnet with his right hand. The car's back side lifted up to air with its own speed. Niffy held the car up standing on its front over his body between his left and right arm. Then, he hit the car's top on the driveway with all his power together with the force generated by the car's own speed. The many parts of the car broken and parted form the car and spread around with shattering glasses and squeezing loud metallic sounds. Its energy generation unit was cracked and it caused an explosion with fire and smoke raised high in the air.

Milton came toward Niffy, "What happened? Why did you try to kill us?"

Niffy became distressed, got into the crying mode. He replied while weeping, "I am sorry for trying to kill you. The command to kill you was from the owner."

"Niffy, I am your owner," Milton pointed to himself with his hand, and continued, "I thought you were programmed not to kill anyone."

"You are the level 3 owner."

"What? Level 3?" said Milton as he stared at Niffy.

Niffy replied, "The level 1 owner is not you. It is in outer space. I was loaded with a kill program that can overwrite my safe-serve character if ordered by the owner."

Milton turned to Aleyna, "We have to get some clothes and get out of here before police arrives." When Milton and Aleyna hurried back into house to get some clothes, Brawny came outside next to Niffy, started rubbing her head to Niffy's leg and purring. Milton rushed to the house holding Aleyna's hand, "Hurry up, hurry! Hurry! GlobCorp is controlling both the police and the army with the androids. We cannot trust them. I am sure they will be here soon after so much noise."

Niffy gently picked Brawny up. After petting her head softly, he put her on the custom-made basket fitted with a tiny blanket at the bottom. It was built with tin-frame bars on his left shoulder. When it is not needed, Niffy could contract the basket to move in and settle within his body without disturbing his activities. When he wanted, the basket would pop up coming out from his shoulder. Brawny sat down in the basket feeling comfortable and calm, watching outside through the bars.

They quickly got out of house with their daily clothes. Milton had his usual informal jeans and a white T-shirt while Aleyna had her skirt and was just putting her blouse on. Niffy extended his stands attached to either side of his legs. Milton could stand on the right side of Niffy's leg extension and

249

Aleyna stood up on the left side, holding Niffy tightly. As Niffy speeded up outside of the residential areas, Milton asked Niffy to establish contact with Shwarz and Asimov through his internal communication system to warn them. He knew they could be in danger as well.

When Asimov answered the phone, he could barely talk as he was running from his robot at home. Asimov never bought any of the GlobCorp's cars. He first learned driving with an automatic gear car when he was sixteen years old. Later, his father bought him an old manual car. He struggled with the clutch and gas pedal for a few months, but he started to enjoy it after he got used to coordinating his left foot on the clutch and right foot on the gas pedal. Since his first car, he always drove a manual-stick car. "I am in a hurry now," said on his phone as he jumped in his car.

"Asimov, you have to get out of your house and stay away from the androids and the cars," Milton shouted to make sure Asimov could hear him. Strong wind was making loud noise on the background as Niffy speeded.

"I already know that. My stupid piece of junk chased me, but I could get into my car. Where are you guys heading?"

"Oh no. You got to get out of the car, Asimov. Cars are also dangerous. My car was blown out while trying to kill us."

"Don't worry about that. I am not driving one of Bernard's toys. This is a real car," Asimov sounded proud of his convertible Mustang.

"Smart choice. Meet us in front of the bitter and sweet place," Milton was worried about the hacking of their communication. He tried to choose his words carefully to avoid potential hackers identifying their location.

"Got you. See you there soon." As they had dessert with bitter coffee this evening, it wasn't too hard for Asimov to understand the location of the coffee shop.

"Call Shwarz, hurry up, Niffy" asked Milton. Niffy called his phone, but there was no answer in Shwarz's phone. Milton was worried. "Let's check on his android. Niffy, establish communication with his android and try to find out what happened." Niffy knew Schwarz's android's id as they have met many times previously. Milton, Asimov, Aleyna, and Shwarz would get together from time to time to have dinner and chat. Milton often took Niffy with him when he went to his place. Niffy established contact with the android internally in a silence mode. Then, he shouted, "You trash can." It was an unusual language for an android to use. Milton was surprised and felt horrified. He could tell something horrible must have happened. He turned to Niffy, "What? Where is Shwarz? Is he OK?"

Niffy sounded sad and could barely reply with a whispering tone of voice, "I am sorry Milton. It killed him and his family."

"Oh no, Shwarz." Milton felt deep sadness and anger. He couldn't believe his friend and his family were murdered.

"I think you need to hear this," Niffy tuned itself to receive a local radio broadcasting news. The woman on the radio sounded furious, "There has been a horrifying murder just a while ago. Dr. Shwarz was one of the rare geniuses in our times. He and his family, wife and two children, have been killed brutally in their home. He has been known with his developments especially on octagonal physics and neural intelligence, which have been used in development of advance robotic systems at GlobCorp. Police chief announced that the androids helping the investigation found evidences that his two other scientists colleagues Dr. Asimov, Dr. Milton and his girlfriend, Aleyna, who were working at GlobCorp, are involved in killing him and his family. Their motives are yet to be known. Mr. Bernard, President of GlobCorp, said that these cold-blooded murderers must pay for their crimes. GlobCorp will do everything in its power to help the police department to catch them and bring to the justice..."

"Turn it off Niffy" Milton wasn't surprised to hear this anymore. The corporation wanted them dead. They knew too much. They were too high risks for the sustainable business and future of the corporation. When they arrived in the coffee shop, it was quiet as the shop was closed. They moved to the side of the shop to wait for Asimov. He arrived with his car a few minutes later.

Asimov parked his car next to them and said, "It is proven that you were right. They want us dead. Obviously, we cannot go back to our places. We need to get out of the city."

"I got a friend from the university. He lives forty minutes North outside the city. He is a friendly guy. We can stay at his place tonight and think about what to do tomorrow."

Milton and Assange would often get in to scientific discussions and arguments while they were studying. Their discussion would sometimes be mistaken as fighting by other passing-by students, but their brain storming arguments helped them to achieve in their studies and strengthened their friendship. Assange often had strong pessimistic views about most of the scientific models and methods that would fire up their discussions.

Milton jumped into the front seat of the car while Aleyna and Niffy slid onto the back seat.

When they arrived in Assange's place, they faced an unexpectedly hostile welcome in front of the door. Assange was holding a rifle and another man next to him was holding a machine gun toward them. Asimov said with a teasing voice, "I have seen friendlier welcome before."

"Assange, what's going on?" asked Milton walking out in front of the car while the others joined him slowly.

Assange pointed to Niffy, "That thing, why did you bring it here?"

"It is mine. Niffy is different than others. He is harmless" replied Milton.

"Keep him away, Milton."

"All right, Assange, he can stay here. Niffy was rebuilt. He is different than other androids," —after pausing for a moment, Milton asked, "But what happened? What are you so angry about?"

Assange slowly moved his rifle down, "This is Charlie, my brother-in-law. He was a captain in the army. Because of these robots, they dismissed most of the army. He lost his job too. These machines are everywhere. They are not trustable."

"I know. The corporation is trying to kill us. They already killed one of our best friends and his family. They killed many others. Aleyna is my girlfriend and Asimov is—"

Assange interrupted him, "Your colleague and all of you are wanted for your friend's murder." He came closer to Milton and gave a hug, "I am sorry for the hostile welcoming, but we don't trust machines. Please come inside. You and your friends are always welcome at my place, but the robot must stay out."

Aleyna took Brawny from her basket to carry in, but she jumped down and wanted to stay outside. They all got in to Assange's home as Niffy waited outside with Brawny. Milton was surprised to see that there were others who don't thrust the GlobCorp. As they were entering the house, Milton ordered, "Niffy, keep your ears and eyes open!"

CHAPTER 16: DARK ERA

Vortek watched the growth of GlobCorp with pride from his spaceship while Serium stayed inside his secured cell. Vortek commanded, "Guards, bring Serium to the deck." Soon, the guards brought him to the main deck with his hands cuffed. Vortek pointed out Earth from the ship. "Look, Serium, this is the Earth you have risked your life for. You wanted to risk the lives of all Zolans for it. I told you they were primitive. Now I am going to prove it. You will soon understand your council friends died for your stupidity."

"What are you going to do, Vortek? You came here for uranium. Why don't you take it and leave?" asked Serium.

"Oh, I already got plenty of it. Our ship is fully loaded, but I want you to see how primitive they are."

"You are out of your mind. You are mad. You got what you want. You should get the hell out of here," shouted Serium, worrying of his mad mind.

Vortek laughed loudly, "Ah ha ha ha huh. No, no. I am not planning to leave soon. I am enjoying this game. I am playing the game fully fair. I obey their laws," —pausing for a moment— "And, guess who is in charge there? Come on Serium, who do you think is ruling this planet now?"

"What have you done? What are you talking about?"

"I haven't done anything at all except taking full control of the management. Now, Earth must obey my commands." Vortek has talked with pride. He was truly enjoying his success and feeling accomplished. He explained how the company grew up and how it took the control of the world's finance. He talked how he managed to sell the androids, how his business was extended to all other industries one by one, and how he got rid of the money, changing one of the fundamental systems.

After hearing all of what he had done on Earth, Serium got deeply worried about Earth's future, but there was nothing he could do to help prevent him. He couldn't think of how Vortek could have possibly done all of this. He felt puzzled, "How could you establish a company and do all that on Earth?"

Vortek said, "It was easier than I initially thought. I got me a business partner down there. Bernard!" He paused for a second looking into Serium's eyes. "Yes, surely, you remember him. I must admit, he has done a much better job in building my company than I thought. See, it is not too difficult to convince a primitive mind to do anything you want to. It is especially easier when the mind is fully dominated by self-centered thoughts and greedy ambitions."

"What a fool," he said, finding it hard to believe that someone would actually make a partnership with such a mad-minded creature. He couldn't stop commenting, "What kind of fool would make partnership with you to betray against his own kind."

"Someone we both know did that, too." Vortek was referring to Serium himself not to interfering with Earth even though there was risk of running out of energy source in his planet. Vortek always considered him as a traitor for not supporting the idea of coming to Earth to get the resources needed in Zola. This was simply an act of treason against his own kind. Vortek added, "You can't really blame him. First of all, he didn't really have much of a choice to accept my proposal, and secondly, one cannot be blamed for having a primitive mind since that is what these creatures are. It is his nature, just like it is the nature of a lion to hunt for food to satisfy its hunger.

Serium got upset and extremely angry at Vortek's actions. He knew Vortek's intentions were horrifying, "These primitive creatures are going to kick your arse, Vortek. You just wait and see," he yelled at him as if there was any chance. He wasn't really thinking that Earth stood a chance against these hundreds of millions of android slaves distributed all over the world. It was a very disturbing and painful fact to accept for Serium that Vortek's corporation was fully in charge of the world.

Vortek said, "I want you to stay in the main deck so you can see everything and witness their primitive nature. As you can see, there is nothing you or anyone else can do to stop me now." Then he ordered the android guards standing next to Serium, "Give him a comfortable chair." The android guards gave Serium a chair and one of them pushed him from his shoulder to make him sit on it. Then, they formed a cell around him within the deck by setting up bars reflecting laser beams. Serium could see everything from the monitors and hear everything going on from his cell.

Vortek contacted Bernard, "Report on the terrorists Bernard. Have you eliminated them?"

"Dr Shwarz is killed and the others are wanted for killing him. They could escape for now. Milton's android is not collaborating with your orders."

"I know that already myself!" shouted Vortek. "Report to me as soon as you find their location," he said, sounding worried.

Serium felt a light of hope, thinking perhaps everything wasn't over yet. As long as there were some who resisted the evil, there would be hope. "Problems, Vortek?" he asked.

"Trust me, Serium, they are no threat to me. They will be found soon and their worthless lives will end."

Then Serium thought about the android not collaborating with Vortek. His hope felt more real as he thought even a machine, one of Vortek's own androids, already achieved understanding of Vortek's madness. He made the right choice to change sides. Vortek's failure in his murder plans was the obvious proof that the hope could grow to create a real chance for the survival of the Earthman.

261

In Assange's house, Assange's wife Suzan, his sister Esra, Charlie, Aleyna, Milton, and Asimov gathered around a large rectangular wooden kitchen table. There were six chairs around the table. They all sit down expect Assange, he brought another chair from the other room for himself.

Assange said, "We cannot trust in these robots. They are in every organization and almost in every house. We have heard on TV that you killed Dr. Shwarz and his family. You are all now declared the most wanted, armed and dangerous terrorists."

"They killed our friends. His android killed them," Milton said. He took a deep breath in sadness. "We have to do something. We must fight them. I don't think anyone is safe anymore. Niffy saved our lives while my car had almost killed us."

Asimov said, "It won't be easy to fight them. People believe anything they hear on TV. We are only few, and the entire country is against us."

Charlie said, "That is not entirely true. I have many friends who served in the army for many years until they were replaced by these machines."

Milton said, "We should talk to them. All the plane crashes were also caused by GlobCorp. I am not sure how, but they have a means to produce strong field of statics. That seems to be the main cause of the accidents. The company is managed from the space. We have been invaded. It pisses me off to think about it. We haven't even noticed we were invaded by some alien slaves we haven't faced."

Suzan's puzzled voice came out, "Aliens? What aliens?"

"Niffy mentioned me once there is a central database in outer space. All androids are commanded by aliens, and their commands overwrite ours. Apparently, these androids have a multi-layer ownership registry system ¬ multiple owners with hierarchy. The space command center is the highest level," Milton said. All of them stared at Milton as none of them was expecting the alien involvement. Their worry and fear grew, knowing that their enemy was not just a giant corporation, but some alien force they had no idea of their powers.

Milton said, "Niffy was being loaded with the command to kill us when he chased us for a while. Then, he overloaded the external downloading mechanism with high-density energy beams and exploded it. They cannot command him anymore."

"Can he access the database?" Assange asked.

"He had very limited access, but I am sure they must have already disabled his access. I'll ask him." Milton walked to the door and asked, "Niffy, can you access the main database?"

"Negative, access denied," Niffy responded from outside the door.

As Milton was walking back to the table, Niffy opened the door with a strong push hitting the door to the wall with a loud banging sound. "You have to hide quickly. A police patrol with two androids are heading this way."

Asimov said, "Car! They will know my car. Is there a place to hide it?"

"Drive it behind the house" Assange suggested.

Asimov drove his car as the patrol car was just appearing from the top of the slope across the house. Niffy said, "I'll handle them."

Milton, Aleyna and Asimov hid in the upstairs bedroom while others stayed around the table. As the patrol car pulled in front of house, Niffy could hear androids reporting to the central station, "We are searching the terrorists in a house at 37 Michigan Road." The androids got out of their police car and approached the patio. Niffy came out to meet them while Brawny was sitting on the patio and watching them from next to the door.

"What are you doing here? How can I help you?"

"Where is your master?" said one of the police androids.

"My master is sitting there," said Niffy showing Brawny. Then as the androids started looking at each other, trying to figure out how a cat could be his master. Niffy whispered, "Relax, I was just kidding, though she is one of my masters. My family is taking a nap. Please don't make noise."

"We want to search around the house, looking for three terrorists," said one of the androids. The other one added, "They are armed and extremely dangerous."

"I know. I saw them on the news. I will report to you if anything unusual happens," said Niffy.

The other android was not convinced from Niffy's words. He said, "We will take a look around ourselves," as he started walking toward the backside of the house. The other android walked beside him to go around. Niffy knew they were not going to miss Asimov's car. There was no way these two androids would be convinced to turn back.

Brawny came running from the patio and stood in front of the androids looking at them with her usual curiosity. She looked at them as if she wanted to be petted. They looked at each other and one said, "We can't touch the cat, it is against our law." In Zola, the laws were strict about harming other creatures. Protecting the nature's balance was the top priority. The animals' lives were not interfered by Zolans or any machines they built. Even though these androids were built for the evil purpose to destroy humanity, they still would avoid directly harming other creatures that were not specifically mentioned in their orders. While the two androids looked at Brawny, Niffy walked with fast steps to reach behind them. As he came close to them, he first grabbed both of their heads and forcefully hit each other. He grabbed the gun from one of the androids with his right hand, using the opportunity for the moment the androids' lost balance from the impact. He held the head of the android and bent backward with his powerful metallic arm. The backward forceful push of the android's head caused him open its mouth slightly. He fired a shot in his mouth exploding the androids head around with a loud noise and some smoke rose up from his blown-off neck.

The other android grabbed his gun to shoot at Niffy, but Niffy managed to fire at his hand before him. The android's right hand got damaged, losing his thumb. His gun was broken with its pieces spread around. The android hit Niffy's head with his left fist. Niffy was thrown to the ground with the force. He fired a shot to the android's head as it was standing, but the bullet barely caused him to move his head only a little.

He came closer to Niffy's head, kicking his face. Then, he put his foot on Niffy's face applying a strong force to smash him. Niffy held his foot and pushed him back. Niffy got up and jumped over the android. Niffy first grabbed him, pulling up and pushed him to the ground forcefully. As he pressed his body to the android's body to prevent him from moving around, Niffy held the android's left hand with his left hand and he put his knee on the android's right hand. Niffy put the gun in his open right eye and fired a shot. The bullet smashed and burned his eyeball, but the android still managed to hit the gun in Niffy's hand. and the gun was thrown away. Then, he hit Niffy's head with his head strongly.

Niffy was shaken with the effect of the force for an instance. Then, Niffy slid himself behind the android while holding the android's neck. Niffy held his jaw with left hand and back of his head with his right hand. He forcefully rotated the android's head turning his face totally behind his body with a squeezing, metallic friction sound. Niffy then rotated his head another half-cycle, turning his face back to the front of his body, which caused his neck to loosen from his body. Some smoke came out from the android's mouth. The smoke smelled like electric cables that got short-circuited and burned.

Niffy was, in fact, smarter than the other androids. It was his higher intelligence, making him stronger. When Milton was repairing him, he fitted Niffy with an additional self-learning mechanism that Milton programmed the chip himself, applying the algorithm he developed during his PhD studies. This additional unit gave Niffy an advantage to learn more things and improve himself in a faster rate than the other androids did.

Niffy ran back to the home, "Come on, everyone, we have to go now. Other androids will be here soon. The two androids are blown off and cannot report back to the station anymore."

As Milton, Asimov, and Aleyna were running down the stairs, Milton said, "Charlie, do you know any place we can get some weapons? We need strong ammunitions."

"I think my ex-army friend can help us get what we need. I'll take the Ute. Follow me with your car," Charlie said as he was thinking of going to General Mike's place. When they arrived at the general's house, he welcomed them. He was happy to see they were all well. The general was one of the few opposing the idea of having androids in the army from the very start. Because of his continuous arguments to prevent the androids from keep increasing within the army, he was made to retire two years earlier than his retirement time.

Charlie saluted him as he got off the car. "General!"

He responded with a relaxed pose, "Relax, Charlie, we are not in the army anymore." He then turned to Niffy, "Excellent work son. I've heard on the news you blew off two of those bastards."

Niffy felt proud. "Thank you, General, I enjoyed it." He wasn't showing the pride because he could terminate two androids, but he was showing the appreciation because the general called him like he was a person and one of them, not just a machine.

They all spent the night at the general's house. Brawny slept next to Niffy as usual. Next morning, Aleyna, Assange's wife Suzan, and sister Esra stayed at home together with the general's wife Dorothy and his daughter Jennifer as the others got on his car and drove away. The general took them to a valley surrounded by hills three hours outside the city. He led them to the base of a hill where a large rock was covered with dust, bushes, and small pebbles around. Charlie asked impatiently, "General, there doesn't seem like anything here."

The general moved toward the side of the rock, almost a meter far from the large rock. He said, "Patience." After he wiped off some of the pebbles and branches from the surface, an old rusted steel box appeared. He took a small key from his pocket and opened the cover of the box. Under the box, there was a small keyboard with numbers on it with a little rectangular digital view like a calculator. He typed a set of numeric password to unlock the secret gate. As soon as he typed the numbers, the huge rock started to move a side, making a sound like a car trying to stop with a worn out brake disk. As it moved aside, a huge space under the hill became apparent. When the gate was opened, it was clear that the large rock, other pebbles, and branches were just attached to the steel door to camouflage the entrance.

As they were walking through the long hallway, the general said, "This is a secret storage facility built in 1942 to be used as a central command center in case if the city was invaded during the second world war. There is no record of its existence anywhere. When they started bringing the

271

androids to the army, they also started giving them the military secrets. I decided to reorganize this place." The main hall of the storage place contained shelves along walls, which were filled with ammunition. There were all types of rifles, machine guns, rocket launchers, bombs, and explosives stored neatly. There were some rooms connected to this main hall built for accommodation, a room built to serve as a kitchen had all the facilities required for cooking. It was full of food including cans of corns, beans, soups, fruits, spam food, flour, rice and others that can be stored for a long time and frozen meat products in a large refrigerator fitted to the corner of the kitchen.

Asimov asked, "How does the power reach to this cave?"

"It has its own generator units," replied General. "I want to show you the other rooms," said the general as he walked out of the kitchen's entrance. The next room was very large and equipped with radio communication units and multiprocessor computers that were built before GlobCorp took over the business along the wall. All of them were amazed by the size of the room and how huge the space was under the hill. There was a large LED screen TV on the wall across the room's entrance and two large sofas, a table and some chairs were in the room. As they moved to the end, there were two other large rooms. When they reached to the entrance of one of the rooms, the surprise was noticeable on everyone's face. Two military vans were parked side by side and one of them was filled with explosives, guns and rocket launchers. Asimov couldn't hide his amazement. "Wow, that's impressive." The general felt happy and tried to hide his smile as he felt patriotic hearing these words from someone with Russian background.

Milton said, "General, this is really impressive. We can use this place as a base. We can coordinate attacks to the androids." Each of them grabbed some machine guns, hand grenades and ammunition. As Niffy could carry the heavier one, he took a rocket launcher. They headed back to the general's home.

CHAPTER 17: MONARCHY ON EARTH

Meanwhile after Milton and his friends left Assange's house, the androids at the police central station reported the event back to Bernard's android and the Vortek. "Two police androids have been terminated. We are waiting your commands."

Vortek contacted Bernard immediately, "Bernard, it is time now. It is time for you to declare yourself as the emperor of the world. Prepare the entire android army and security forces. Whoever and whatever come in between you and your kingdom, you must crush them. Remember, you cannot show any weakness if you want to hang on to your kingdom."

Bernard was excited about the news that he was to rule the world with his army of androids. He thought there had to be many people who would be willing to support him since his corporation was so powerful. He was sure that most of the people would certainly stand on the side that had a better chance of winning in a conflict. He responded with a proud and excited sound, "Yes, sir, it is an excellent time. I'll ask the army to be ready for any opposition, but first, I'll smash these few terrorists."

Bernard commanded the android who was assigned as the general in the army, "Prepare all your forces. Collaborate with all other security units to capture the terrorists. Prepare to suppress any opposition to my ruling. Send one thousand armed androids to control the surroundings of the White House. Tell them to wait for my commands." As the army and security forces were preparing to act to suppress any possible demonstration or action against Bernard's declaring himself as the emperor, Bernard got into his car and headed for the airport to go to Washington DC. Androids in the army units based in Washington DC were quickly organized and took their positions around the White House as Bernard settled in his private jet waiting for him at the airport.

He contacted one of the androids, "Ask all members of the cabinet to go home and stay at their home until further notice. Tell them that there is a code-red security breach. It is necessary for their safety to stay inside their homes. We will inform them when the situation is resolved."

Bernard arrived at Washington DC three hours later with his two personal androids. He met the president and said, "Mr. President, I am deeply sorry for interfering your work and causing disturbance, but you and your family should vacate the White House temporarily. My androids identified a serious terrorist threat."

The president asked, "Police and army can handle it. Why are you here?"

"I am afraid some high-level authorities in both army and security agencies are involved in a large-scale act against the US government. We have to handle it using androids. I promise you personally, the androids will stabilize the situation as soon as possible. They will inform you to return back once the security is established." Bernard assigned two androids for each parliament members and two for the family of the president to ensure they would stay at their homes.

After the White House was fully evacuated, Bernard called for a media meeting. He made his speech aired live for the public in front of media members, watching with curious eyes not knowing what was all this about.

"People of Earth, today is the day for us to unite! Today is the day to get rid of the geographic borders and to unite as one. I, as the emperor of this world, promise to lead you toward a truly peaceful and wealthy future. Today, we come to a point in time that we have enough power to establish the peace worldwide. We have enough technology to eliminate poverty and unemployment from the surface of this Earth. All I ask in return from everyone is to give our new system a chance, to give a chance for the peace and to give a chance for ending the poverty. We must respect our system just as we must respect each other. Those who oppose us will face the power of heavily handed justice."

A female reporter stood up from the back row and laughed. "You emperor? What the hell do you think you are doing? Is this a joke?" she said and she walked to the entrance of the media conference hall where several androids were standing by the door. One of the androids stepped in front of her and punched her face with his powerful metallic hand. The android's fist came out from behind her head covered with blood. In front of the media and the entire world watching on TV with frightened eyes, her lifeless body fell on to ground. Many screamed in horror while the others froze, couldn't move and couldn't say anything. Bernard, with an unaffected cold heart approached the microphone, "I assure you, it is not a joke. The laws will be implemented equally for everyone worldwide." Then he left the media conference room.

Milton and his friends saw everything on live TV broadcasting. One thing was clear anymore, people of earth were no longer free. They were slayed by their slaves. Earth was enslaved by the evil corporation. "I can't believe that bastard Bernard could do this. We have to kill them, we must kill him and his machines," Asimov said.

Milton said, "We must plan our acts well, we are only few."

"People in the army and security forces are minority compare to the androids. We cannot expect they could help us. We must assume they have to obey the orders," the general said.

Milton said, "We cannot stay here too long. I am sure they will look at every house for us. We should move to the base." Dorothy was enjoying chatting with Suzan and Esra. They rode on the general's vehicle together with Charlie.

Dorothy liked the warmth and calmness of Brawny and carried her to the van with them. Asimov asked Aleyna to drive his car, and he wanted to hold down on to his M249 automatic. Asimov, Jennifer and Niffy squeezed in on the backseat as Milton sat next to Aleyna.

When they were just leaving the house, an army van appeared behind them. At first, they turned toward the house, but androids saw them leaving the house and turned back to the road to come after them. Aleyna was following the general's vehicle in front. The general's vehicle was a big old four-wheel drive. They couldn't speed enough to lose them.

Aleyna saw them in her rearview mirror. "We are being followed. They are coming pretty fast." Milton turned back and asked Jennifer to change seats. He could jump back over the seats, taking advantage of Asimov's convertible. Asimov and Milton pointed their rifles toward the van.

As the van got closer, Milton, Asimov, and Niffy started firing their machine guns to the vehicle. While they were shooting, a helicopter appeared on top of them. Milton looked at Niffy and said, "We can handle the van, you take care of the chopper," as he pointed with his eyes to the rocket launcher lying over Niffy's feet. The androids in the van were shooting back at them. Asimov shouted, "Aleyna, open the trunk." His car's trunk was connected to an internal switch allowing it to be opened from the driver's seat by pressing a button. As soon as Aleyna pressed the button, his car's trunk popped up and shielded them from the bullets.

Jennifer lay down to make space for Niffy's launcher. The chopper was getting closer on top of the general's car to stop them. Niffy fired a rocket to the chopper. The chopper exploded with fire and smoke. It broke into many pieces and spread all around the road.

As they were shooting at each other with the military van following them with a fast speed, Asimov extended his gun outside toward the side of his car and could managed to hit their left front tire with a few bullets. The van lost its balance. The right side of the vehicle was thrown up in to air as the left tire collapsed. The van tipped over its frontend and tumbled. As the van tumbled up with its speed, the fuel tank was exposed. Milton fired a series of shots to the van's fuel tank. The tank caught fire and exploded loudly, rising fire and smoke high on the sky.

When they arrived in the valley, Charlie turned the TV on to see the news. While they blew up the helicopter and the military van, a TV network cameraman captured the fire and smoke rising from the freeway to the sky. Broadcasting the images of fire and smoke on the air took public's attention. People were getting out and gathering on the streets of the city. As people were gathering, many police and army vehicles were surrounding around the city. The security vehicles continuously announced for everyone to go back to their homes and stay inside. Cameras were showing the streets. A young man in the crowd took the camera's attention. He was carrying a large cartoon holding with his both hands above his head with this: GOT NO KING.

Milton and his friends knew these androids would not take it easy on the crowd. This gathering would cause disasters. They were cold steel machines and would not care about the emotions and pain of the people. They certainly would not have an idea what *freedom* meant for people. The androids in one of the police car noticed him with the big placard protesting the emperor, which was an intolerable act for their commands. They came next to him and one of them transformed its right arm to a sharp sword like long blade and hit hard on his head splitting into two from the top middle.

281

He stood motionless for a moment as a thin line of blood came down from the middle of his forehead down to his nose and mouth. He did not have time to scream, or to feel the pain; died instantly and fell down as all his blood was bursting out in all directions along the cut.

Everyone saw it on tv broadcasting got horrified by the scene. Nobody could find a word to say. Milton broke the silence and shouted, "We've got to get out now and help them. Those machines will slaughter them." He was standing with worries and angry feelings, but he knew he had to stay calm and think wisely no matter what the situation was. The crowd on the streets got bigger and bigger. They were gathering on one side as the security forces gathered across them. There were only a few people among the army and police forces. Some of the people in crowd had hand guns and some had personal rifles. These guns could not give much harm to these androids with steel bodies. Milton said, "General, could you please support us with the radio communication from the base?"

"Huh, do I look like someone to sit here and watch you guys from TV. I am going there to do my job son," said the general as he started arming himself with big strong bullets for his machine gun. Milton noticed women picking up large rifles too. He approached to Aleyna and said, "What do you think you are doing? You ladies stay here. It is too dangerous there."

Aleyna said, "If we don't destroy them, it won't matter where we stay. They will find us and kill us all anyway. We have the right to fight for our lives as much as you do."

Milton said, "But you don't even know how to use it?"

Aleyna said, "Yeah, I can certainly pull the trigger."

"No, you really cannot," said Milton and added, "not when the safety is on and never point the gun to us." He pushed the gun downward to the side of Aleyna. Then, he showed her the safety mechanism. They all grabbed a few hand grenades, bullets and various guns. The general put many other automatic machine guns on the back of the military van.

Asimov took two large machine guns around his shoulders, put three handguns that could shoot large bullets around his belt, an army knife squeezed in his belt, a knife inserted in his boot, and fitted hand bombs around his body. He said, "I am leaving with my own car. I'll hold them until you arrive. Those people need help now."

As he started moving to his car, his eyes got locked on Jennifer's beautiful brown eyes. In that instant she looked back at him and could see a sparkle of love and his failed efforts trying to hide his weakness, his emotions for her. He was ready to sacrifice his life with no hesitation to help those he hadn't even met. She could tell by looking at his face how he tried to avoid getting caught of his stare and turned his face other way quickly. That was all for his manly proud of prioritizing to sacrifice his life to save others over revealing his personal desires.

She felt uncomfortable and disturbed in her heart to letting him go and not knowing what could happen there. She was sure in her mind she had to be with him in this war that could be their last few hours in life. She rushed quickly after him and jumped in his car.

Milton said, "Niffy, let's go with them." Milton and Niffy jumped in the back seat of Asimov's car as the others were coming with the van.

When Asimov reached the city, they saw the horrifying scenes of slaughter. So many people were killed mercilessly. There were human limbs, cut arms, legs and half cut bodies over the streets covered in red blood.

A dozen androids came in front of a group of crowd and opened fire with machine guns. Blood of men, and women were spilt all around; the body parts were broken up and spread around with the impact of large bullets. Asimov came from the side of the road and crashed into the line of androids that didn't notice Asimov's fast-approaching car as they were too busy murdering unarmed people with their noisy weapons. Milton, Niffy, and Jennifer started firing their machine guns.

The androids were caught by surprise as they were not expecting any resistance with heavy arms. They jumped out of the car and threw a few of the extra machine guns to the people who managed to escape android's bullets at the side of the road, taking cover behind buildings from the androids. Niffy stood up and threw a hand grenade toward a group of four androids shooting at them behind a security vehicle. The security vehicle exploded and destroyed in fire together with the androids. Other androids were continuously shooting at them. They ran behind a nearby building to take cover.

The scene of blood and death of so many people affected some of those who were in the security forces. A female officer noticed the android standing next to her was trying to target an eight year old girl caught accidently in the middle of war while passing by. The girl was trying to hide behind a corner of a building, but from the side of the android, it could shoot her easily. She pointed her gun to android's head and shot him on the head with her powerful gun. After blowing off the android's head, she looked into the kid's eyes and winked. In an instant, a series of gun fires were heard. The police officer's body covered in blood fell down on the pavement.

Asimov and Jennifer were shooting at one side to prevent androids coming closer as Niffy kept shooting the opposite direction. Milton ran toward the next building's front and threw himself to the tiny space in front of the building's entrance to take cover. He shot the two androids who just killed the police officer.

The number of androids around was increasing every minute. Asimov's ammunition was finished in one of his rifle. Whilst he threw it away and took the other one, he asked Jennifer to provide cover for him. He ran across to the next building's entrance to get closer to a group of androids shooting at them while Jennifer continued firing bullets to prevent androids targeting him. After getting closer to the androids, he threw two hand grenades one after another. Androids were blown in pieces, and their parts spread around the building. He came back next to Jennifer in a cheerful mood and asked, "What is a pretty girl doing in a battlefield like this?"

She replied with a smile, "Turn around your face, let me see if you got hit on the head."

Suddenly, they heard the sound of a chopper appearing on top of the building next to them. They had no place to hide from the chopper as it approached over them. Niffy, from across the street was firing shots at it, but it wasn't enough to stop them. Niffy's side of the helicopter was covered with steel. Niffy couldn't get any of the androids in the chopper to his target. There were many other androids on the other side of the street shooting at Niffy and preventing him to get to the other side of the chopper. The chopper had strong bullet proof glass in front; Jennifer's firing bullets weren't doing any damage. Asimov could see an android on the chopper was targeting Jennifer. The android suddenly fired a shot at her. He jumped and pushed Jennifer on her shoulder and threw himself over her. As she fell down, she heard Asimov's sigh, "Uhh." Asimov was shot on his right shoulder and couldn't hold his gun anymore. The android saw him dropping his gun to the ground.

Androids were all around the streets, almost everywhere. Milton was continuously shooting from the building's entrance space at the androids shooting at him from behind the building two blocks down on the street. He threw a hand grenade over two androids and blew them in pieces. But as soon as they were destroyed, two more of them replaced their position almost instantly and started shooting back at him. There was a group of five other androids taking cover on the street behind their security vehicle and shooting at him. While he continued firing bullets, he ran to the next building's entrance shooting the two androids. As he was shooting continuously, his gun made a *click* sound and stopped firing. He was out of ammunition. He threw his last hand-grenade to the security vehicle with five androids staying behind. The blast destroyed three of them together with their vehicle.

He grabbed a case of ammunition to set in his gun. When he was just inserting the ammunition, he suddenly felt the strong metallic grab of an android on his shoulders from behind. The android came from inside of the building while Milton was standing next to the door facing the opposite direction, outside across the streets. The android was working to handle the building's general services, electrical work, plumbing as well as building's general security. As all other androids, this one's service program was also overloaded with the high-level security program to carry out orders from Bernard and Vortek. All the androids were communicated regarding Bernard's strict orders to crush any demonstration against him. This android also became a part of the android army to join the war against humans who opposed the new system.

As the android dragged him in to the hall of the building, he dropped his gun from the pain of the powerful force on his shoulders. The android picked him up and threw him forcefully across the wall. Milton fell down to floor, suffering in pain. As android was coming to him, he quickly grabbed the stool next to him and hit it. The stool broke, but the android didn't seem to feel anything. He grabbed Milton up again and said, "I am going to tear you off in small piece..." While he was talking, Milton reached the knife on his belt behind. This was a special army knife. The sharp edge was attached to the holder with a spring system. With a touch on the button, the sharp blade could be thrown away by the force of an internally fitted spring. Milton quickly moved the knife's sharp edge to the android's mouth and pressed the button. The blade of the knife moved through the android's throat causing a light scratch on the seal corner of the safety unit. The android knew what happened. With the effect of the surprise, he threw down Milton. Milton ran out and threw himself to the ground toward the outside from the door. The android blew up.

Meanwhile, the chopper approached over Asimov and Jennifer after they saw Asimov drop his gun. When the android was pointing to target Asimov and Jennifer with his machine gun, they thought that was the end. Asimov held her hand, relaxed and felt ready for their final moment. Just when they were about to be shot, they heard a whizzing sound. With the sound, a fire ball hit the helicopter and split it into many pieces with fire and smoke, spreading the pieces around in the sky. Glasses of the buildings around the chopper fell down shattering. The propeller of the helicopter hit the building, and fell down together with many pieces of metal and glasses.

Jennifer noticed the blood coming out from Asimov's shoulder. She tore a piece off the bottom of her skirt and rubbed around his wound. While he was settling to sit at the side of the wall, she kissed his cheek. "Thank you for saving my life. I can't believe you took a bullet for me."

Asimov tried to hide his pain. "Well, who wouldn't, for such beautiful eyes!"

Jennifer lightly pushed on his left shoulder. "You, silly joker –"

A van appeared from the corner of the street. It was the general's van. When the van stopped next to them, Charlie walked from behind the van holding the missile launcher smoking in his hands. As they continued fighting more and destroying some androids, more androids were coming around. Milton ran back closer to Asimov and Jennifer's side. The androids were a lot more than they could even imagine.

The androids fighting weren't just those in the army and police, but all the androids had the fighting skills. The androids were capable of using any weapons supplied from the army.

CHAPTER 18: A LIGHT of HOPE

Vortek was watching everything through the androids' vision from the main deck of his ship together with Serium. When the helicopter was shot down by the humans, Serium couldn't hide his cheer and shouted, "You'll lose, Vortek." Vortek got mad at Serium's cheering the humans. He turned to him with anger, but replied with a calm voice. "I can see you really like these creatures. I have an excellent plan for you. Since you believe they are so civilized, I will let them decide your destiny. They will make you taste the pain with their barbaric and primitive minds. They will cut you in pieces, torture you while you will be begging them for your life. But as you will learn soon, your begging for these barbarians will not help you."

Vortek commanded to the androids next to him, "Give him some Earthman's clothes. Put him in one of the ships and send to the center of action, to his fan Earthians."

He turned to Serium and said, "I will cease fire and make sure they will not die before they kill you torturing." He ordered the cease-fire to the androids on the ground but asked them to keep their positions. He added, "You see, they are no threat to me. I can kill them anytime I want. I will wait to see them kill you first. I will finish them up later. You can think of it as your own revenge, and you will appreciate me when you are dead." He made a sickening laugh as the androids took Serium to the ship.

On the ground, the shooting stopped as ordered by Vortek. Milton and his friends didn't know what was going on and why they stopped shooting at them. Suddenly, a bunch of lights appeared in the sky moving fast toward them. Milton and all others came next to each other and watched the light coming toward them. As it got closer, they noticed it was a small flying object that they have not seen before on Earth.

The space ship landed on the street just thirty meters away from Milton and his friends. The people who survived the androids' bloody shootings watched the ship with fear and curiosity. The people around had no idea about the existence of aliens or their involvement with the corporation. Some people were shouting, "Keep your cover, everyone. This might be carrying more androids."

A voice was heard saying, "It is carrying weapons, stronger weapons for machines!"

Another from the crowd shouted, "It is a bomb, people. Stay away. It is a bomb."

While speculations continued, a door opened from the spaceship and a few stairs extended out. Nothing happened for a few minutes. Nobody wanted to get too close to look inside. Then, Serium walked out of the ship while his hands were cuffed behind him with the laser handcuffs. Milton and his friends were facing Serium and could not see he was handcuffed. As he came to the end of the stairs, his handcuffs disappeared. He walked and stepped on the ground in the street in front of people's curious look. Androids were just standing still waiting for commands from Vortek. Milton knew that everything was planned from the space out there. It was obvious in his mind that this spaceship was coming from the same place the killer androids came from.

Milton ran to Serium and punched his face with all his strength. Serium fell to the ground harshly, with bleeding lips. Milton wasn't able to think straight as his mind was affected seeing so many dead people around. His friend was also lying injured. Serium said, "No, no, I am not your enemy." Milton hesitated for a while and stopped. The fortune-teller's words passed through his mind in an instant, *A hope from far - far*

295

distance... Then, he thought, *No, there can't be such things.* As his mind wandered in thoughts for the instant, someone from the crowd fired a shot at Serium while he was trying to get up. He got shot on his left thigh and fell to the ground again.

Then, a woman came running and shouted with her Japanese accent, "Stop, stop that. He is not an android. He is a human just like any of us. He had handcuffs. He must be a prisoner." She came from Japan to study in the United States seven years ago. After she finished her study in finance, she decided to live in Chicago. She saw that Serium's hands were cuffed behind him, but it disappeared as he walked down from the ship.

She said to Milton, "If you kill him, you are no different than these machines," pointing to the androids in security forces. She kneeled down beside Serium and said, "Are you all right? We need to stop bleeding."

"Thank you," he said as he groaned in pain. Yuki took her jacket off and rubbed around his wounded leg. She asked him to hold it tightly over the injured part.

"Vortek sent me here expecting you would kill me," said Serium.

Milton sat next to him and asked, "Who is Vortek? Who are you and Where did you come from?"

"Vortek is the one causing all these troubles. My name is Serium. I am from a planet far from here in a different solar system. My planet is called Zola. I was the leader in my planet. Vortek was one of the ten council members who help in ruling the planet. We lived in peace and harmony for many years. Vortek killed all other council members and convinced everyone that I killed them. He wanted to rule the planet and the universe. I and other council members opposed to him to come and interfere the Earth's destiny." He paused to moan in pain and coughed for a while before he continued, "GlobCorp is just a puppet corporation controlled by Vortek. He brought me here to show me that I was wrong."

"Wrong in what?" Milton interrupted him.

"In believing that the people of Earth are civilized and have good in them. He wanted to prove me wrong by getting me killed by you," said Serium as he suffered in pain. He breathed heavily due to the bullet's wound.

Milton said, "We don't know if what you are telling us is the truth or not. We'll talk later. He took a handcuff from one of the blown-off android's body nearby and put it on Serium's hands. "Did you bring it here?" asked Milton, pointing to the ship.

"No, it was controlled from the mother ship," he replied.

Milton said, "Let's go aside, it is not safe here, we don't know when these machines will start firing at us again."

Vortek didn't want to kill them at that moment. He was watching everything from his deck. He said to his assistant, "There is no doubt they will kill him. We just need to be patient for a while. Ask all androids to leave the area."

The captain looked surprised with Vortek's command, "Why don't you let the androids kill them now?"

Vortek replied with a cool attitude, "When they kill Serium, we will have the proof of an obvious fact; the fact that these humans are cold blooded murderers. At the moment, they are no threat for my androids. I will kill them after I have the record."

The captain thought for a while not clear of what Vortek's plans were. He said, "I don't see why we would need the proof."

Vortek said, "There would be no resistance for us back at home when we rule Zola and Earth."

All the androids left the area soon. They were all surprised not knowing why. Milton asked to Serium, "What's going on? Why are they leaving?"

Serium had no idea what Vortek was doing. "I am not sure. Vortek was expecting you to kill me, but you didn't do that and his plans must have changed. It is not easy to guess what he thinks."

Milton said, "You need to come with us."

Since Milton wanted to take Serium with him, Yuki said, "I am coming with you. I want to join you in fighting these machines. I want to know about him too." Yuki felt something about him that others haven't noticed. Their weapons were,

299

in fact, no match for these androids. Their chances to beat the androids seemed less than slim. She thought Serium could help them. Since he is from the same planet, he might know what to do, how to defeat them. Besides, he looked intelligent and peaceful person. She wanted to look after him and help him to get well soon.

Milton soon recognized his mistake to seeing him as enemy and being impatient in judging poorly. He helped him walk to their van to show a kind of apology for. However, he thought he had to be careful and keep the handcuffs on until he is sure of his intention. He didn't mind Yuki coming with them. They all got into the van and Asimov's car to return back to their base.

CHAPTER 19: MASSACRE

When they arrived at the base, everything seemed calm. Asimov looked like he was getting better already. He was lucky the bullet just went through his right shoulder muscles without causing any permanent injury. They all came to the main hall and sat on the floor as Milton walked out. Yuki followed him and said, "You really should uncuff him. His hands were cuffed when he landed. I saw it with my own eyes. If he were with the enemy side, there wouldn't be handcuffs."

Milton replied, "There can be tricks. We have to be cautious until we are sure which side he is at." He took some first aid kit and gave it to her. "I think you should clean and rub his wound, and we should talk with him."

They came to the main hall. While Yuki bandaged his wounds, Serium explained everything. He said, "People at Zola are at great danger, but we must fight against Vortek to gain freedom here."

Milton said, "It is not easy to defeat his army of androids. They have steel-cast bodies."

"Unfortunately, it won't be easy, but I am sure there has to be a way to defeat him" Serium said as he held his lower jaw with his right hand, staring at the floor to gather his concentration to find a way to defeat the androids. He knew it wouldn't be easy. He couldn't see any way to defeat such a big army of androids. Milton and the others were convinced from his explanations that Serium was not the enemy. It became obvious to them he wanted to help. Milton unlocked his hand cuffs. They made some soup from the cans for dinner. All of them were feeling exhausted from the fight, and they fell asleep soon.

The general was up early with the sunrise as usual and he turned on the TV. He couldn't believe what he was seeing. The TV broadcast of the retreat of androids in Chicago encouraged people in all around the world to get together and fight for their freedom against robots. In Europe, millions of people gathered on the streets and wanted to destroy the androids. In many countries —China, Japan, Russia, Turkey, Brazil, Peru and many others— demonstrators gathered in the cities early in the morning. In the United States, people were gathering in the streets in all cities. The general couldn't believe what he was seeing. He woke the others up. He said, "This is not good, they cannot fight androids. They will all be slaughtered. We have to do something. We have to help them."

Soon the demonstrators with light guns or unarmed appeared to be surrounded by androids. It was obvious that these machines could kill them easily. Seeing so many demonstrators, Bernard got scared of his kingdom. He expected to get public support as he was the most powerful man on Earth. However, many people were prepared to fight for their freedom rather than being part of the victorious side. Many of them would even prefer to die than to continue life under Bernard's ruling. He contacted Vortek to ask his opinion.

Vortek was also not totally happy. Although he got as much uranium as he wanted, he noticed it was not very likely that he could get a record of the humans brutally killing Serium. He said to Bernard, "I suggest you follow the way I recommended you before. You cannot show weakness and mercy to those who come between you and your kingdom. When necessary, as it is the case now, you must show your full power. Kill all those who oppose you. I gave you full control of androids to do that."

Bernard was totally lost in his thoughts, not sure what to do and not knowing if this is the best way he should follow. However, he thought Vortek was always right so far. He helped him a lot. For Bernard, Vortek was a great leader and great success idol. He decided Vortek's words all make sense: as an emperor of the planet he should show his power when needed. Now was definitely the time that was needed. Bernard said, "Yes, you are right, Vortek. I will crush them like bugs and I want you to see I am in full control of my kingdom before you leave."

Vortek smiled, "You need to do it pretty soon Bernard. I don't know how much longer I will stay. I started to get bored, but I'll stay for a while to see how you go."

Bernard ordered the androids, "Kill them all. Kill whoever gets on the street to oppose my ruling!" His order spread throughout all androids. Even the androids serving at home started to observe their master's behavior at home to identify if they were opposition or wanted to do any action against the new monarchy.

Jack was the captain of the police Special Weapons and Tactics team, which is also known as the SWAT team. He was recently forced to retire just like most of his colleagues being replaced by androids. He was staying at his home with his wife. He heard five gun shots and screams coming from outside near his window. When he looked out, he saw his neighbor's four year old boy lying facedown on the garden shot from behind. He could see their housemaid android was holding a pistol with smoke coming from its front end. Then, he looked up to their window and saw splashed streams of blood. It was obvious their android killed them. His wife came to the kitchen's door and asked him, "What's going on?"

"You stay in the kitchen and close the door" Jack said with an excited loud tone. She entered back in to kitchen and closed the door. Jack knew the androids serving at the houses were not supposed to be able to kill the humans. He was always suspicious about the androids. He always knew his suspicions were the main reason for him to be forced to retire. Now, he could see the life had changed, everything was different.

His android heard his excited voice and came down. "Anything wrong, master? You don't look so good," the android said.

Jack noticed his android had already transformed his right hand into a sharp blade. He immediately changed his mood as he noticed his android was preparing to kill him. He responded with a calm voice, "No, nothing is wrong. I was just wondering what happened to these guys next to us," pointing out to window by slightly moving his eyes.

"They were opposing the new system. They were against our emperor and the law was implemented to set the justice" the android replied as if it was proud of the emperor.

Jack said, "Oh, how foolish. Our great emperor provided us with the technology and a lot of great things, like you, to appreciate. I guess it is hard to please everyone." As soon as he said so, he saw the android transformed his arm back to the regular arm and hand shape. His android was named as Can-O. He asked trying to keep his cool tone of voice, "Can-O, speaking of —pausing momentarily— the Emporium. I remembered now, I got a book long time ago about our new system. I don't remember the name exactly, but something to do with monarchy. Bring it to me, I want to read and know more about our great system. It is upstairs, in the bookshelf."

As soon as Can-O went upstairs, Jack ran downstairs where he kept his large rifle that was capable of shooting strong bullets. He grabbed his rifle and start running upstairs. At the same time, Can-O looked through the bookshelf searching for a book, which had the word monarchy in the title. When he saw the book titled *Brutal Monarchy*, he knew instantly Jack was no fan of its emperor. He ran down immediately. When he got half way down the stairs, Jack came out holding his big rifle.

"I don't need a slave anymore. I will use you as a trash can. You would serve me better that way as it suits with your name," jack said, and fired two shots one after another to his head. The large bullets blew Can-O's head off. Can-O's body fell down the stairs next to him. He dragged his body at a corner of the room. He took a piece of towel paper and wiped his gun's front end and put the smashed paper over the android's headless neck.

In New York, where a TV station was showing most of the broadcast from, androids surrounded the crowd of thousands of people. The androids did not even bother shooting at them. Their hands had the ability to transform to a sword-like blade extension to make it easier for them to perform their serving duties in the kitchen, or so it said in their operating manual. They got inside the crowd and cut people like they were vegetables. Androids with strong, sharp steel blade spilled floods of blood on the streets. They were not distinguishing, women or men. They killed whoever got in their way while the entire world watched the massacre in horror on TV. The general turned off the TV. Nobody could watch this horror any longer.

Assange screamed with almost a crying tone, "It is our fault. We should have never gone downtown. We should have just stayed in. We gave them wrongful hopes, and we let them down."

Suzan approached to him, "No, Assange, no" —as she hugged him tightly and cried— "It is them, androids. They would do this regardless of what we did."

At the corner of the hall, Serium felt deep sadness. As a leader, he always tried to keep his emotions hidden, but these horrific scenes were overwhelming for him to handle. He looked around the room and could see how everyone was feeling down with no hope of the future. He was always sure the good will would not be lost and surely had to win, but evil was winning this time.

CHAPTER 20: A GOOD IDEA

Serium stared down in the room filled with hopeless silence and thought what could possibly stop this evil. He said with a whispering tone of voice as if he unconsciously spoken out loud what he was thinking in his mind, "If we had a control program for machines or some type of control breaking, we could perhaps upload to androids and try to stop them."

Suddenly, Milton moved his head up and said, looking at him, "Do you mean like a virus, a computer virus, to mess them up?" He knew Assange was expert on the computer viruses. Assange could possibly program a surprise virus to interrupt the android's decision making process.

"Perhaps, that might be what I am referring to," Serium said as he was not sure what the computer virus meant on Earth. There was no such thing in Zola called *virus* for a machine, but what he knew was that some programs could impact or prevent the others not to work as intended. Vortek, in fact, used a virus to wipe out the research data from the computers when his androids murdered the scientists. However, Vortek had studied the life on Earth and technological systems during his entire trip from Zola to Earth.

Serium wasn't as much familiar as him about the computers and technologies used on Earth.

Assange responded, "These androids are no computers. A computer virus is not likely to harm them and even if we had the right virus, we cannot access the main unit. How can we possibly upload the virus on them?"

"They work with computer chips just like any other computers. The only difference is that their programming methods are much more advanced," Milton said.

Serium suddenly felt hope in his friend's eyes, "Yes, they work with chips" he said as he tried to stand up holding his left thigh with his hand. "We could try to access the main ship," he continued, looking at Niffy. "Niffy, can you access the main database?"

"No, they disabled my access," Niffy replied.

The general led them to the room that he called engineering room. He said, "Perhaps, we could use one of these computers here." Then, he went out and came back with a metallic stick. He said to Serium, "This will help you to stand up," as he handed the stick to him.

Serium was impressed by the gesture coming from someone with a high rank in the society. He felt comfort that he was on the right side in this war against Vortek. He thought Vortek's claim for the humans' primitiveness was only in his rotten mind. He turned and said, "Thank you General, this would certainly help."

Serium scanned through the computers with puzzled eyes since he didn't know how these machines on Earth could function. He turned to Milton, "Is there a way to bypass Niffy's coding unit and connect him to these machines?"

Milton knew exactly what he wanted to do. He experienced Niffy's horror chase when he downloaded and resolved a message outside the Niffy's data downloading unit. He said, "That's a brilliant idea. Connecting Niffy to the PC by bypassing his own-coding unit will confuse androids. They wouldn't be able to identify Niffy while connected."

"There is a code through a level of secret access to the androids including the ones working as general staff at the mother ship. The androids specifically built to bring to Earth wouldn't have the code, but the others that are produced with our usual process, would have the code. It is required by our constitution. The code is revealed to only Zola's leader," Serium said. He paused for a while thinking in silent before he continued explaining, "Since Vortek hasn't been through the official ceremony and not declared as the leader in accordance with our traditions and laws, he wouldn't know about it. If we could upload a program to one of the androids, he could share the program with the others before executing the program. The program should aim to activate their self-destruction mechanism" he focused his eyes in the corner of the ceiling to densify his thoughts.

Assange got overly excited. He suddenly hugged him and patted on his shoulder. "That's a great idea" he said before jumping on the chair in front of a notebook computer. "That can work, has to work." Milton attached one end of the cable inside Niffy's left ear and the other end to the notebook. He opened a command window that was used in early models to interact with the computer. He started coding the virus that would activate the android's self-destruction mechanism in the main ship in space. He was an expert on the virus programs, but it wasn't easy to build a virus that could cause the androids to misidentify an un-existing damage in their secured units and cause the self-destruction mechanism to activate.

Milton looked doubtful about it as he was also attacked by his car. He said, "I am not sure if this can solve all our problems because androids aren't the only ones killing us. What about cars?"

Serium replied quickly, "Don't worry about the cars. They must have the same internal communication system as androids and exactly the same self-destruction mechanism. The virus that will spread through their internal communication system will spread to the cars and all other machines produced as well. The car's self-destruction system will have exactly the same impact as on an android's chips."

Assange turned back, looking worried, "Well, if the cars explode while travelling, it might kill many -"

The general interrupted him, "They have to be stopped at all cost because they will kill the entire human race if they are not stopped."

Assange stayed quiet for a while, thinking what he could do. He tried to think how he was going to program it while he was listening to them and watching his monitor. He talked to himself whispering, "Hmm? Unless, hmm...?" while scratching his head.

Milton heard his whispering and asked impatiently, "What is in your mind?"

Assange replied with a gesture showing some pride, "My program is going to first interrupt their main processing unit. The cars will stop. The androids will be dysfunctional before the virus causes their self-destruction mechanism to activate. This will give people travelling a chance to escape."

The general asked, "How long would that be?"

Assange replied, "It is impossible to tell precisely, perhaps few seconds."

Milton said, "Yes, that would certainly help. We have to hope people will be able to escape before the cars' self-destruction mechanism gets activated."

Dorothy said, "I can announce on the radio to warn them to stay away from the cars. That would help at least some people who can hear us on their radio."

The general said, "Yes, that would be great. We do not have much choice anyway. If the cars can be destroyed, they must be destroyed as soon as possible."

While Assange started focusing on the monitor, Milton said, "I have to go back."

Aleyna asked, "Where? We can wait here until the virus is uploaded. Stay here!"

"I can't just sit here and watch them slaughter everyone. We have to fight," he said. As he was saying that to Aleyna, the general, Charlie and Asimov were already picking up guns and ammunitions.

The general said, "We are not needed here. They can work on uploading the virus. We go out and give our fight." Then, he turned to Asimov and looked at his injured shoulder; blood stains were visible from his bandage. "I think you should stay here. Provide us communication, Asimov. That would help us more."

Asimov loaded a bullet in his machine gun's mouth holding it with his left arm. "Just a bullet won't stop me from all this fun, General. I don't need two hands to blow those bastards' head off."

They got on the van and headed to the city. Assange first connected to his laptop back at his home through remote login. He transferred some of his own previously built programs. Before all these troubles started, he had been working on a project to develop a hacking program called Devils Enemy, a virus to download information from governments and large corporation's database. He never trusted militarily powerful governments and big corporations. He has always suspected of their involvement in criminal activities worldwide. As these corporations and governments were being controlled by evil androids, it was not possible to rust them or the media. Mainstream media has always acted like a puppet for the governments even before androids have taken the control. He wanted to show the world powerful governments and corporations' criminal and murderous activities and expose them to the worlds. He strongly believed the world was entitled to know the truth. He thought he could save time by modifying his existing programs.

The general's wife Dorothy knew how the military equipment worked including the radio communication. Her husband had taught her from time to time about handguns, automatic assault weapons, and other military tools. He often said to her," We can never know what could happen in the future. It doesn't harm to know even if you would never need to use them," to encourage her learning. Dorothy turned on the radio communicators. She wasn't sure what to say at first. She took a minute to think what to say. She had to find a name for themselves as why people should believe an announcement on a radio channel. Those who the announcement is being made on behalf of needed to be someone or something people could take seriously. She started announcing, "Attention to all travelers on the road! Your car may stop temporarily on the road while travelling. Please leave your car as soon as it stops. Stay away from it. This is GlobCorp's central office. We are informing all our valued customers about a defect on our vehicles that could be dangerous. Stay away from your vehicles until further notice. Get out of your cars as soon as it stops." She repeated the announcement several times and waited beside the radio.

Aleyna made some strong coffee and served a cup of coffee to those stayed at the base. Serium wasn't sure what

318

to do with it. He observed others drinking it for a while. He hesitated to give it a try, but he finally decided to take a sip. As soon as he put it in his mouth, he spat it out instantly, "Phew" spreading coffee drops around. It was clear he didn't like the bitter taste of coffee as the others laughed. Yuki went to kitchen, carrying her coffee. She soon returned with a cup of tea in her right hand while holding the last few gulp of coffee remaining in her cup with her left hand. Serium was not very keen to try another adventure, but Yuki wasn't giving up easy. After seeing Yuki's insistence for him to try the tea, he felt like he had to try. Finally, he got a sip of tea, he looked calm and recovered from the shock of the bitter coffee taste. He looked at her eyes showing his appreciation, "Thanks, Yuki. This tastes much better." he said with a smile.

About ten minutes after Dorothy turned the radio on, she heard a sound. "Is there anyone who can help me? Androids killing neighbors and anyone who tried to go out. I need support."

Dorothy replied, "What is your location?"

"I am in Rockford. My name is Jack"

"I am Dorothy. I'll check for help and get back to you. Stay tuned on this channel," she said and changed the radio channel to 3.4, which her husband could hear from the van.

She said, "Base calling v1, do you hear me?" She paused for a while as there was no response and repeated, "Copy V1, base calling."

The general answered, "I hear you clear. Copy, this is v1." Others looked strangely to the general as his formal talking with his wife sounded abnormal.

"Can you get to Rockford? They need help," she asked.

"We are close there, we can get there in few minutes," the general replied.

"Jack is waiting for your support. I'll let him know. I am out now," Dorothy said.

"Roger," the general responded and turned the van to the city of Rockford, which was on his way from their base Monroe to Chicago.

Unfortunately, their radio communication was recognized by the androids. The android in charge of the army asked his assistant android, "Gather one hundred androids to search for them. Find and kill them all!" They got on the way to search for the base immediately. They could identify that their location was somewhere around Monroe.

When the general arrived at one of the residential roads, they saw some houses had broken windows and doors with damage that looked like a war zone. Jack saw the headlights of the old model cars and he thought this must be the help he asked for. GlobCop's new model cars had a softer bluish looking light horizontally installed in front of the car. As they were driven automatically, strong headlights were not needed. He used his flash light to signal toward the cars at a distance across his house.

Then General saw a light was flashing to them from a window across the road. They decided to park the car at a side road two blocks off the house to avoid getting attention from the androids in the neighborhood. They walked up to the house covering themselves beside the walls at dark. When they arrived at the door, Jack opened the door and whispered, "I am Jack, wait a second here, please." He turned back into the home and kissed his wife as he asked her to stay inside. He came out and walked to the other side of the wall carefully setting his back to the wall. There were two androids there standing on the other side. Jack whispered slowly, "They killed the neighbors. They are now discussing what to do."

Milton said, "I'll go to the other side. We shoot them at the same time from both sides."

The general said, "I am going to check out that house," as he pointed a house that had lights on across the road. Charlie and Asimov went with the general.

After Milton reached the other side, Jack and him fired at the androids from both side and shot them down. Milton said, "You should get your wife out and come with us. I am sure other androids already know about the ones terminated and many will come here soon." Before even Milton could finish his sentence a big convoy of police cars appeared across the street heading toward them. They both ran in to the house. Jack introduced his wife quickly while running to the side window, "Lucy, Milton! Milton, Lucy my wife."

Meanwhile the general, Charlie and Asimov were covering themselves behind the front patio's wall and shooting toward a house. There were five androids there gathered from the neighborhood. Charlie threw a hand grenade over the androids that destroyed two of them in the explosion. The impact from the explosion of the grenade caused their self-destruction mechanism to activate. The grenade's blast joined with the android's own explosion to cause a loud noise. The blast made the other three androids surprised for a moment, which gave them a good chance to shoot them. After getting hit by several bullets, all the remaining androids were terminated.

Charlie noticed the police vehicles approaching to Jack's house, "Oh, no! We have to move now. Our friends are in big trouble." They all ran to the side of a house closer to Jack's house. Charlie ran into the garden of the house on the other side and climbed on the top of the roof from a tree. Asimov stood in one side of the neighbor's house whilst the general stood up on the other side to support their friends inside. Fifty of the one hundred androids arrived in police cars and slowly surrendered the house. Asimov was worried about the situation as they were outnumbered. He thought, "My dear friends, if you are going to do something with the virus, please hurry. We certainly need a lot of help, especially Milton."

Meanwhile, the other fifty androids continued moving toward Monroe to find their base. They were not aware of the androids coming for them. Although the androids didn't know their exact location, they had a lot of equipment to identify any radio wave, advance sound detectors and thermal spectacles to search for humans.

After police vehicles parked one after another around the house, androids got out of their vehicles and took position to shoot at the house, taking cover behind their cars. Charlie could see the androids clearly since their side toward him was open. He targeted the head of one of the androids with his machine gun. As he focused his eye on the target, his finger pulled the trigger, firing a few bullets almost simultaneously. The destruction of the android caused a surprise for the other androids. The androids didn't know where the shot came from and what to do. While they started looking around, Charlie used his opportunity to destroy another android shooting on the head.

In the meantime, the general and Asimov started to shoot from the opposite direction, destroying several of them. Androids then noticed they were being shot from the opposite direction and they moved to the other side of their vehicle, exposing themselves from Jack's home side. Jack had an impressive collection of weapons accumulated. His interest on the weapons was not only a hobby, but a part of his professional life in the SWAT team. Milton, Jack, and his wife could see the androids settling within their visibility range. They started shooting at the androids with automatic machine guns from inside before androids could target their friends.

Although they could destroy six of the androids, their numbers were just too many to terminate them all. Some of the androids went behind the house and they started shooting into the house from the back wall windows. Milton moved backside, keeping himself low below the window level. He responded to the androids with firing bullets. While the shooting continued, a hand grenade flied off from the window into the house. They all ran toward the kitchen and laid down as the grenade exploded inside the house. Then, Jack and Milton crawled toward the window side and they also threw hand grenades to the androids, blowing three of them off in pieces together with their vehicles.

As the shootings continued, both from the androids and from Milton and his friends, a chopper's sound was heard. Charlie started firing at the chopper. One android was visible from the open side of the chopper and Charlie hit it and made it fall from the chopper. After the android was destroyed, the chopper turned toward him. He continued shooting at the chopper, but his bullets weren't strong enough to bring it down. Then, the chopper fired a rocket. Unfortunately, he died instantly.

The general and Asimov both watched the rocket's explosion with fire spreading around as the top corner of the roof where Charlie was on was blasted off into smaller pieces. There was no time to grieve for their friend. With the shock of losing his friend, the general attempted to get closer to the chopper and shot at it from the open site. Asimov noticed him moving and quickly ran to the general. Just when the general was coming into android's target, he jumped over him and tackled him to the ground. They could hear the sound of a series of bullets fired from the chopper's machine gun passing by near their head as they fell down. "No, General.

We need you in this war. If you go out, we will lose you. We will lose the war without your help. We have to stay alive. We must keep fighting these bastards," said Asimov with a frustrated tone of voice.

As soon as he finished talking, the general fired a few shots with his right arm beside Asimov's head. An android came from the side of the house Asimov left and was about to shoot them. Asimov couldn't see it while his face was downward. The general was facing toward the direction of the android. Asimov turned and saw the headless steel body of the android. As he stood up, he said, "See, General, that's what I am talking about. We need you alive." Asimov ran back to his position as the general could get over the shock.

CHAPTER 21: DEVILS ENEMY

The other fifty androids reached the location of the base. They started searching the source of the radio communication from the top of the hill. Brawny ran to the hall and suddenly stopped. She straightened her ears started staring toward under the door as if she sensed something was moving outside. Niffy heard their noises on their communication systems. He warned the others whispering, "They found us! The androids are here."

They all got quiet. While Assange continued working on the virus Devils Enemy information exchange system, Serium and the others went to the storage room to pick weapons, ammunitions and grenades. Assange asked Dorothy to turn off the radio not to make any sound. They started waiting inside. Serium said to Niffy, "When the virus program is close to completion, dial the android 583 in the mother ship with access level 3 and request secure entrance gate." Serium knew the android 583 was the ideal candidate to infect the virus because it was responsible for the communication within the ship. It had access to download and upload information from all the other androids.

Niffy acknowledged the command and asked, "Yes, I am ready to receive the access code for the gate."

Serium said, "The code is 1-1-1-0-0-1-1-0-0-0-1-0." Then, he put his right hand on Assange's shoulder. "We have only a limited time. It won't be long before they find a way to enter the base. I am not sure how long we can hold them, but it cannot be too long. I will go to the other room across to divert their attention and gain time. I think we should lock this door."

All of them left the engineering room, leaving Assange and Niffy. Brawny also ran back into the engineering room as she usually felt comfortable staying next to Niffy. However, her senses made her nervous this time. Even when she got into the room, standing next to Niffy, she looked scared and tried to hide at the corner in a tiny space behind the computer desk. Serium went to the room across, which was built for resting while Yuki and the others followed him. Serium said, "It is best if you ladies go to the back room," referring to the large room where they kept the vans and a lot of weapons.

Aleyna said, "He is right. We should split. We should position in different rooms to divert their attention. I will go to the kitchen. You ladies can go to the room across it."

Yuki said, "I will stay here."

Assange's wife, Suzan, said, "I will go with Aleyna, too."

Dorothy, Jennifer and Esra walked to the big room across the kitchen where Aleyna and Suzan went in. They sat in front of the entrance, watching toward the hall's main entrance. They all silently waited for the androids to enter. There was a cold silence in the room filled with fear and worries. Aleyna looked at Suzan's eyes that fear was strong. She held her hand gently and said, "We'll hold them out of the hall. I am sure Assange will stop them."

Niffy kept one of the machine guns with him. Assange moved the sofa behind the door. He laid the table down in the middle of the room close to the wall. He put the computer down behind the table. Assange continued working on the virus while sitting on the floor. Niffy stood in front of the table, turning his left side toward the computer. He tried to secure his connection on his left ear to prevent a direct hit in case the androids fired shots in to the room. Assange asked, "What are you doing?" while Niffy was settling himself in front of the table.

Niffy replied, whispering, "I have a steel body. My body can stand their shooting better than the table." Niffy noticed Assange's strange look at him with disapproving eyes. He added, "we don't have time to argue, you have to continue programming." Assange smiled Niffy's words sounded like a person making decisions rather than just taking commands. He turned back to work saying, "My dear friend Milton must have done a great job on you." He knew they were running out of time and started focusing on the program.

Suddenly, the noises from outside the hall stopped. Aleyna and Esra thought that they must have given up searching them and left. Serium waved his hand toward Aleyna and Esra as they appeared at the entrance and said "Stay back, keep your cover! Stay back!" He was not sure what was happening and why the noises stopped, but he was sure the androids wouldn't give up on a mission until either the mission was complete or they were terminated. As soon as Aleyna and Esra went back and hid at the entrance of the rooms across each other, a loud explosion sound came from the main entrance of the base. Entire base was shaken as if it was a large earthquake. Serium was right about them; they hadn't given up. They were setting bombs to blow out the entrance door of the base. Fire from the explosion filled up almost the entire hall while the huge thick entrance steel door was blown across toward the kitchen. The flames of the blast was off as fast as it came on.

When the smoke settled down, androids appeared at the entrance. They started to enter to the hall. Serium fired the machine gun repeatedly and terminated three of the androids shooting them at the head. Androids also started firing machine guns through the hall. Aleyna and Esra started firing shots from the back end of the hall. Since they were shooting continuously, the ammunitions in the guns ran out; When Aleyna ran out of the ammunition, Suzan continued shooting while Aleyna reloaded her gun. In the big room across, Jennifer was shooting when Esra needed to reload her gun. While they were all shooting with machine guns, one of the androids threw a hand grenade in to the hall. Luckily, the grenade passed the entrance of the room Serium and Yuki were standing and didn't reach to the entrances at the far back. The grenade exploded filling the hall with fire and smoke.

Aleyna screamed to Serium, "You can't stay there. You have to run here, I'll cover you." She noticed androids could easily throw bomb to the room. They were also able to progress moving forward slowly. Aleyna got out of the entrance and lay down continuously shooting from the side wall as Serium held on Yuki's shoulder, and they ran back toward her. The visibility in the hall was low due to the smoke and dust created from the explosion. Suzan was also shooting from the entrance since Aleyna was in the hall. When they got close to the entrance, Serium and Yuki threw themselves to the Kitchen entrance and Aleyna rolled herself across to the other room while Esra continued shooting to make cover for her. When Aleyna rolled into the entrance was about to get up, "Aaahhh!" she screamed in pain.

Aleyna got hit on her left foot, and she could barely pull herself in to the room. She sat aside, holding her foot and sobbing in pain. Jennifer brought a bandage and wrapped it around her injury. The androids were too many for them to stop. They continued shooting, but one hit of a bullet wasn't enough to stop them. As the ones in front kept getting hit by bullets, many others were entering and were able to progress slowly in the hall. As the androids got closer to the other room's entrances, an android threw a hand grenade to the room Serium and Yuki had just left. The sound from the explosions and the shootings were loud, filling the entire base with echoes.

Pressure was built on Assange as he knew he had to finish the virus very soon as he could hear loud fighting noises outside the room. While shootings continued, they heard an android hitting the door to force it open. But he couldn't open the door by pushing with his steel body.

Some of the androids passed their door and advanced toward the back end. Yuki and Dorothy was shooting to stop them advancing. A few androids in front were terminated. However, the others continued shooting. Suddenly, "Ouhhh!" Dorothy screamed; she was hit by a bullet and fell down toward the hall. While she was falling down, the androids targeted her and rained bullets on her. Her lifeless body covered in blood fell down into the hall in front of her daughter and her friends.

Jennifer cried out, screaming, "Nooo, Mom, noo!" Aleyna held her left hand with both of her hands while she tried to get out to hold her mother. Suzan hugged and grabbed her tightly to stop her from getting out. The androids were getting closer and closer at every moment.

Niffy said, "Get ready, they are going to blast the door." Assange's sweat was running from the side of his head down his cheeks. He kept his silence and continued working with focus.

Niffy dialed to android 583 in the mother ship "Access request for level 3 – secure entry gate" through his internal communicator.

The android 583 responded "entry code required."

Niffy sent him the code "1-1-1-0-0-1-1-0-0-0-1-0" as Serium told him.

Android 583 responded "Access granted."

While Assange tried to hurry and rush to finish the virus, a loud explosion blew off the top half of the door across the other end of the room. The bottom part of the door was blasted off in pieces and flied to the middle of the room.

Meanwhile, Milton, Jack, and his wife Lucy were trapped in the house. Asimov and the general continued shooting at the chopper hovering over the roof, but their bullets didn't seem to do any damage. The androids were shooting from all around the house. Milton went to the back room and responded to the androids behind the house with machine gun. The chopper backed up from the house, moved to the front. It fired a rocket instantly to the window where Lucy was standing next to. While Jack watched with frightened eyes, the rocket entered the house, shattering the windows through her body and exploded. Many shrapnel pieces were spread and filled the room with smoke. The roof of the living room collapsed down over Lucy's broken-up body. Milton shouted out, "Jack, are you OK?" There was no response. He screamed again repeatedly, "Jack? Jack?" No response.

Milton walked back toward the living room while firing few sets of shots through the back window. When he turned to the room, he was shocked by the view of the room looking like a pile of rubbish, dust, and cement with the smell of rocket burns. He turned his eyes to Jack, standing still while blood drops were coming down from his shoulder leaking down his right hand and dripping on the floor. He noticed Lucy's body under some large broken cement pieces and dust.

He held Jack by putting his arm around his left shoulder and slowly pulled him away toward the other room. Jack was hit by a piece of shrapnel on his right shoulder, but he couldn't even scream for the pain of his injury. He was frozen from the unbearable pain of seeing his wife die with the horrifying rocket blast.

Milton saw the androids were already moving in to the garden, passing through the broken-down fences. They were heading in to the home from the collapsed walls of the living room. He thought of Assange for a moment and said to himself, *Come on Assange, if you are going to do anything, you'd better do it soon*. Milton went to the back room and sat behind the wall near the door with Jack. They started firing their machine guns over the androids that were closer to the collapsed walls. A few of the androids were shot down, but two of them were able to enter the house.

When one of the androids came and stepped on the pile over Lucy, Jack couldn't stay in his position. He quickly ran out, shooting at him and yelling, "Get your cold feet off my wife." Milton couldn't stop him. Jack was able to shot down the android standing over her body. Milton terminated the other android entered the room. Unfortunately, the other androids reaching close to the house fired many shots at Jack and killed him there instantly.

Asimov and the general were also surrounded by many androids. They were shooting with their machine guns continuously, but the androids started to get closer to them. Asimov was exhausted from continuous shooting with one hand. Their hopes of the future and the future of the world were fading away more and more at every moment.

In the base, the androids blasted out the door of the engineering room. Suddenly, Assange screamed, "Done! It is finished, Niffy." Niffy was shooting at the androids entering the room. Several androids entered, shooting at Niffy all together with their heavy machine guns. Within seconds, smoke started to come from Niffy's ears and the lights in his eyes disappeared. His body fell down to ground while Assange watched him helplessly. He lowered his head down and put his hands on his head to cover his both ears. He was expecting to be killed in any moment. He thought even Niffy couldn't stand long against these androids with powerful guns.

He waited, waited, and waited a few more seconds while each second felt like an hour. He wasn't shot still alive, and there was total silence in the base. The androids were looking confused as if not knowing what to do. They dropped their guns and kept looking at each other. Assange slowly walked through the door between the lost-looking androids. As he passed through them, he held his breath. He was scared of waking them from their ecstasy state back to the reality. As soon as he reached to the main hall, he called the others shouting out loud, "Everyone, ruuuun, get out now." Yuki helped Serium and Suzan held Aleyna with her one arm while holding Jennifer with the other. She wrapped her arm around Jennifer's forehead and eyes to prevent her from seeing her mom as they passed by Dorothy's body. They all went through the androids holding their breath not to take their attention. They all took deep breaths when they reached outside.

Back at Rockford, several androids had already entered the room while Milton was shooting. Suddenly, he noticed the androids were not returning his shots. When he pulled his head out of the entrance, he noticed them dropping their weapons and looking at each other purposelessly. Milton walked out from the room, looking for his friends. The general and Asimov came in a slow pace. Milton quickly ran beside them and started looking at the androids twenty meters away. The androids soon started to explode one by one. Some cars parked around the neighborhood also exploded with smoke coming out from their hood. Within a minute, all androids around them were blown away.

From outside the base, Assange and the others watched the androids explode and die out. Assange noticed at the time Dorothy was not there and Jennifer was crying. As he looked with puzzled eyes to Serium, Serium told him Dorothy was killed. He then noticed Brawny was missing too. While the general, Asimov, and Milton were returning back, they saw many people on the streets walking. At least, that was a good sign for many people survived the car explosions.

They arrived at the base shortly. Their losses were too many, most of them sat aside, with crying eyes, putting their head down. Serium had never experienced such dramatic emotional down feeling in his life. Esra cried out screaming in pain as if her hearth was being torn off. While she cried in pain, she remembered how Charlie would always comfort her by hugging her and resting her head on his chest. When she rested her head on him, she would always feel his warm heart as he would kiss her hair gently. Her memories of affection and love kept increasing her pain. She couldn't control herself, just kept crying out. Suzan and Aleyna hugged her to console her, but her pain was too great to calm her down.

The general hugged her daughter as she was crying in tears. The general had been trained to suppress his emotions and to perform his duties under any circumstances. No matter how difficult and painful the situation would get, he had to focus on achieving his duties just as required in the army. However, even he, the great general, was unable to control his pain and to prevent his tears. He walked inside while Jennifer also followed him. They saw Dorothy's body covered in blood, some pebbles, and dusts. He held her, hugged and cried while Jennifer sat beside him, crying and holding his arm. Suzan and Assange sat beside them, trying to console them.

Milton hugged Aleyna, to comfort her as she sat on the ground, wounded in her feet. Milton, then looked around scanning with his eyes, but he didn't see either Niffy or Brawny. He went inside looking for them. He saw Niffy lying down motionless. He kneeled beside him and put his head down trying to avoid crying as he thought he should help others to ease their pain. It wasn't easy for him not to think about Niffy and Brawny, how great their hearts were, and they shared many good memories together. He couldn't stop thinking how Brawny would meet him in front of the door when he came back home from work every day. He thought of how Niffy would take care of them both, doing shopping, cooking, and cleaning the house. Even though he didn't want to cry, he was unable to prevent his tears leaking through his eyes.

After a while, the general managed to suppress his pain and said while wiping his tears off his eyes, "We will always remember those who gave their lives to save others. They will always live in our hearts. We have to be strong and get back to work as they would want us to do so. Millions of people's lives depend on us. They need our help."

Serium said, "We should get to the ship and bring it here soon."

Milton walked to the hall, "Do you think it would be still there?"

Serium replied, "If the connections of the power unit to the main engines haven't been pulled out, it would have been already gone. However, if we wait too long, Vortek may send a ship to carry it back. We have to hurry." When Serium had landed with the ship, he laid down under the main unit box on the back of the ship. He managed to open the box containing the cables while his hands were cuffed behind him. Then he pulled out the cables transferring power to the engine.

Assange and Suzan led the general and Jennifer aside and laid down Dorothy's body carefully. The general then entered the large room as he said, "I'll get the carriage to attach to the van to carry the ship."

Milton heard a soft sound, "Meaw". Suddenly, Brawny appeared from in between broken pieces of the tables at the corner. Everyone felt a slight cheer seeing her alive. Aleyna picked her up and hugged her. Milton and Aleyna petted her together. Then Jennifer took her in her arms.

Milton put his hand on the general's shoulder and said, "Please, General. I'll bring it with Assange." He got worried about the general. The general looked too exhausted and powerless, affected from the tragedy of losing his wife after living together for many years. Milton went to the next room to get the carriage outside.

They attached the rectangular metallic carriage that had small thick wheels to the van in front of the base. Milton looked at Serium and Asimov as they looked like suffering with their injuries. They both seemed to be exhausted from living too many disasters in a day. He walked next to Asimov and whispered, "You and Serium should stay here and take care of our friends." The general refused to stay back and joined Milton and Assange to go back to Chicago with their van.

Serium said, "I should come with you Milton. You don't know about the space ship. You might need my knowledge."

Milton agreed, "Yes, I think you are right. We might need your assistance."

Suzan said, "I'll go and drive around to look for survivors who might need help."

Yuki was sitting on a piece of rock next to the entrance of the base her head down and crying for her friends and worrying about her family back in Japan. She had no idea if

344

they were still alive there. She stood up slowly, wiping her tears from her cheeks, "I'll help you," she said to Suzan. Suzan brought out two bottles of potable water and first aid kits to set them in Asimov's car. Suzan and Yuki headed to the city to help the survivors.

There were piles of ruins of houses, concrete cements, bricks, broken glasses, and metal pieces around caused by androids. There were also a lot of broken, exploded cars with black smoke stains along the way. In the city, there were many bodies of dead people lying around and parts of exploded androids spread all around the streets. Milton parked the car next to the ship. When they got off the car, Assange couldn't stand the scenes and felt sick. He put his arm to the car to keep his balance and rested his head on his arm. He felt nauseous from breathing the air filled with dust and smell of human remains. He couldn't avoid vomiting.

In the mothership, when the virus was uploaded, the android standing always next to Vortek reported, "The androids are uploaded with a virus transforming to all androids."

Vortek reacted with anger, "What? Did you get virus?"

The android replied with a steady mechanical voice, "Virus is affecting only the ones that are built with a self-destruction mechanism."

"Oh no!" said Vortek with an obvious disappointment in his eyes. He ordered, "Ask all non-staff androids to jump off the ship immediately." He noticed the androids would explode soon. The androids that were built to serve within the ship didn't have the self-destruction mechanism. It was fit only on the androids brought to be delivered to Earth. Some of these androids remained in the ship as they didn't need to sell them. They could raise sufficient financial resources to build the android production factory without selling the remaining 173 androids. These androids couldn't perform the orders because they had been already uploaded with the virus that caused confusion in their processing unit and disabled their functionalities. Other androids loaded them in a carriage and dumped them out to the empty space. The androids exploded one by one in the dark space.

Vortek was angry and disappointed. He thought his plans to take control of Earth were spoiled by a few primitive humans. He whispered to himself, "A stupid virus caused it all?".

The captain was standing next to him, "Excuse me?" He couldn't hear what Vortek was saying. "What is your plan now?"

Vortek looked at him and said, "Well, we are done here, Captain. We have sufficient resources of energy for thousands of years. We can return to Zola and start building powerful weapons. We will enslave them next time."

The captain reminded him, "How about Serium's ship? Do you want to send a ship to bring it up?"

Vortek replied, "No, Captain. A damaged ship is not worth wasting our time. Let's keep moving." Vortek was worried that they could launch a rocket attack to their ship. Since he lost all his androids on Earth, he could not take the chance to face a military attack against the mother ship.

The captain ordered to the android standing next to them, "Get the ship moving to our destination, home planet."

On Earth, standing beside Serium's ship, Milton said, "It won't be easy to push this thing over the carriage."

The general dragged out two extended pieces of metallic sheets from the carriage to the ground to serve as tracks to pull the ship up and said, "Yes, if there was a place to tie the front part of the ship, everything would be much easier." From their view as they were standing, all around the ship's surface looked smooth and shiny. There was no place to tie anything.

Serium said, "There is a holder under the ship in front, but it is covered. I could open the cover, but I need something with a flat edge, something with strength..."

Milton took a screw driver and showed him, "Would this screwdriver work?"

"Perfect" said Serium and repeated in his mouth, "Screw - driver? Huh?" He tried to memorize its name while he stared at it. In his planet, they wouldn't use any tool because everything would be done by the androids. He grabbed it and lay down, putting his head under the ship. After a minute, he said, "Give me the end of the chain." General handed him the end of the chain and the lock to tie the chain. He soon moved his head out from under the ship to his side and got up, "Ready."

The general said, "Now leave it to me and stand aside." He reached toward the side of the trailer facing toward the inside and pushed a button. As soon as he did so, the chain started to pull itself up to the carriage. The ship was soon completely loaded on to the trailer. The general secured it by tying the chain around. They headed back to the base carrying the space ship on the trailer.

The public still didn't know everything and weren't sure what was happening. All the androids were destroyed, but everyone was cautious to get out again. The general called the president from his home and explained how the world was all set up by aliens. The androids and cars were sent to destroy us. Then he said, "Mr. President, all androids have been destroyed. Mr Assange with the help of his friends has uploaded a program and destroyed the androids. I think it is time for you to take back the control of the country and inform the world." He also called his colleague, the general in Washington Dc. He asked him to organize the army to find survivors and help people who suffered from the war.

While Milton gathered Niffy's body and put it aside, he whispered to him, "Thank you, my friend. You saved us, you saved the world. I promise when you wake up again, you will feel much better and stronger than before."

Aleyna, Suzan, and Yuki returned back all, looking exhausted. Their tiredness was not just physical that they worked hard to help the victims, but it was also a mental exhaustion of seeing many dead bodies, heavily injured people, destroyed homes and ruins left behind from the war caused by the androids. They organized a ceremony to bury Dorothy and show their respect for all others who lost their lives, including their friend Charlie, Jack, and his wife Lucy.

The next morning, they woke up with the sound of a chopper approaching. They quickly grabbed their machine guns and came out of the base. They took cover behind the entrance and waited as the chopper landed. A military official and two soldiers came out of the chopper and approached to the entrance. The general Mike recognized his colleague from Washington. He couldn't believe the general could find him and came so soon from Washington. The general saluted him by putting his right hand on his hand as all military personal would do to their superiors saying, "My commander!"

The general Mike wasn't sure why he called him his commander. He was also a general. He saluted back, "General." Then, he put his hand down and asked, "I suppose you found this place from my phone calls. Why did you come all the way here so suddenly?".

The general replied, "Yes, Commander, we traced the call. The president sent me to inform you that you have been assigned as the Minister of Defense and the commander of the US army. We started to regroup the army, police, and social services to help survivors."

Milton asked, "How about Bernard? What happened to him?"

The general replied, "He was arrested and put in jail. The court will decide his future."

The general Mike said, "The war is over. I am not in a state to command the US army. I will join the rescue team to search for survivors and help."

Serium said, "General, this was just a battle. You must start preparing the army immediately. You have maybe one year, or two at most, to get ready for a much bigger war yet to come upon Earth."

CHAPTER 22: THEORY OF ORIGIN

Synopsis

There have been various theories about the origin of life, Earth and the human formation. Among the most well-known ones are the Charles Darwin's theory of evolution, the big bang theory proposed by Georges Lemaître, and the generic religious view on creation. Although, Darwin's theory and the big bang theory have been widely acknowledged through decades, the majority of people believing in a religion have continued to strongly reject both of the ideas on evolution and the big bang. The main underlying reason has been the fact that in either of the theories, there were no links or no room for things to be created by a supernatural power or event creating things from nothing. There has always been missing links, unexplained facts, and unanswered questions about the formation of Universe, the Earth and the life.

The Theory of Origin proposes a new view for the *big picture* about the creation of the universe and clears the contradictions between the religious view and the scientific view. The main cause of the contradiction is not considering the cyclic process of the universe or nature. Life-cycle is well known and acknowledged as a localized idea on the Earth focusing only the cyclic process of living things on Earth. In reality, the life cycle extends to the life of planets and the universe itself.

Although the big bang and the evolution theories are accepted to be the explanation of the major events of formation of the universe and humankind, they are, in fact, smaller parts of a much larger cyclic process of formation. These theories are also flawed in contradicting with some facts as discussed in the proceeding sections in this chapter.

One of the main unexplainable parts or the unconvincing reality about the big bang theory was that too many specific conditions had to happen by chance for the universe, Earth, and human life to form. So many of the critical conditions happening by chance has been the difficulty that most people found it hard to believe or accept although scientific environment provided some evidences, which are somewhat second-degree evidences. There has not been a complete and strong first-degree evidence for either the big bang or the Darwin's theory of evolution.

Another question that challenges both the Darwin's evolution theory and the religious view in claiming that humans being created in *perfectness for survival or evolved to perfectness for survival* is that "are we really in the most ideal, perfect, way for life?" Although the religious view believes only God is perfect, the main underlying belief is still that humans are created in the best possible way since God would not make mistakes, or there couldn't be any better way to create us than how God thinks or knows. Human's perfection has been a perfectness perhaps one can call it "a secondary level of perfectness" based on the main formation of the belief that God has the ability to create us in the best possible way and not make things wrong. However, it is very easy to prove that we could have been created in a better way. For example, we could have stronger body structures like some insect types have such as ants or we could have the ability to fly without needing equipment or the ability to move very fast under water and stay for a long time, etc. Surely many other examples can easily be produced on this subject.

These questions and arguments clearly illustrate that we, as currently existing, are not really created as perfect as we could be or not really evolved to the perfectness as claimed by the evolution. Another important question is that, "Is there really God's involvement in all this?" And if yes, why the science especially the scientific theories of evolution and the big bang have been always in a contradicting state with the God's creation. There has not been a convincing theory offered by science to provide answers to all the questions.

The Theory of Origin proposed herein provides new enlightening views to those questions and can be considered as a bridge between the view of God's creation and the scientific view of Darwin's evolution theory and the big bang theory. This theory also clearly demonstrates why the natural balance on Earth and in the universe must be preserved at all cost. All these facts bring out three crucial factors for us in our daily lives:

1. Preserving the environmental balance
2. Acknowledging the existence and necessity of the natural forces ("nature" here includes the outer space [universal] events and phenomenon in addition to the nature on Earth), which leads us to respect the nature
3. Respecting for the right of all living creatures to live and to co-exist

The story in the book was developed around the Theory of Origin. As the story progresses around the universe, the mysterious links between the theory and the story surrounding the planet Zola has been revealed.

Introduction

The big bang is defined as a cosmological model of the initial conditions and subsequent development of the universe that is supported by the most comprehensive and accurate explanations from current scientific evidence and observation as stated by Feuerbacher, B.; Scranton, R., (25 January 2006, Evidence for the Big Bang. TalkOrigins. http://www.talkorigins.org/faqs /astronomy /bigbang.html#evidence. Retrieved 2009-10-16) and by Lemaître, G. (1927 Un univers homogène de masse constante et de rayon croissant rendant compte de la vitesse radiale des nébuleuses extragalactiques. Annals of the Scientific Society of Brussels 47A: 41. French - Translated in: A Homogeneous Universe of Constant Mass and Growing Radius Accounting for the Radial Velocity of Extragalactic Nebulae", Monthly Notices of the Royal Astronomical Society 91: 483–490. 1931). As used by cosmologists, the term big bang generally refers to the idea that the universe has expanded from a primordial hot and dense initial condition at some finite time in the past, which is currently estimated to have been approximately 13.7 billion years ago and continues to expand to this day as discussed by 4. Komatsu, E.; et al. (2009, Five-Year Wilkinson Microwave Anisotropy Probe Observations: Cosmological Interpretation; Astrophysical Journal Supplement 180: 330. Bibcode: 2009ApJS. .180. .330K) and more information can be found in wikipedia (http://en.wikipedia.org/wiki/Main_Page).

Georges Lemaître (1931, The Evolution of the Universe: Discussion. Nature 128: 699–701. doi:10.1038/128704a0 and in the reference above dated 1927) proposed what became known as the big bang theory of the origin of the universe, although he called it *his hypothesis of the primeval atom*. The framework for the model relies on Albert Einstein's general relativity theory and on simplifying assumptions such as homogeneity and isotropy of space. The governing equations had been formulated by Alexander Friedmann (1922, "Über die Krümmung des Raumes", Zeitschrift für Physik 10: 377–386. doi:10.1007/BF01332580 German - English translation in: Friedman, A. 1999, "On the Curvature of Space". General Relativity and Gravitation 31: 1991–2000, doi:10.1023/A:1026751225741). After Edwin Hubble (1929, A Relation Between Distance and Radial Velocity Among Extra-Galactic Nebulae, Proceedings of the National Academy of Sciences 15: 168–73, doi:10.1073/ pnas.15.3.168. PMID

358

16577160,

http://antwrp.gsfc.nasa.gov/debate/1996/hub_1929.html) discovered that the distances to far away galaxies were generally proportional to their redshifts, as suggested by Lemaître in 1927 this observation was taken to indicate that all very distant galaxies and clusters have an apparent velocity directly away from our vantage point: the farther away, the higher the apparent velocity. If the distance between galaxy clusters is increasing today, everything must have been closer together in the past. This idea has been considered in detail back in time to extreme densities and temperatures, and large particle accelerators have been built to experiment on and test such conditions, resulting in significant confirmation of the theory, but these accelerators have limited capabilities to probe into such high energy regimes. Without any evidence associated with the earliest instant of the expansion, the big bang theory cannot and does not provide any explanation for such an initial condition; rather, it describes and explains the general evolution of the universe since that instant.

The observed abundances of the light elements throughout the cosmos closely match the calculated predictions for the formation of these elements from nuclear processes in the rapidly expanding and cooling first minutes of the Universe, as logically and quantitatively detailed according to big bang nucleosynthesis.

Fred Hoyle (1948, "A New Model for the Expanding Universe". Monthly Notices of the Royal Astronomical Society 108: 372, http://adsabs.harvard.edu/abs /1948MNRAS.108..372H) is credited with coining the term big bang during a 1949 radio broadcast. It is popularly reported that Hoyle intended this to be pejorative, but Hoyle explicitly denied this and said it was just a striking image meant to emphasize the difference between the two theories for radio listeners ("Big bang' astronomer dies" BBC News. 22 August 2001. http://news.bbc.co.uk/1/hi/uk/1503721.stm, Retrieved 2008-12-07). Hoyle later helped considerably in the effort to understand stellar nucleo-synthesis, the nuclear pathway for building certain heavier elements from lighter ones. After the discovery of the cosmic microwave background radiation in 1964, and especially when its spectrum (i.e. the amount of radiation measured at each wavelength) sketched out a blackbody curve, most scientists were fairly convinced by the evidence that some big bang scenario must have occurred.

The evolution theory was proposed by Charles Darwin in the book called *On the Origin of Species by Means of Natural*

Selection or the Preservation of Favoured Races in the Struggle for Life (1st ed.) (1859, London: John Murray, http://darwin-online.org.uk/content/frameset?itemID=F373& viewtype=text& pageseq=1, retrieved 2009-01-0924).

Darwin proposed sexual selection, driven by competition between males for mates, to explain sexually dimorphic features such as lion manes, deer antlers, peacock tails, bird songs, and the bright plumage of some male birds (1871, The Descent of Man, and Selection in Relation to Sex (1st ed.). London: John Murray, http://darwin-online.org.uk/EditorialIntroductions /Freeman_TheDescentofMan.html. Retrieved 2008-10-24). He analyzed sexual selection more fully in The Descent of Man, and Selection in Relation to Sex) Natural selection was expected to work very slowly in forming new species, but given the effectiveness of artificial selection, Darwin stated "I can see no limit to the amount of change, to the beauty and infinite complexity of the co-adaptation between all organic beings, one with another and with their physical conditions of life, which may be effected in the long course of time by nature's power of selection." Using a tree diagram and calculations, he indicated the divergence of character from original species into new species and genera. He described

361

branches falling off as extinction occurred while new branches formed in "the great tree of life with its ever branching and beautiful ramifications."

Natural selection in mathematical models is expressed by genetic algorithms. Evolution Theory Model is composed of two operators: mutation and crossover. The model has an objective function, or fitness function, to define the best fit and the operators are used to produce candidate solutions. Among these candidate solutions, a proportion of solutions is kept for reproduction while the others are degraded. The solutions that are evaluated as "better" based on the objective function are more likely to be selected for reproduction.

Mutations are the random changes in DNA sequence of a cell's genome and are caused by different factors such as viruses, radiations, mutagenic chemicals, transposons, and errors occurring during DNA replication. Mutation is used to increase the diversity of genes since the optimal solution may not exist within the existing genes. *Crossover*, or recombination, occurs by randomly mating the existing members to produce new ones. The new solution would have a gene that is composed of the two parents' gene.

In Darwin's theory, the objective corresponds to the ability to survive in life. The genes that have a more chance to survive in an environment would be preferable in nature. If we consider an extreme case, for example, the movie superman, it is obvious that superman would have the better chance of survival than any human being. That means we cannot be the optimal result of such a fitness function, which is the ability for survival. More realistic view is that if we were to evolve in a way to have the best chance for survival, we should have evolved to something less fragile, stronger, perhaps smarter, and having other abilities such as being able to stay under water for a long time or fly. Then, the obvious question why we evolved to how we are today as human still remains unanswered by the evolution theory.

Although the big bang provides some insight for the universe, it doesn't provide information on the individual planet's formation and life. It cannot provide a convincing explanation on how and why all the specific conditions that are required for life could get together to form the planet Earth. Chain of events such as having hot magma on the central core, having certain quantity of ice on Antarctica and Greenland, the perfect mix of gases forming breathable and livable environment on Earth and other life conditions are not likely to be formed by fully random set of events. Theory of Origin proposed in this book clears the fogs over these issues.

Theory of Origin

Billions of years ago, even long before the universe was born, there was nothingness. As a starting point, let's simply assume that a creation event have taken place at first to form the universe, planets and at least one specific planet with livable conditions just like Earth. At least in one of these livable planets, a human or human-like creature with high intelligence was created. Let's call this planet as Planetorg, meaning the original planet. In Planetorg, there was the intelligent creature, other creatures for harmony, and the plants to provide food for the creatures. Each creature had a function, mission, to contribute for the ongoing existence of the universe (or one can call the universe as nature). *The ultimate purpose* has never been the survival of a certain creature, but *the survival of the system*. The **key element of the system** is the **universal balance**, which involves balanced chemical compositions in very tiny structures like micropes, the balance in life styles and also the balance among planets and galaxies life such as the gravitational inward forces versus the outward forces of the rotation velocity, or the expansion force of the galaxies versus the inward binding forces of dark

364

matter within empty space in the universe. The **key concept of the system** is the **universal life cycle**, which is not just a local life cycle within a planet, but life cycle of galaxies and planets within universe.

The intelligent creature had the DNA structure and perhaps the shape of the modern human. We may not even know the shape because our evolution process to this original creature may have not been completed, yet. However, assuming the current shape of human wouldn't invalidate the generality of the system's theory even if the full development may not have been completed. In this original assumed creation of the universe, everything was in perfect harmony due to the optimal balance state, which was necessary for the survival of the universe.

The, "nature" was part of the creation, including the planet's internal structure, atmosphere and the structure of the universe. Given the context of the nature, the movements of the planets, stars, and small meteors in the universe, weather conditions in any planet were considered as natural phenomena or natural events. There was a strong purpose in natural events, and this purpose was to preserve and to protect the optimal balance state in the universe. For the nature, its purpose has always been the top priority, and anything else is the secondary in importance. In order to preserve the existence of the universe in the original state, *the key* has always been *the optimal balance state* in the universe, in the condition of the individual planets and stars.

Since the natural phenomena have the most crucial role to preserve the balance, it would be normal that the nature would have the super powers to perform and to serve for its own duty. Whenever there becomes a situation of imbalance or leading toward the imbalance, nature would take control by performing necessary actions, which could be very drastic for all creatures depending on the level of change in the balance. These actions could be as simple as just a few light rains or some snow, but they could also be strong storms, flooding, volcanic eruptions, large-scale freeze of open oceanic water, or crashing large meteors and even planets to destroy and re-built the balance system. *Natural events* are like *repairs and fixations* for the problems. It is similar to human situation when one gets sick, needing a surgery, the person would go to the doctor and get surgery. We do that even if we often know it is a painful process, but it is necessary to reduce the pain in the long run and may even extend our life span. Natural events can also be painful and

366

even disastrous for the locations that they occur, but it is a reformation process, fixation of a damaged part, and a refreshing action for the global balance.

There can be no doubt the intelligent human race on the Planetorg must have created highly developed and technologically advanced society. They lived in piece and comfort for some years, which could be thousands or even millions of years. The time frame is impossible to guess for us as they were the very initial creation of a cyclic process. However, one thing is for sure that advancing technology would have caused damage on the balance of Planetorg's physical and chemical structure. Most of the elements in the planet's contents would have been taken out to build tools and equipment for the comfort of the society living in much more advance level than today's modern world. Huge production factories and equipment would slowly change the chemical balance of the atmosphere of the planet as well as the physical balance of the planet's crust.

At some time, the balance on the planet would be disturbed so much that it would be impossible to fix it through events on the planet such as storms, icing, or any other natural activity specific within the atmosphere of the planet. The situation is equivalent of a local optima case where the evolutionary algorithms would be trapped and cannot get out of it simply by applying crossover method using existing population. Here in the planet's case, existing population would mean the existing tools of the nature, including the population of the creatures, within the atmosphere of the planet to establish the balance. In the mathematical model of evolution algorithm, a mutation would be necessary to diversify the genes and generate fresh new genes of populations to get rid of the local optima trap. This process corresponds to a severe drastic outer space action of the nature to re-establish the optimal balance. The most probable drastic activity of the nature in this case is the crush of a large meteor, perhaps similar to the size of the planet, with the planet to start a fresh reformation process.

Such an enormous impact of a huge meteor to the planet would produce huge explosion, energy, and heat. A large portion of the planet would turn to dust, and some of free hot magma would spread in space. The smaller pieces of magma would instantly freeze and turn to solid particles in space. The magma layer in the core of the planet must have had the same or similar composition to that in Earth, which is composed of melted silica (45% - 70%), iron and magnesium

(2% - 32%) and others (oxygen, aluminium, and alkalines including sodium, potassium, and calcium). Even in such an enormous explosion, some portion of the liquid hot magma would spread in space at the instant of the crash forming ponds of magma and not necessarily all of it turning to dust particles. Then, these ponds of magma would gather back moving toward each other and sticking to form larger magma ponds. The magma would not cool off immediately because huge amount of heat is produced during the crash. Only the surface of it would solidify forming a layer of crust, which further helps keeping the internal heat. This movement of magma ponds toward each other after explosion is caused by their gravity force, which is the result of their heavy density.

Another big portion of the planet would be separated from the main body due to the impact of the explosion caused by the crushing force. This portion could either travel in space to far distances to other solar systems until it either crushes with another star or planet, or settles in an orbit in the same solar system or a different one.

Another possibility is that the freed portion could stay even in the current orbit of the planet. As it rotates, some of the dust particles may attach to this piece, making it larger

369

each time this portion is passing by around the crash zone, but the majority of the particles would form a massive dust cloud behind it moving around the orbit together with this large piece. At the same time, a large magma pond formed by recombining the spread magma would be covered by the dust particles. As the large magma gets attached with particles, it gets larger and totally covered with the attached particles. This getting-together action reforms and reshapes the planet. Since the core magma is not lost and other molecular (microscopic size) particles from the living human already exist, conditions to reform the life would be established. The freed part of the planet could form a moon by time. However, this initial cycle of explosion and reformation may not be forming the moon and the Earth, or it may even not be within our solar system. It may be in a totally different system, but forming a cyclic structure similar to the Moon and the Earth's movement in this solar system.

If the broken free portion of the planet is still a very large portion (in fact a planetlike size) and moves free to the outer space, it may crash again and create enormous energy and huge fire balls in the empty space. This energy can initiate the formation of a solar system in a way similar to the big bang theory. The difference, in this case, is that the big bang is not creating the universe by a random set of events and some unknown energy, but it is be creating a new solar system from the energy that is formed due to the activities within the already created (or existing) universe. If we assume this solar system would enlarge by time just as in the theory of the big bang, the newly created universe would make the actual system of universes similar to the shape of lattice leaves growing over each other. The life in this new solar system could be possible since the molecules from the original human and plants would exist as trapped within the tiny particles. However, to be able to reform the life, the molecules trapped inside the tiny particles have to exist for recreation of life without turning to a total fire and energy. At this points, the series of events and all things are not as random as they appear to be. That is clear once the understanding of the original optimal balance condition is established. There is a purpose in all this and thatre- is establishing the optimal balance condition.

After the explosion (crash of the planet and a large meteor), there would be either a single planet reforming from the particles attaching to each other around the core magma or a planet and a moon forming at the same time. Although the original human are turned to dust and microscopic-sized particles during the big explosion, the DNA code of the human couldn't be lost. The genetic information of the human and its DNA coding would be preserved in molecules inside even the very tiny particles of Planetorg. It may take a hundred thousand year or more for all the dust particles to re-gather and attach back to each other to form the second-generation planet with its atmosphere.

Once the planet's reformation is fully completed and the planet becomes ready for life again, the tiny microscopic particles that were trapped inside small rocks or crystals of minerals would come back to life. The theory of evolution would start taking place in a way similar to Darwin's theory. However, the aim of the recreation and reproduction of the genes is not to gain the best survival ability, but to create the original human and original system with the other creatures. The reason to aim that is to bring the nature back to its original state of the optimal balance condition.

This does not mean other the planets in the universe, if had life, would have exactly the same creatures. All the creatures in the original system may not be formed in every reformed live planet. Having different variety of living things in different planets does not invalidate the theory.

Although the aim of the microscopic creature formed from human DNA remnants would be to create the original human, it is not an easy process just to form the human shape straight away. That is the reason the nature goes through the evolution process aiming to create the human whose genetic codes are known to the nature. Many varieties of the living creatures in the planet would, in fact, be formed from the same source just like us. These creatures are still from the same source, Planetorg, and can exist in the balanced state. Obviously, there would also be other creatures' DNA trapped in the tiny particles and their DNA remnants would attempt to form these creatures also in a similar process. That would even diversify the population more and more whilst improving the general condition towards the optimal balance system. Diversification does help the balance system and the more living things diversified, the better balance system would be formed.

Through the cyclic process of evolution, all the creatures are connected to each other from the origin, and at least this connection must create the respect of the living creatures for each other's life. Normally, the respect among all creatures for the other's right to live would come from the understanding of the existence of the optimal balance state for the universe that is necessary for all creatures to exist.

Conclusive Remarks

The Theory of Origin took its name from two main facts. The first one is that very tiny microscopic creatures go through the evolution process to create their original form, which is mainly the originally created first human (this is for the human DNA). There could also be other creatures in the original optimal state and those creatures may also be formed through evolution at the same time. Another one is that when any condition changes in the universe or in a planet from the originality, the nature will always take charge and use its superpowers to turn the conditions back to the original condition at the time of creation. The original condition was the perfect harmony and universally optimal balance condition.

After the initial creation, nature takes the control in the universe and over individual planets to preserve the original balance. To achieve this very difficult task, nature is fully equipped with super powers. Human is, in fact, a part of nature itself. However, when the balance is harmed by any way, nature must take corrective actions, and these corrective actions can have disastrous consequences for human and all other living creatures on that planet. That is the reason that all creatures must show respect to the nature, contribute to a balance state in anyway and never forget its duties. Respect means behaving in a responsible way to eliminate or minimize the damage to the planet's environmental balance.

The proposed theory also leads to the indestructibility property of humans due to the reformation process. This is one of the aspects of the theory that contributes in creating this fascinating story.

www.ingramcontent.com/pod-product-compliance
Lightning Source LLC
Chambersburg PA
CBHW051320250626
47155CB00007B/2391